Shopping
for Women

By the same author

PHILIP OAKES

Shopping for Women

ANDRE DEUTSCH

First published in Great Britain in 1994 by
André Deutsch Limited
106 Great Russell Street
London WC1B 3LJ

Cataloguing-in-publication data for this title
is available from the British Library

ISBN 0 233 98861 0

Printed in Great Britain by
St Edmundsbury Press, Bury St Edmunds, Suffolk

For Ilsa Yardley

Acknowledgements

My thanks to Dr Desmond Morris and Dr Devra Kleiman for their zoological advice, especially with regard to giant pandas. Theirs was the information. The speculation is all mine.

When in trouble
Or in doubt,
Run in circles,
Scream and shout.

Twentieth century English. Anon.

one

Patrick Lamb stared at the mountains unfolding below him on the starboard side and smiled bravely at the air hostess. She did not return his smile. In his limited experience with Koreans – a mere week, including three days in Beijing when he had consulted them at hourly intervals while he waited for the weather to clear – they had only smiled when the news was bad.

'Sorry, thick fog. No plane,' they said. Followed by the smile. 'Sorry, no flight today.' An even bigger smile. 'Weather closing in. Maybe tomorrow.' Smiles all round. Lamb's own face had ached with the strain, but now he felt he was making progress. The hostess had not smiled at him when he boarded the plane and it was unlikely that she would smile when he disembarked. She was not a diplomat. She inhabited the real world.

He risked another glance at the mountains and instantly wished that he had not done so. They were not particularly large, but they seemed very close. Up to now he had seen them only in paintings, landscapes in which jagged peaks, tufted with bamboo, rose like turrets from a serene countryside. He had not believed they were really like this. Artists were given licence to invent, but those crags, those fangs of granite that glistened in the early morning sunlight were more hostile than the sternest imaginings. He saw a river flowing across a sandy plain, a walled hamlet, a flock of birds like ticks on a page. His ear-drums popped and he swallowed painfully. The cabin was not pressurized and each throb of the engine seemed to loosen the straps of gristle that hinged his jaw. He yawned and wagged his tongue from side to side. At that moment his eyes met those of the hostess. Her expression did not alter, but Lamb knew without doubt that she thought he was mad. He braced himself in his seat and rehearsed his explanation. He spoke schoolboy French and a few words of German. The language barrier, he realized, was formidable. There was no one he could ask to interpret.

He was one of seven passengers. Behind him sat a colonel in the North Korean army who nursed a piano accordion, swathed in plastic, on his lap. There was a Pakistani husband and wife, both wearing suits of pale gabardine, vaguely military in cut, but without insignia of any kind. There was a two-man delegation from Beijing who spat incessantly into paper handkerchiefs. And there was Lottie Moffat, Lamb's photographer, not of his choosing and, as far as he could tell, indifferent to the fact. She looked over the back of her seat and wagged her finger. It was a greeting, he supposed, but it reminded him most strongly of the signal he used to summon a waiter in a noisy restaurant.

He leaned forward to catch her question. 'You okay?'

'I'm fine,' he said. 'It's just my ears.' He tugged at the lobes and realized that, once again, the hostess was watching. He imagined the conversation that night when she related the perils of the flight to her nearest and dearest. 'A madman from England. Crazy roundeyes.' He could not hope to persuade her otherwise. His pantomime was bound to be misunderstood. Turbulence cuffed the underside of the plane and he gripped the arms of his seat. He had never enjoyed flying. Even the best journeys invoked a sensation which lay midway between terror and boredom, and he offered a silent prayer that soon he would be standing on solid ground once again. Even foreign ground. They had been on their way for a week. In Moscow they had missed the direct flight to Pyongyang, which meant a stopover of two days before going on to Beijing where, they were assured, a plane would

2

be waiting. That much was true. It had waited in plain sight on the tarmac while fog curdled thinly around the perimeter. Twice they had checked in. Twice they had been sent back to the hotel. When, at last, they took off it had been in heavy rain. Now they were heading into snow. Patrick drew a deep breath and resolved to be cheerful.

'What time do we land?' asked Lottie, taking the seat beside him.

'About an hour from now.' He glanced at his watch. 'Too late for lunch, I'm afraid.'

She groaned dramatically. 'I'm starving.'

Her appetite amazed him. In Moscow she had eaten caviar and blinis and yogurt and stuffed cabbage in such quantities that the waiters in the tourist restaurant had gathered round to watch. In Beijing she had demanded duck and crispy pancakes for both lunch and dinner, with seaweed on the side and toffee bananas to follow. Not surprisingly, she was a plump girl, twenty-two years old, with long, blonde hair and she could pass, thought Patrick, for his daughter. Bearing in mind their relative ages, she could actually be his daughter. But, at forty-three, he had no children and, since the decree was made absolute three months earlier, he had no wife either. He realized, with a small surge of pleasure, that he had not thought about Cassandra for a full twenty-four hours. It was too early for self-congratulation. All that it meant was that one anxiety had been displaced by several others. But the change was welcome. It did at least offer variety. One of the unreported aspects of a disaster which continued for some time was its monotony.

'Do you think they'll lay on transport?'

'They're bound to.' Although, thought Patrick, if North Korean efficiency maintained its normal standard, they could be making the rest of their journey on foot. He was not a born traveller. Other places and other customs made him apprehensive, and recent experiences only confirmed his prejudices. He opened his brief-case and again checked his travel documents. His own face stared up at him from his passport. He wished that he liked it more, but the scanty hair, the snub nose and the thickening jawline did nothing to earn his respect. He did not look like a leader of men.

He looked what he was: overweight, middle-aged and un-happy.

'I could have done better than that,' said Lottie.

'Better than what?'

'That picture. It's terrible.'

'I thought it was official policy,' said Patrick. 'To make you sorry you dared to be photographed. Humiliation guaranteed whenever you show it. A reminder not to step out of line.'

'Is that what you really think?'

'Now and again,' he said. 'It depends on what's been happening. Some days are better than others.'

'How about today?'

'Don't ask.'

An hour later they landed at Pyongyang. The main airport was closed and the plane sledded through cloud on to the runway of a small military airfield. A cold wind, peppered with snow, blew across the tarmac and plucked at the wind-sock that trailed from a solitary flagpole. A row of DC3s hedged the perimeter, their windows and propellers lagged against frost. Was this a museum, Patrick wondered, or was no one aware that the war of thirty, or was it forty, years ago was over? He pulled up his coat collar as a small, smiling man in a dark overcoat trotted forward to meet them. 'Welcome,' he said, shaking their hands in turn. 'My name is Mr Lee. You are the first Britishman I have encountered. I hope I speak well enough for you.'

'Perfectly,' said Patrick. The cold was intense and his teeth chattered. Mr Lee's coat looked threadbare and his shoes, on which brass buckles winked, were wet through. His smile, though, was radiant and he ignored the snow which pecked at his face and hair. 'You must correct me if I make mistakes,' he said. 'I study Linguaphone records many years old. Idiom may be out of date.'

Patrick nodded stiffly. He felt as though he had taken root on an ice floe. Already his feet were numb, his face was becoming rigid and he hugged his brief-case as though it contained some secret element, an electric coil which pressure would bring to life.

'For God's sake,' said Lottie, 'let's move.' She barged

4

past him and ran towards a low, wooden hut whose yellow lights they glimpsed across the barrens of the airfield. Mr Lee scampered behind her, uttering cries of distress. The words were indistinct but somehow, Lamb discerned, a breach of etiquette was being committed. Could it be, he wondered, that in this hell-hole of a country, freezing, primitive and reactionary though it undoubtedly was, women did not, by inalienable right, come first? It was almost too much to hope for. He bent his head to the blast and lurched after them.

They met outside the door of the hut. Mr Lee held the door knob fast and shook his finger in Lottie's face. 'Mr Lamb is leader of delegation,' he panted. 'Important we establish precedent.'

The wind howled and Lottie blinked at him through snow-clotted lashes. 'Just open the door,' she said.

'You understand?' said Mr Lee.

His lips, Patrick observed, had turned lilac verging on blue, but his grip on the door knob was unyielding. Lottie stared at them both in disbelief. 'Is this for real? We're going to die out here.'

Mr Lee clung to the door knob. 'You understand?'

'I understand,' said Lottie.

The door swung open and heat billowed out to meet them. Coke stoves, glowing like molten ingots, stood at either end of the hut and their fumes made Patrick catch his breath. He dried his eyes and saw the reception committee standing in line. Two women wearing red and green robes presented them with bouquets (he recognized peonies, azalea, twigs of spruce), and a man in a long, black overcoat and a fur hat shook his hand. Mr Lee bobbed his head. 'Please to meet Mr Kim, government minister responsible for conservation in People's Republic.'

'Delighted,' said Patrick. He tugged at Lottie's sleeve. 'And this is Miss Moffat.'

Mr Lee giggled. 'Like nursery rhyme.'

'I beg your pardon.'

'English poem,' said Mr Lee. 'Little Miss Moffat sat on her tuffet, eating her curds and whey. Is that correct?'

'More or less,' said Patrick. He did not dare look at Lottie.

'You must tell me,' said Mr Lee. 'What is a tuffet?'

5

There was no time to reply. Mr Kim took his arm and led him to a table on which there was an array of glasses. He spoke rapidly to Mr Lee who handed them round. 'Mr Kim drinks to the success of your mission,' he said. 'Down the hatch.'

It was unlike anything that Patrick had tasted before. He registered turnip and petrol and some other vaguely vegetable essence which reeked of the silo and numbed his tongue. 'Ginseng,' said Mr Lee encouragingly. 'To make you live a thousand years.'

Patrick licked his lips in disbelief. 'Will it really?'

Out of the corner of his eye he saw Lottie's face, screwed up as if she was about to vomit. It was not the time for sympathy. This was a diplomatic occasion and she had to pull her weight. He smiled at her fiercely and clinked their glasses. 'Get it down,' he hissed. She glared at him without speaking and took a token sip.

As far as he could tell only Mr Lee spoke English, but he could not be certain. Before leaving London he had been briefed by the foreign editor. 'Don't trust them for a second,' he advised. 'I doubt whether your room will be bugged. They've not got enough people to listen in all the time. But watch what you say. Don't call them gooks. Don't let slip that you think the president's a bastard. They wouldn't care for that.'

Mr Kim refilled his glass and bared long, yellow teeth in a smile that outranked that of Mr Lee. A reciprocal toast was called for. 'To the People's Republic,' said Patrick and, for an incongruous moment, he remembered his mother. 'Politeness,' she had always told him 'costs nothing.' It was a universal axiom, he thought, but she had never visited North Korea or tasted ginseng.

They drove to Pyongyang in separate cars, long black limousines with lace curtains at the rear windows and fresh flowers in clip-on vases attached to the doors. Lottie was shepherded into the first car, while Patrick was led to the one behind. He was wedged between Mr Kim and Mr Lee and the door was slammed shut. There was a strong smell of fish and garlic which intensified when Mr Lee opened his mouth. In the gale on the airfield and the fug of the reception it had not been apparent, but in the confined space of the car Patrick was in no doubt what Mr Lee had consumed for lunch. The drivers wore peaked caps and dark aviator glasses and blew their horns at anything that approached. Traffic was light. They passed small, shaggy oxen hauling carts piled high with cabbages, and gangs of women chipping ice from the roads. As the cars drove by they saluted with their shovels. 'They salute anything that looks official,' said Mr Lee. 'They are not educated.'

It was two in the afternoon and a blood-red sun hung low in the sky. Mr Kim chain-smoked, lighting one cigarette from the stub of another. 'The minister would like you to inform him on environmental issues,' said Mr Lee. It was clearly a mouthful to deliver and a look of relief flitted across his face as he completed the sentence. 'There are many questions,' he continued more briskly. 'I have made out a list.' Patrick's heart sank as he took a notebook from his pocket and flicked the pages. 'Acid rain in Wales,' Mr Lee began. 'Bovine tuberculosis. Is it transmitted by badgers? The disappearance of the sand eel. Why should this be?'

'Hold on,' said Patrick. His head ached and the ginseng still clung to his gums. He was in no shape to face up to this kind of quiz. His briefing, to say the least of it, had been inadequate, and he doubted whether opinion qualified as information. Mr Kim lit another cigarette, deepening the blue haze within the car. Air pollution, thought Lamb, was unlikely to appear on the questionnaire. He attempted to wind down a window, but Mr Lee slapped his wrist with one finger, as if correcting a child. 'Too cold,' he said. 'Freeze bollocks off.'

'I beg your pardon,' said Patrick.

Mr Lee looked anxious. 'Is idiom incorrect?'

'Not incorrect. A little racy perhaps.'

'What is racy?'

'Vulgar,' said Patrick. 'Rude.'

Mr Lee covered his mouth with the flat of his hand. 'Oh my! I did not know. Please explain.'

Patrick stared through the window, but the scudding landscape offered no inspiration. 'Bollocks means balls,' he said at last. 'Balls are testicles.' He pointed to the crotch of Mr Lee's trousers. Mr Lee understood what had been said and he was appalled.

'As a matter of interest,' said Patrick, 'where did you hear the phrase? Was it on Linguaphone?'

'Not Linguaphone. Linguaphone is polite. Jack Blazer taught me.'

'Jack Blazer?'

'You will meet him. Not today, but later. He is a bad man.'

There was a burst of static from Mr Kim and the interpreter launched into a long and aggrieved explanation. Clearly, he felt that he had lost face. Now and then he seemed close to tears. Translation was going to be a problem, Patrick realized; matters of taste even more so. He should have said nothing. He was not in the business of scoring points and it occurred to him that by being tactless he had adversely marked Mr Lee's card. It was not so. 'Bollocks,' said Mr Kim, stretching the syllables between palate and tongue. 'Boll-ocks.' His forefinger, tarred with nicotine, darted towards Mr Lee's groin and then briefly probed his own parts. He was celebrating a new word, Lamb realized, and he was making a joke. Concern for the environment had been postponed. For the moment they were all chaps together.

Soon they were driving through the city suburbs. It was not a gradual approach. One minute they were in open country; the next, they were hedged in by apartment blocks, some of them still being built. The scaffolding, for the most part, was timber; tree trunks with the bark still attached. Men in hard hats mixed concrete and hoisted sheets of steel mesh. Naked light bulbs jigging on lengths of grimy flex glared through gaps in the breeze block walls. They crossed a bridge. Beneath it lay a row of small boats, locked in ice. The sky was a clear apple green, flecked here and there with black snow clouds. As they turned into a square where their hotel faced them across a terrace of flagstones, a wedding party posed for photographs by the entrance. The groom held on to his top hat. The bride's veil billowed above her head. Lottie dived out of the front car, camera in hand. As she peered into the viewfinder, the driver of the car deliberately stepped in front of her.

'What's happening?' asked Patrick.

Mr Lee clicked his tongue. 'Not possible,' he said. 'Permission has not been arranged.'

'Who's going to object? It's only a wedding.'

'Permission is required,' said Mr Lee.

'Who gives it?'

'Difficult to say.'

'Ask the minister,' said Patrick. 'Let's see if he has any pull around here.'

Mr Kim uttered one short sentence and the car door was flung open. Unhurriedly, he stepped on to the pavement and indicated that Patrick should follow. The driver got back into the car, the wedding party regrouped and snow fell like confetti. 'Can I take pictures now?' asked Lottie.

'That seems to be the idea,' said Patrick. The speed with which the situation had changed was awesome, he thought. Nothing had been said, no signal given. All that it took to turn no to yes, black to white, was the presence of one man. He stood to one side, hands in his pockets, a fresh cigarette between his lips. The wind ruffled his fur hat. Occasionally he stamped his feet. It was like being on a film set, thought Patrick, where, just as a gag, a visiting celebrity was urged to join the crowd. His looks were unremarkable. He was dressed like everyone else. He wore no badge, no distinguishing mark. But somehow he was conspicuous. He stood out. He had the power and that was what people recognized. Lottie stepped back to include him in a wide shot but Mr Kim turned on his heel and walked into the hotel.

'Finish now,' said Mr Lee.

There was no discussion. The wedding party fled across the square. The cars were unloaded and they followed their bags through the swing doors. The change in temperature was dramatic. Suddenly they were in Africa. Patrick felt the moisture being blotted from his face. There were flowering shrubs, a fountain which fell into a basin of cobalt tiles, and a tank of tropical fish, in front of which sat Mr Kim. He joined them at the reception desk and flipped through the hotel register. No one tried to stop him.

'Your passports, please,' said Mr Lee.

It was always a nasty moment, thought Patrick, even in a country where the customs were familiar and the water safe to drink. Here it was like surrendering not only proof of identity, but identity itself. He watched their names, framed in blue and gold, slide into Mr Lee's brief-case. In the space of a second they had become non-persons, swallowed by the state.

'Tonight,' said Mr Lee, 'there is a banquet in your honour. Many important guests wishing success to your mission. I will call for you at eight o'clock. Rest until then.'

'I'm not tired,' said Lottie. 'I thought I'd look around. Take the air, you know, see the sights.'

Out of the corner of his eye Patrick saw Mr Kim shake his head. The movement was barely perceptible, but there was no mistaking the message. 'Tomorrow perhaps,' said Mr Lee. 'Today is not possible.'

'But I'm not tired,' said Lottie. She poked Lamb in the ribs. 'Tell him we're not tired.'

Patrick met the full voltage of Mr Lee's smile and knew it was a waste of time. One had to learn to read the signs. Small smiles meant a minor inconvenience. A blinder like Mr Lee's spelled a total impasse. All the same, he went through the motions. 'We're not tired,' he said.

'Not possible,' said Mr Lee. 'Too cold.' He made a pantomime of shivering in his blue denim. 'We take care of our guests.' He picked up his brief-case and slid the register over the desk. 'Please sign your names. Then I take you to your rooms.'

'Tomorrow we see the sights,' said Lottie.

'If it can be arranged.'

Mr Kim shook their hands (his own was dry as a bone) and watched them mount the staircase. The carpet was acrylic, a tide of canary yellow which flowed brilliantly from the landing above. The colour was unfortunate, thought Patrick. It reminded him of meals unwisely chosen, drinks recklessly consumed. What, he wondered, would be the menu at the evening's banquet. When he reached out to touch the banister the shock made him gasp. It was as though he had jammed his finger in the mains.

'So sorry,' said Mr Lee. 'Static electricity.' He pointed to the carpet. 'All stored up there. When you touch banister you complete circuit.'

10

Patrick felt his heart pound as if it had been used as a punch-bag. 'You should have warned me.' His fingers stung and his legs were shaky. The entire country was a health hazard, he thought. He would not even wish it on Cassandra, although she would most likely pronounce it stimulating. It was strange how discomfiture brought her to mind. Happiness never had the same effect. But anxiety, embarrassment, any of the infinite forms of upset spirited her from the closet where he had confined her to shimmer like a hologram over things gone wrong. He wished her gone and lumbered up the stairs.

His room turned out to be a suite, twice the size of Lottie's. 'You are leader of delegation,' explained Mr Lee.

'We're not a delegation.'

'More than one person is delegation.'

'But it's much too big.'

'Good place to hold meetings.'

'What meetings?'

'There are always meetings,' said Mr Lee. 'Always matters to discuss.' He indicated the packs of cigarettes strewn around the bedroom and living room. 'These are for guests.' He pointed to the refrigerator. 'Beer and fruit juice in there. Drink now and rest.'

He bowed his way out and Patrick resisted the impulse to lock the door behind him. More than anything he longed to be somewhere else; failing that, to be alone. Too much was being organized around him. It was like being in the army or back at school. Other people were presumed to know best. The bureaucrats were in charge and there was no appeal. At the same time, he thought, diplomacy would grease the wheels. The smoother the arrangements, the sooner they could leave. He must not lose sight of the objective. 'Don't worry about the pictures,' he told Lottie, 'you'll get what you want tomorrow.'

'What's all this about permission?'

'It's just their way,' he said. 'It's how they think. It's not a democracy. They're not used to people doing as they like. They have to be persuaded.'

'How are you going to do that?'

'Delegate negotiates,' said Lamb. 'How does that sound?'

'Stupid,' said Lottie. 'I think the whole thing's stupid.'

She sprawled in an armchair, yellow like the stair-carpet, and kicked off her shoes. Her face was flushed and her eyes bulged with tears. Not for the first time, Patrick wondered what he had done to deserve such a colleague on such an assignment. It was not a serious question and he already knew the answer. In journalism, or at least in this particular ghetto of journalism, it was the age of the bimbo and Lottie was one of its star performers. The picture desk thought so and so did the Admiral. 'A pretty girl who takes pretty pictures,' he told Patrick. 'Just what the paper needs.' Not that he was one to interfere, he went on. Editors were hired to edit, writers were required to write, but his success as a proprietor lay in knowing what people wanted. It was the rule he lived by. It had made him rich and it paid everyone's salary. Patrick would do well to remember that. 'And keep your dick to yourself,' he added. 'I want her on the job, not in the club.'

There had been more on the same lines. Six thousand miles away and a month later, Patrick recalled every word of the conversation and fresh sweat beaded his palms as he thought of his given role. Mr Kim would recognize the labels that he wore: lackey, running dog of capitalism. There was probably a wall chart, like those used to identify aircraft in silhouette, on which he figured abjectly and unmistakably. At whatever speed or altitude he flew, his outline was known. He could not disguise what he was.

Outside the window darkness had fallen. Tall street lamps quartered the square and snow filtered down through cones of light. It was like a prison yard, he thought, a place of correction. Nothing moved. There was no traffic on the roads, no distant glow of shop-fronts or factories to indicate that a capital city was going about its business. 'Will we be here long?' asked Lottie.

'I shouldn't think so. Long enough to get ourselves organized. It's up to them really.'

She sighed heavily. 'Do you know exactly where we're going?'

'North,' said Lamb. 'They didn't tell me the precise location. I don't suppose it has a name. Somewhere in the wilds.'

'It has to be better than here.'

'Better pictures anyway,' he said.

Her hair, he noticed, was standing on end as though it was being tugged by unseen magnets. He brushed his hand over his own head and realized that it too was bristling. 'It's the static,' said Lottie. 'I've got some gel if you want it.'

'Why doesn't theirs stand up?'

She shrugged. 'Diet. Natural oils. Maybe they don't shower as often.' She squinted round the room. 'Maybe they just watch TV.'

In one corner a small black and white set was showing what appeared to be a documentary. A stout, sullen man wearing a pale uniform with a Prussian collar strolled across a building site, surrounded by men in overalls and hard hats. He pointed to a crane, then to a bulldozer and everyone applauded. In the next sequence he watched combine harvesters attack a cornfield and again offered his advice. In quick succession he supervised a team of surgeons attaching clamps to a pulsing heart and a nursery class in which small and tidy children danced decorously around his entourage. Patrick zapped the remote control but the same programme was showing on all channels. The dancing children dissolved to a mountain peak wreathed in cloud, which in turn gave way to the man himself. A roll of fat bulged over the back of his collar; otherwise, thought Patrick, it was a fair approximation of what God looked like. 'Our respected and beloved leader,' he said. 'Soldier, scholar and all round good fellow.'

'Is he the president?'

'The very same.'

'I want to go home,' said Lottie. She picked up her shoes and padded to the door. 'Time for a zizz. Wake me when you're ready.'

Patrick unpacked his bag and stripped down to his shorts. The room was airless and the windows were sealed. On the television set the programme had looped and once more the president crossed the building site. The crane performed its waltz and the bulldozer bit into the rubble. Patrick turned his back on the proceedings and lay down on his bed. When he closed his eyes he thought of Cassandra. The omens were not propitious, he thought. Spelling out the situation would not improve it, but putting it into words might make it less

13

daunting, fractionally less absurd. He decided to give it a try. I am in North Korea, he began. I am looking for a panda when I should be shopping for women. There were three hours to go before dinner, but he had plenty to think about.

two

It was on the day his divorce was made final that Patrick Lamb went shopping for women. He did not approach the enterprise gladly, but with a sense of foreboding, as though in some great bureau in the sky a computer had completed its calculations and coughed up a docket on which was inscribed his appointed task. Three years of marriage to Cassandra had all but destroyed his self-confidence. For the past year they had lived apart, meeting only at editorial conferences, fewer and fewer as *The Arbiter* galloped downmarket, exchanging messages through their solicitors like grumpy ventriloquists for whom dialogue had become too difficult. The truth was that they disliked each other. It was an understanding which had crept up on them, as if they had not at first realized that they belonged to different species, or, rather, sub-species. They were both journalists and they both had the same master. But there the resemblance came to an end. Cassandra was the paper's agony aunt ('counsellor' was how she described herself) with a readership approaching five million. Her column was called Open Heart and, even in his despair, Patrick acknowledged that nobody did it better. 'Her talent,' he told friends, 'is to write trash brilliantly.' He tried hard not to sound envious. His own name appeared on a column of gossip called Lamb's Tales. It was urbane and worldly in a way which implied that the writer was above the hurly-burly which was its meat and the chances were, thought Patrick, that it was due for the chop. Urbanity was no longer on *The Arbiter*'s menu. He saw his reputation dwindling while Cassandra's rose. It was nature's way, he told himself, but the admission gave him no comfort. It was a commodity which was becoming harder and harder to find.

The morning's post brought the document which announced that their marriage was over. There was no going back. He sipped his coffee and stared out glumly at the fine September morning. His living room overlooked Battersea Park. Already the leaves were changing colour and through the open window he could smell the nutty fragrance of autumn. There were other smells too. A mile down river there was a factory where barley sugar was refined and when the wind blew from that direction the reek of burning sneaked into every room and remained there like smouldering waste, wadded into every corner. He had been unaware of it when Cassandra lived there. He had been drunk on flesh. For the first twelve months her physical presence had been sufficient to override any disagreement and her appetite and enthusiasm for sex had equalled his own. There were times when they were dressing to go out for dinner when her passing scent had the effect of a spoken command and he would strip off the clothes she had put on so carefully and they would make love on the floor while outside the taxi waited and the phone rang unanswered.

One evening he came into the bedroom and watched her complete her toilet. She was naked with her back turned towards him and he stood in the open doorway while she sprayed herself with perfume, allowed it to dry, then sprayed herself again. He still did not speak as she sat on a low stool by the dressing table and dipped her finger between her legs. He saw it glisten in the lamplight before she stroked it first behind one ear, then the other. She changed position and saw his reflection in the mirror.

'What were you doing?' he asked.

'You saw.'

'But why?'

She stepped into a pair of briefs and snapped the elastic

16

against her hips. 'You like it,' she said. 'It's what turns you on.'

It was true; he could not pretend otherwise. But it was not for his benefit alone. He had a sudden vision of men all over London frisking behind Cassandra like dogs pursuing a bitch on heat. He could not bear to see himself as one of the pack.

'I don't fancy going out tonight,' he said. 'It's been a heavy day.'

She did not argue as he had expected. 'Suit yourself,' she said. 'It's nothing special. I won't be late.'

He went to bed at midnight and in the morning when he awoke he was still alone. Cassandra was asleep in the spare room, lying peacefully on her left side, the bedclothes undisturbed. She had told him once that she never dreamed. Waking, she could instantly resume a conversation that she had been conducting seconds before she closed her eyes, as if picking up a brief which, momentarily, she had set aside. It was unnatural, he thought. But it explained her energy and her mindless confidence. Her brain was actually disengaged for hours on end and so suffered less wear and tear than the competition. Also, because her sleep was dreamless, she was never plagued by night fears and anxieties. Confidence bloomed in the vacuum.

He pulled back the sheet and slid into bed beside her. She wore only the briefs which he had seen her put on the night before and, trying not to wake her, he rolled them down to her ankles. Her skin was flawless. Even her toe-nails were perfect. He eased the briefs over her feet and turned her gently on to her back. Her hands were clasped, but he pulled them apart so that she lay flat like a patient anaesthetized for an operation. She breathed lightly and evenly. At the vee of her belly her hair was coiled in tiny, dark springs and he kissed her, leaving a fleck of saliva below her naval. He stroked her breasts with the tip of his index finger and saw the nipples rise. I love you, he thought. I want you. Carefully, he propped himself over her with both arms rigid and then, centimetre by centimetre, lowered his body until their skins touched.

Her eyes snapped open. 'What do you think you're doing?' she asked.

He froze in position. No answer that he could think of seemed adequate. He cleared his throat. 'I was just seeing how you were.'

'And how am I?'

'Fine,' he said. 'As far as I can tell.'

He straightened his arms, but she did not move. 'Did you want to have sex?' she enquired.

'In a manner of speaking. I wasn't thinking of it like that.'

'Were you going to wake me? Or did you want it to come as a lovely surprise?'

'I expect you'd have woken anyway,' said Patrick.

'I expect I would. In mid-career, so to speak.' She spread her legs. 'All right then. Get on with it.'

'Not if you don't want to.'

'Are you asking me?'

'No,' he said. 'Yes, I am.'

'Go ahead,' said Cassandra. 'Don't let me interrupt.'

'You're sure?'

She said nothing, but stared over his shoulder as he inched himself down. For the next five minutes she remained inert. When he kissed her she allowed him to forage in her mouth with his tongue, but she did not respond. She was dry until he moistened her with his wet fingers, but she did not wince or protest when he forced his way inside her. Patrick was reminded of a variety act he had once seen in which a man fought with a life-sized dummy, tucking its head beneath his arm, reeling from a simulated blow, working for two until he crammed his opponent into a box and closed the lid. He cried out when he came, not in ecstasy but frustration, then lay spent and miserable, while beneath him the sheet turned clammy.

'Have you finished?' Cassandra asked.

He nodded wordlessly and she rolled from underneath him and padded to the bathroom. He heard the lavatory flush and the hiss of the shower. He felt sorry and sad and misunderstood. His intentions, he knew, had been loving. But she would never believe him. He had made a wrong move which had become a disaster. He would not be forgiven and Cassandra had served notice of the fact. What she had given him, by design and with intent, was The Worst Fuck in the

18

World. It was an achievement of sorts, difficult to engineer and impossible to forget. It deserved capital letters, if not a memorial plaque. He pulled the sheets over his head and wished that he was dead.

A week later Cassandra moved out. The separation was formalized; the divorce set in motion. There was no one he could ask for advice without revealing domestic details he preferred to keep secret. Friends lowered their voices when he came into the room. Women, in particular, looked at him as though his flies were undone. Word got around, he thought. If he was not a criminal, he was a casualty. Shaving, he caught an expression on his face – wounded or simply baffled – which reminded him of his father. He had first noticed it when he was a child and now he knew the cause. Without doubt, it was domestic. Most accidents, he reminded himself, happened in the home.

The shopping list was Amos Bennet's idea. 'The world's full of women and you need a replacement,' he said. 'Decide what you want and go for it.'

Patrick shook his head. 'That's not the way it works.'

'Why not?' demanded Bennet. 'She's deserted ship. Look for another hand. See what's available. You're in a buyer's market.'

Bennet lived on the floor above. He was in his late sixties, an author of satirical novels who was occasionally interviewed by young women from newspapers and television who, he claimed, were inflamed by his reputation as a male chauvinist. 'If I bang on the ceiling I expect you to come running,' he told Patrick. 'All these young scrubbers really want is a bit of leg-over.'

In print his forte had always been a comic hyperbole which made Patrick wonder whether he was joking still. He was not known for his sensitivity. In fact, when he thought about it, Amos was an object lesson in how not to deal with women. Years ago, his wife had left him. She had gone away, ostensibly to visit friends for a few days, but eventually Amos became aware that beds were unmade and the refrigerator was empty. He telephoned the most likely places where his wife might be staying and at last ran her to ground. She was unaccountably embarrassed. 'Didn't you read my note?' she asked.

'What note? What did it say?'

'That I was leaving you.'

'Where did you put it?'

'In the tea-pot,' she said. 'The one you always use.'

There was a short pause. 'I probably drank it,' said Amos.

It was a unique claim to fame, thought Patrick, but in no way did it qualify Amos to give advice. In fact, Amos made all his pronouncements from a state of siege. He was not only suspicious of women. The likelihood was that he feared and disliked them too. If women triumphed in his novels it was invariably by unfair means. They were either unnaturally pliant or viragos. Whatever unease he felt was concealed by an icy bluster, the sort of rudeness, Patrick assumed, with which feudal lords had addressed their serfs. He had a handsome, rather haughty face which, for most of the time, wore an expression of disgust, as though he had been caught picking his nose and elected to bluff it out.

His trouble was, thought Patrick, that he had not always succeeded. Amos longed for honours. He saw himself as a man of distinction, a grand old party destined, if not for a baronetcy, then some unassuming, sober-sounding title which would cushion his later years and bring automatic respect. An OM would do nicely. It was an exclusive order; no hacks need apply. Each year as the List was being compiled, he awaited the official invitation. Was he prepared for his name to be put forward? Amos knew the form. His acceptance speech was ready and waiting. But the call never came.

It was a conspiracy, he thought. His enemies had put it about that he was not a fit and proper person. His ongoing sexual career was no secret. It gave him a certain style, but only among newspaper hacks and a few of his contemporaries. Reported at second hand, it made him sound seedy and greedy, not in the least dashing, merely the victim of a bad habit. He would never be Sir Amos, he thought bitterly, and the women of both sexes were to blame. He was envied and resented in equal measure and it was not fair.

'What you need,' he said, 'is a nice little arrangement. No involvements. Someone who knows her place.'

'I don't know about that.'

'Why not?' Amos stared at him belligerently. 'You'll have to learn not to be so bloody pathetic. You're probably the sort of wet who enjoys being walked over.'

It was not true, thought Patrick, but Amos was right in one respect. He was not looking for confrontations. He was exhausted by ill humour, and the idea of a mistress, skilled in the art of company, who would exercise his mind and body without seeking any emotional return was appealing. On the other hand, he could not imagine it improving his morale. Purchasing power proved nothing beyond the fact that he had money in the bank; not much, as it happened. He had to rely on personality, or at least on charm. He had to learn how to put it to work.

He folded the letter from the court and returned it to its envelope. Cassandra, no doubt, was already filing her own copy and he resolved to be just as methodical. Making a list was the first step. He spread his notebook and popped his ball-point.

1. Find agreeable woman [he wrote]. Same age as self or younger. Nationality/colouring unimportant.

2. Accept all invitations to dinner, parties, weddings, funerals even. Remember grief heightens sensibilities.

3. Check deaths, divorces, separations. Look for someone of like mind.

4. Consider joining sports club, political party, protest group.

5. Query above. Avoid caring women. Make no promises.

It was sketchy, but it was a start. The most elaborate thesis began with a rough outline. Perhaps it was too rough. What mattered most was what he least wanted to write down. The truth was that the woman he sought was one who would like him, admire him, even desire him. As pre-requisites went it was pretty basic but it was a lot to expect. He closed the notebook and sheathed the ball-point. The day was wearing on and there were things to do. Patrick stifled his doubts and resolved to shop boldly.

The Arbiter office was no place to start. It was built of ginger brick and sat, like an over-done loaf, behind the main road in Clapham. The windows were made of reflector glass, a job-lot, Patrick suspected, turned down by an hotel on the Costa Brava. There were white cement sills which had already streaked the walls as though birds had sat in line to release their droppings, and the entrance was framed by two corrugated pillars which supported nothing but a cube of royal-blue plastic inscribed in gilt, 'Falkland House'. The unveiling had been performed by the Admiral's wife. The Prime Minister had sent a letter of congratulation which was given pride of place on the front page.

Patrick parked his car behind the scrolls of razor wire which surrounded the building and took the lift to the fourth floor. It was an ascent into hell. There were acres of desks surrounded by cubicles in which listless young women stared at computer screens. Few people appeared to be speaking to each other, but the air was filled with a ceaseless electronic babble. The cubicles were shoulder high, so that whatever was taking place inside them could be witnessed by anyone who cared to look. But no one did look. It was as though the occupants were wearing blinkers which restricted movement and vision. There was hair-cord underfoot, scored with grime and curling away from the walls. The ceilings seemed to be made of the same material as the styro-foam cups which littered every desk. Pots of hanging plants trailed down the stairwell, but as Patrick passed by, a woman in a brown overall hauled up each rope of greenery and dunked it in a bucket brimming with detergent. At first, he had found the sight alarming. Now he understood that every plastic surface in the office was entitled to its weekly shampoo.

In one cubicle, larger than the rest, a conference of some kind was taking place. A fat man wearing a club tie was systematically tearing up a sheaf of photographs, throwing the shreds in the air so that they rained down on the heads of a group of men in their shirt-sleeves. 'You call those tits?' Patrick heard him shout. 'I've got better knockers

22

on my front door.' It was not the day, Patrick decided, to ask favours of the picture editor.

His own cubicle contained a chair, a desk and a word processor. Far below he looked down on a parking lot, packed with dinky cars. There was a distant glimmer of river, a flash of railway line. But even on a fine day the prospect was sullen. On a patch of waste ground someone was burning rubber tyres and a column of smoke rolled towards Blackfriars. Through the haze Patrick sometimes imagined he could see *The Arbiter*'s old office, now occupied by a Japanese bank. When the Admiral had bought the paper he had announced that they would not be following the competition to the wasteland of Wapping. The celebrations were short-lived. The move to Clapham had followed within six months.

His telephone rang and he picked it up with a sinking of the heart. It was a reaction which had become more or less habitual. 'Is your passport up to date?' asked Dominic Downey, personal assistant to the Admiral.

'I think so.'

'Better make sure,' said Downey. 'We've got a little job for you. The Admiral wants you to go to North Korea. There's a panda he'd like you to pick up.'

three

'Mr Kim asks about your proprietor,' said Mr Lee. 'Why is he called the Admiral? Was he perhaps a famous sailor?' Patrick smiled across the banqueting table, its cloth starched like a skating rink, and put down his knife and fork. The chicken on his plate had been served with its head still attached and he had not yet decided how to deal with it. Was it regarded as a special delicacy? Would his hosts be offended if he left it uneaten?

'It's a nickname, a joke,' he said. 'Someone made it a long time ago.' Or rather, he cautioned himself, that was the legend. It was now an integral part of the Admiral's equipment but he could not guarantee how much was truth and how much was fiction. In the authorized version the name was first uttered by an airman named Harry Miller who was knocked out by the wholly unfancied J. P. Nelson in the third round of an inter-services boxing tournament at the Albert Hall. When he came to, Miller was told of his defeat. He was not greatly surprised, but he could not recall the name of his opponent. 'It was Nelson,' said the team coach, 'a bleeding sailor. You should be ashamed of yourself.' 'Not just a sailor,' said Miller, who did not wish to enter the records as a near-champion, thrashed by a nonentity, 'that was a bleeding Admiral.' It was a pretty tale, thought Patrick, and it bore re-telling.

He parcelled it out to Mr Lee, sentence by sentence, and studied the reactions as the interpreter re-enacted the fable. At one point he mimicked an upper-cut and Mr Kim clapped his hands. Patrick marvelled at the pleasure he had inspired. Few authors were granted such instant satisfaction.

What he could not tell was the rest of the story. How, years later, Dominic Downey had run Harry Miller to ground and hired him as the Admiral's valet. The day he took up the appointment he was photographed shaking hands with his employer who was wearing boxing gloves. The picture appeared on page one of all the Admiral's papers. It was a demonstration of public relations, painlessly arranged and splendidly orchestrated. Miller had turned out to be a lousy valet, but he and the Admiral made a good double act; old sparring partners, the winner helping out the loser. It helped to transform the public image of the Admiral from shady entrepreneur into rugged philanthropist, although there was an extensive past to refurbish: sanctions-busting in Rhodesia, arms sales in Biafra, a land grab in Brazil. The Admiral had played his part. He did not want merely to be rich. He realized that respectability, or rather the crusty rectitude fashioned for him by Downey, was a way to become even richer. Investors warmed to the character he assumed: the honest adventurer, not above cutting a corner or two, but a man to rely on when the chips were down. Was this the portrait that had been presented to Mr Kim? Did he believe it to be authentic?

Across the table he imitated Mr Lee, jabbing with his left fist and hooking with his right. He leaned over his chicken – head still attached, noted Patrick – and smiled broadly. 'The old one-two,' he said.

'So you do speak English?' said Patrick.

'Waiter's English. I worked for two years in London. Dim sum. Fried rice. Sweet and sour.' He wrote on an imaginary pad and shrugged his shoulders. 'A long time ago. Very rusty.'

But still sharp as a tack, thought Patrick. He made a mental note to take care what he said in ear-shot of Mr Kim. Everything would be snapped up and quite possibly used against him. The wartime motto was still true. Careless talk cost lives or, at least, reputations. He wondered if Lottie understood as much. She had slept for nearly three hours and her skin glowed. He tried not to feel envious. It was not her fault that his head ached and his stomach heaved with apprehension. As bimbos went she was agreeable enough. She might even be an asset if she was properly deployed. 'Miss Moffat was chosen by the Admiral to come here,' he said. 'Personally. He admires her work. He hopes you will give her every assistance.'

Lottie heard her name and looked up. She was gnawing her chicken head and there was a shine of grease on her chin. 'Ask him about pictures,' she said.

It sounded a touch peremptory, but it was time to move things along. 'We need to plan a schedule,' said Patrick. 'Where are we going to pick up the panda? How far do we have to travel?'

The translation unwound while waiters removed the chicken debris and brought in lettuce leaves daubed with soy paste. Mr Kim selected a leaf and chewed it thoroughly before replying. 'Far,' he said.

'How far?'

Mr Kim spread his hands, inching them apart as though they were tethered with elastic. 'A thousand miles. Maybe more.' He frowned and spoke rapidly to the interpreter.

'Where bamboo grows,' said Mr Lee. 'What pandas eat.'

For no good reason Patrick's sense of apprehension quickened, as though, invisibly, the ground was crumbling beneath his feet. He knew that pandas fed on bamboo shoots. He had expected to travel a fair distance to collect the beast. But something was being left unsaid. Back in London the plan had seemed simple. He recalled Downey's preliminary briefing before he was led in to face the Admiral. 'The thing is,' he told Patrick, 'we've struck a little bargain. We're buying some newsprint from these orientals and they're giving us a panda. Buckshee. The black and white job. Absolutely genuine.'

'A giant panda?'

'As big as they come,' said Downey. 'Practically extinct and priceless with it. And we'll be giving it to London Zoo. As you were. The Admiral will be giving it. A grand ecological gesture. Good for them and good for us.'

Patrick thought of the publicity to be garnered from the gift. More than that: there was surely a niche in the Honours List awaiting the man who presented a giant panda to the nation. 'Better for us,' he said. 'Provided it's all kosher.'

'Why shouldn't it be? Everything's taken care of. Import licence, quarantine. It's all been seen to. All we have to do is collect it.'

'Why me?'

'Why not you?' said Downey. 'What else are you doing that's so important?'

The Admiral had put it just as bluntly. 'You'll be earning your keep,' he said. 'More than you've been doing lately.' He was a short, squat man with a red face, ribbed like a hot water bottle. His nose was concave and he had tiny eyes. In the portrait which hung in the entrance of Falkland House he wore a naval uniform which somehow gave him an institutional look. 'Apart from that,' he said, 'we need a touch of class in the writing. Isn't that your line of business?' He raised his hand before Patrick could answer. 'It *is* your line of business. That's what you're paid for. Just don't get in the way of the pictures. Let the dog see the rabbit. Make sure little Lottie gets what she wants.'

It was easier said than done, thought Patrick, as he watched Mr Kim munch his way through another lettuce and soy parcel. Further down the table little Lottie was watching him just as intently. 'We need to decide on a date,' he said. 'When do you think we could collect the panda?'

Mr Kim dismissed the interpreter with a glance. 'Not collect,' he said. 'Catch.'

'I beg your pardon?'

'Panda is in the wild,' said Mr Kim. 'Whereabouts have been established. Not captured yet.'

Patrick stared at him glassily. He could barely trust himself to speak. Diplomacy was called for. The newsprint, he supposed, was being bought at a cut-price rate. 'A little bargain,' Downey had called it. But the panda was the cherry on the cake. The Admiral expected him to deliver it, as specified. He could not go home without it. The waiters returned with soup, sliced beef and a rice cake, stuffed with more soy. There was a happy clatter of spoons and forks, but his appetite had vanished. He downed a glass of ginseng. Momentarily his mouth was numbed, but the relief stopped there. 'How long will it take?' he asked.

'Not long,' said Mr Kim. 'One month. Maybe two.' He spoke briefly to the interpreter.

'Panda very elusive,' said Mr Lee. 'Difficult to find. British saying applies: we live in hope. Is that correct usage?'

Patrick nodded. He had never been an optimist and no silver lining rimmed the clouds that hung over him now. The prospect of spending a month, perhaps longer, in a country so alien and so utterly boring plunged him into despair. He caught Lottie's eye. 'There'll be some delay,' he said neutrally. 'It seems the panda still has to be caught.'

Looking back, he was not sure what reaction he had expected. Tears, at least; a tantrum perhaps. Instead, she smiled brilliantly. He could not believe it. 'Did you understand what I said?'

'We're going to catch a panda.'

'Not us, exactly,' said Patrick.

'Yes, we are,' she said. 'Isn't that terrific. Think of the pictures.' She clapped her hands and everyone stopped eating as if they expected an announcement. She did not disappoint them. She pushed back her chair and raised her glass. Patrick tried to wave her down, but it was too late. The room was hushed. Only she could break the silence. 'I give you a toast,' she called. 'To your panda which will soon be ours.' She tilted the glass and drank deeply. There was a moment's pause and then, to Patrick's amazement, the guests followed suit. 'Panda,' they murmured, testing the word as if they were biting on a coin which might be counterfeit. 'Panda,' they repeated, more confidently, as it proved not to be a dud. 'Panda!' they shouted, as Mr Kim nodded his approval.

Patrick felt slightly dazed. He had no idea what rules of protocol had been breached. But he was aware that, yet again, PR had triumphed. Mr Kim could have nipped the celebration in the bud. But he had chosen to let it go ahead. He did not give the impression of being an indulgent man, unless, for reasons unknown, he was indulging Lottie. Or could it be that he was indulging himself? His smile was secretive, as though it reflected some inner amusement. Most likely he had further revelations to make. Knowledge was power and, in his ignorance of what lay in store, Patrick felt weak at the knees. He looked imploringly across the table. 'We need to work out some details,' he said.

Mr Kim's smile broadened and Patrick saw the glimmer of gold as his teeth clamped down on a cigarette holder. Mr Lee leaned forward but he was waved aside. 'Tomorrow,' said Mr Kim, 'you talk to Jack Blazer.'

As they drove to the theatre Patrick remembered where he had heard the name. It was Jack Blazer who had taught Mr Lee to say 'bollocks'. No further explanation had been given, but he was certainly no favourite of Mr Lee. They sat side by side in the back of the limousine, a rug tucked over their knees. Mr Kim had taken chàrge of Lottie. Her toast had made her the star of the show. People had lined up to shake her hand. 'You see,' she told Patrick, as he helped her on with her coat, 'all you need to do is get them on your side. Old Kim's a sweetie really. Just leave it to me. I'll get things going.'

It was just possible that she might, he thought. Lottie was young, but her guile was drawn from an ancient female fund which gave unlimited credit, no questions asked. All women subscribed to it. Scheming came naturally to them. They lied as easily as they drew breath. They were opportunistic, ruthless and amoral. Not all of them, he conceded, or, at least, not all of the time. Lottie was on his side. He had to remember that. Whatever line she was now handing to Mr Kim was for their common good. An act of faith was necessary, but it was not easy to make here and now. He rubbed a small hole in the condensation that masked the window and peered into the darkness.

'Most people gone to bed,' said Mr Lee.

'But it's not late.'

'People like bed. Keep warm and make babies.'

'Will Jack Blazer be in bed?'

'Very likely,' said Mr Lee. 'Best place for him. Nowhere for him to make mischief.'

'What sort of mischief?'

'All sorts.' Mr Lee quivered with a brief but intense fury. 'You will find out. You will see.'

'But who is he?' demanded Patrick. 'Where does he come from? What is he doing in Korea?' The car skidded on a patch of ice and Mr Lee cheeped with alarm, like a canary whose cage had been capsized. He rapped on the driver's window but the head in front of them did not turn. It was like an executioner's car, thought Patrick. They were speeding through the night in a distant city. There was no British embassy. His passport had been impounded. He had not been able to let the office know where he was. He could disappear without a trace and no one would care. Accidents happened. He felt the tremors of an approaching cock-up, something seismic, still far-away, but unmistakably headed in his direction.

'Jack Blazer is British. Like you,' said Mr Lee. 'He fought against the People's Republic and was taken prisoner. He chose to remain.'

Patrick did sums in his head. The Korean War had been in the Fifties. 'He's been here for forty years? He wanted to stay?' The idea was difficult to entertain.

'Ask him yourself,' said Mr Lee. 'Jack Blazer talks and talks.' He jerked his head in disapproval. 'Makes fun of Linguaphone. Makes mischief.' His lips clamped shut as if further opinions were too risky to release and, without warning, he gripped Patrick's thigh beneath the blanket. 'Say nothing,' he begged. 'Jack Blazer is honoured guest. You will meet him tomorrow.'

The car swung into a lighted square and drew up outside a building armoured with slabs of granite. Everything shone. The stone reflected the glare of chandeliers. The pavement was immaculate. In the background Patrick saw women with brooms and shovels. Mr Kim flicked the ash from his cigarette and one of them scurried forward to catch it, almost before it touched the ground. He led the way through pneumatic doors and men wearing blue uniforms bowed them into a room full of flags. In one corner stood a bust of the Great Leader, and his portrait, done in several sizes, hung on each wall. There were also photographs in which he clasped the hands of black men and brown men, bemedalled soldiers and

30

air force generals. On a leather-topped table a visitor's book lay open and beside it there was a drinks trolley. 'Champagne,' said Mr Kim and thrust a glass into his hand.

Patrick's eyes felt as though someone had scattered sand beneath the lids. His legs ached with fatigue. They were promised an opera which, he calculated, would not be over for at least three hours. 'Cheers,' he said. If he fell asleep he prayed that he would not snore.

Lottie tugged at his elbow. 'Did you find anything out?'

'Not much. Did you?'

'He keeps saying he'll see what he can arrange.'

'They haven't a clue,' said Patrick. 'See how they smile. It's not a good sign.' It was not the moment to elaborate, but his theory was bearing up. On all sides teeth were bared in expressions of extravagant good will. North Korean dentistry was on display and the standards, to say the least, were variable. Mr Kim had the most gold. There was also enough stainless steel, patching molars and canines, to furnish a small kitchen. They smiled, he decided, not only because they were embarrassed or mistaken or to demonstrate their good intentions, but simply to mark time. Life itself was on hold. The next move had yet to be signalled. The smile was like a pilot light which showed that the machine was still operational, but the broader it became, the greater the hazard. It was a smile of unknowing and he felt his own lips curl in imitation.

Mr Kim raised a finger, the crowd parted and they were led to their seats. It was a strange experience. The theatre was full, but not a head turned in their direction. It was as though they were invisible. Patrick breathed deeply. There was a strong smell of wintergreen. Coughs and sneezes spread diseases, he thought. But the audience was silent; a thousand throats were locked in anticipation. The house lights dimmed and twin screens on either side of the stage glowed like the panels of a lantern. They bore titles, projected in French, Arabic and English. 'Man of the Mountain,' Patrick read aloud.

'Name of opera,' hissed Mr Lee. 'Dialogue appears as it is sung. Guests in audience can understand as story unfolds.'

It was an ingenious device, but hardly necessary, Patrick decided a while later. The plot was basic. Rugged partisan

31

hero, suffering under the yoke of Japanese oppressors, risked the contempt of friends and family by posing as a collaborator, while secretly working for the resistance. There was a doll-like heroine who sung in a shrill soprano. There was a torture scene in which the hero was tied to a stake and flogged. There were off-stage explosions as a troop train was ambushed and there was a glorious finale in which dryads dressed in khaki danced around the lovers while behind them a mountain top pierced the billows of dry ice and a red star shone over all. There had been no interval and his bladder was bursting. 'Wonderful,' he said. 'Unforgettable.'

Mr Kim looked at him keenly. 'Not too long?'

'Not a bit,' said Patrick. He had managed to doze through the second and third acts, but no one had noticed. In fact he realized yet again that apart from the official party no one seemed to notice him at all. As he made his way to the foyer the audience parted like fish, responding to a pressure wave. 'Thank you,' he said, as they stepped aside. 'Thank you,' he said more loudly. No one replied. In the men's room it was the same. The stalls cleared as Patrick advanced. Only Mr Lee kept him company, whistling softly between his teeth and staring at the graffiti-free walls.

'Why don't they answer me?' asked Patrick.

Mr Lee tugged at his zip. 'They are not used to visitors.'

'Are they forbidden to speak? Is it government policy?'

'Of course not.'

'I just want to say hello to someone.'

'That can be arranged.'

'Not like that,' said Patrick. 'Nothing official.' He imagined some poor sod, dragged in from the street and told to make conversation. It would be like a royal garden party, with the agenda set in advance and security men at everyone's elbow. 'I just felt like being sociable,' he said. 'You don't have to make a meal of it.'

'A meal? What kind of meal?'

Patrick sighed. 'It's just an expression. I mean you don't have to put yourself out.'

'Out?' said Mr Lee. He took a notebook from his inside pocket and waited, pencil in hand. As he sought to explain,

Patrick thought briefly of Jack Blazer. He began to see why he had taught Mr Lee to say 'bollocks'.

The following day he knew for sure. 'The little bugger never stops asking questions,' said Jack Blazer. 'It's like I was running a quiz. What do I mean by "upsadaisy"? If I say "right you are" is it like "We'll be all right on the night"? Why isn't "balls-up" in the OED? He never lets up. He wants to be teacher's pet. I just thought I'd make him sweat a bit for his marks. I never could stand a smart arse.'

'He thinks you made him look ridiculous,' said Patrick.

'Too bloody bad,' said Jack Blazer. 'He'll get over it.' He pushed a large, oval tin across the table. 'Have a biscuit,' he said. 'Chocolate Chip Cookies. I get them through Beijing. And toothpaste. And whisky.' He pointed to the bottle. 'Care for a drop now? The sun's over the yard-arm.'

Patrick shook his head. The ginseng and champagne that he had drunk the previous night still seethed in his bloodstream. In an hour's time a whisky would be very nice. But work came first. 'I'm supposed to ask you about the panda,' he said. 'Mr Kim said you were the man to talk to.'

'Too bloody right,' said Blazer. 'There's no point in talking to that lot. They couldn't organize a bunk-up in a brothel. Get Blazer to do it. That's what I'm here for.' He peered through the window. 'That's a nice bit of crackling you brought with you. Does she belong to anybody?'

'Not to me,' said Patrick. Below them the garden fell away to the shore of a lake. It was mid-afternoon and the sun was setting behind a row of pines. By the water's edge there was what looked like a shrine and he could see Mr Lee pointing out some detail of a stone lion to Lottie, whose camera, he noted, was still in the car. 'No pictures,' Mr Lee advised them. 'It has not yet been arranged.'

'But I spoke to Mr Kim,' said Lottie. 'He promised.'

The first big smile of the day appeared on cue. 'Very soon,' said Mr Lee. 'All the pictures you want.'

But not here, thought Patrick. Jack Blazer had his own villa in what Mr Lee called the Writer's Village. At a guess it had fourteen or fifteen rooms and staff to run it. Already he had seen a maid, a cleaner and a cook. Higher up the hillside there were other villas, many of them larger than Blazer's establishment. All had their own gardens, their own stand of trees. Along the shore-line he could see boat-houses and landing stages. The paths had been swept clear of snow. It was very different from the tower blocks they had passed on their way out of Pyongyang. The huddled masses did not live here. In a classless society this was a haven for the top brass. He could understand why Mr Kim was reluctant to promote it worldwide.

'She'll be getting chilly out there,' said Blazer. 'Does she know enough to come in from the cold?'

'I should imagine so.'

'Pretty girl,' said Blazer. 'You don't see many like her in these parts. She even smells different.' He stroked his nose reminiscently. 'Women here smell of cooking oil, like they've been working in a chippie. It's something in the soap. Not nice.' He polished his nose again. 'Mind you, you get over it. Needs must.'

He was short, squat and perfectly bald. Hair twirled from his ears like horns and tufts of the same colour, a pale flax, protruded from each nostril. It was as though his head had been stuffed and the excess was working its way out. He wore a blue serge uniform, buttoned at the neck, and highly polished boots. 'Army issue,' he said. 'British army. They nicked 'em when they put us in the cage. Fifty thousand pairs, they reckon. They've still got some in store. The genuine article, WD stamped. I've been wearing them for forty years. Not the same pair, mind you. I get a new issue every three years.'

Patrick studied the brilliant toe-caps. They would have passed inspection at Aldershot. 'Why did you stay?' he asked. 'Didn't you want to go home?'

'Not much point,' said Blazer. 'They had me down as a deserter. It was a bit of a cock-up really. I'd been on the loose for about a month when they picked me up. Not our lot. The other side. I made a few broadcasts. Peace in our time and all that. You know what it was like.'

Patrick shook his head. 'I was too young. It's too long ago. I was only a kid.'

'Well, I'm telling you,' said Blazer. 'I just wanted out. No more bombs. Nobody shooting at me. So I quit. And then they said I was a traitor.' He stared into the garden where Lottie and Mr Lee had turned towards the house. 'As if it mattered,' he said. 'As if anything a poor bloody squaddie said on some Mickey Mouse wireless meant a light to anybody. But I knew I'd be for it if I went home. So I stayed put. End of story.'

Lottie and Mr Lee were climbing the steps to the patio that marked the garden's end. Their breath hung about their heads like cumulus. They walked faster to reach the comfort of indoors. And the comfort was considerable. Patrick gestured around the room. 'But what about all this?' he asked. 'How did you qualify?'

'Doing this and that,' said Blazer. 'I made myself useful.'

A maid brought them tea and put logs on the fire. 'Shall I be mother?' said Blazer. He poured condensed milk into his own cup and drank noisily. 'Lottie,' he said, staring at her over the rim of the cup. 'I knew a girl named Lottie. Worked in an office at Catterick. Well developed. On the same lines as yourself.'

'Built to last,' said Lottie. She was wearing a black sweater and stretch pants. There were gold studs in her ears and an Alice band held her hair in place. 'Was she special?' she asked.

Jack Blazer nodded. 'One in a million.'

'Did you keep in touch?'

'No chance,' he said.

She covered his hand with hers. 'Never mind. You can keep in touch with me.'

It was so effortless, thought Patrick. Even when it showed, the technique was faultless. All it needed was a little speeding-up. 'When the job's done,' he said. 'When we've got the panda.'

'Don't worry about the panda,' said Blazer. He squeezed Lottie's hand and heaved himself to his feet. 'It's all laid on. Transport, equipment, personnel. All we have to do is find the bloody thing. There's people looking now. Trackers. They've been at it for weeks. They'd have been at it a lot sooner if someone had got their finger out.' He shot a venomous glance at Mr Lee. 'They think they can just order one up. Panda, One Giant. As if they were sending off a coupon.' He cocked his head suddenly. 'Do people still do that? Shop by post?'

'All the time,' said Lottie.

'Daft way of doing things,' said Blazer. 'You never get what you expect. I wrote off for a swozzle once. The gadget ventriloquists use. That and a book of instructions. How to throw your voice in five easy lessons. Put it under your tongue, they said. Amaze your friends.' He grinned at the memory. 'I swallowed the bloody thing. Two pound ten it cost me. Straight down the karzi.' He pointed at Mr Lee, whose shoes, Patrick observed, were steaming in the heat from the fire. 'That's what you need, my son. The interpreter's friend. Something to give you the gift of tongues.'

He crossed the room and threw the switch of a light-box standing in a corner. 'Here's where we're going,' he said. 'North west as far as you can see. Lots of scenery. Mountainous country, bamboo forests, giant rhododendron, very pretty in summertime, so they tell me. Advance unit in position. Signs of panda reported.'

They studied the map together. 'What signs?' asked Patrick.

'Droppings,' said Blazer. 'Pandas eat five times more than they can digest. So they never stop shitting. All of it full of bamboo.'

'How do we get there?' asked Lottie.

'Plane, helicopter, trucks.' Blazer traced the contours on the map with a stubby finger. 'Mules, most likely, at the very end.' He dug Lottie in the ribs. 'How d'you fancy it? Sleeping under canvas. Meals round the camp-fire. Looking for panda shit.'

'Wonderful,' she said.

In the glare from the light-box, the horns of hair seemed incandescent and Blazer's expression was rapt, as though he was already seeing the mountains stacked around them. 'The tracking's like it always was,' he said. 'Bloody hard through bamboo. Then it's all down to science. Anaesthetic darts and that. In the old days the locals used to kill them on spear traps, straight through the heart, no messing about.' He switched off the light-box. 'They still do,' he said. 'They don't understand about protected species. They like a go at the old *bei-shung*.'

'What's that?'

'White bear,' said Blazer. 'That's what the Chinese call it.'

The room was in semi-darkness. Flames licked the chimney back and, as they watched, the last trace of the sun, a hoop of red like a paring of orange peel, dropped below the horizon. The rush of night was instant and overwhelming. 'I could do with that whisky now,' said Patrick.

Blazer poured drinks all round. 'We'll get you kitted out tomorrow. Then we'll get a weather report.' He clinked his glass against Patrick's, then Lottie's. 'Here's to Operation Panda,' he said.

'To all of us,' said Lottie. 'Mr Lee, too.' She drew him into the circle, her arm around his waist.

Jack Blazer bowed his head. 'Right you are, petal.' He kissed her soundly on each cheek. 'Ready for the off, as the bishop said to the actress.'

As he showed them to the door a woman wearing an embroidered shift, flowers on brown silk, came from the rear of the house. She waited, with her back to the wall, and as they passed Patrick detected a distinct smell of cooking oil. 'Meet the wife,' said Blazer. They exchanged smiles, but there was no more to the introduction.

They drove into the darkness, snow-covered rocks suddenly looming in the headlights, trees baring their white flanks. 'Do you suppose they've been married long,' said Lottie.

'Thirty years,' said Mr Lee. 'Special permission was required.'

Needs must, thought Patrick. Under the blanket he reached for Lottie's hand and held it tight.

four

What he could never explain to his friends was why he needed to marry Cassandra. Most of them loathed her on sight, a reaction which, at the time, he found incomprehensible. She was a small, dark woman with pained eyes and a tremulous mouth. Her breasts were large and prominent and she had a habit of smoothing her skirt between her thighs as if to reassure herself that everything it concealed was securely in place. The first time they met was at a lunchtime party. 'Who's that?' he asked his host, an accountant named Tommy Hammond, who dealt largely with journalists warring to the death with the Inland Revenue.

'Are you interested?'

'Possibly.'

'Take care,' said Hammond. 'A dangerous lady, that one.'

'She doesn't look dangerous.'

'Two husbands down. One to go.'

'You mean she's divorced?' asked Patrick, feeling uncommonly clumsy.

'At present she is. Number three's already lined up.'

Patrick studied her across the room. She was leaning against a bookcase, glass in hand, listening to a television interviewer whose trademark was a large, spotted bow-tie which spanned his collar like a giant moth. Early in his career, Patrick recalled, his ties had been of a conventional size, but they had grown in proportion to his telly fame. He was one of Hammond's celebrity clients, not that Tommy was a scalp-hunter, but he preferred someone known to someone insignificant. It was better for business, he explained. Like followed like and a prosperous clientele meant healthy profits. Patrick, as he was frequently reminded, was meat and two veg; not one of the star attractions, but sustaining. 'I'd advise caution,' said Tommy. 'We don't want to see you getting into trouble.'

He did not listen. He waited until the interviewer addressed his monologue to someone else, then moved in. 'I've been watching you,' he said.

'I know.'

'Do you mind?'

'Why should I?'

Standing close he was aware of her scent, or rather two scents, one supplementing the other. She inclined towards him as though blown by a strong and persistent wind and instinctively he offered his arm. She seemed insubstantial. Her hair framed her face like soft, black fur and her eyes were liquid. He felt his heart actually shift within his chest and there was a lump in his throat. He swallowed hard, but it did not go away.

'Is something wrong?' she asked.

'Nothing.'

'You look strange.'

'I feel strange,' said Patrick, not daring to pause in his confession. 'I think I've fallen in love.'

She did not laugh, but moved closer. 'With me?'

'I can't be certain. It's never happened to me before. What do you think?'

She ran the tip of her tongue across her upper lip. 'It's possible.'

Even when he learned that she was joining *The Arbiter* as one of the Admiral's new pace-makers he was not deterred. The very idea of the column, he thought, was a joke. But he did not put himself to the test by studying it too closely. 'Far be it from me to rock the boat,' murmured Felix Benn, a diary editor with whom he lunched the following week, 'but do you honestly think you have anything in common?'

'Enough,' said Patrick.

'Your lifestyles are rather different.'

'So they should be.'

'She's hardly your kind of writer.'

'That doesn't matter.'

Benn drew a copy of *The Arbiter* from his pocket and opened it at the centre spread. 'What your friend writes,' he said, 'is licensed illiteracy.'

He was a fat, placid man whose acerbities were normally confined to the diary he edited, and his sharpness on what Patrick had expected to be a matter for congratulation was unexpected. 'Look before you leap,' said Benn. 'Take a good, hard look.'

The shock was considerable. Cassandra's photograph headed the page and beneath it were strewn a series of paragraphs, each enclosed in a pink, heart-shaped blob. Most of it was opinion – strident, breast-beating and contradictory. The remainder was advice – bossy, hectoring and brusque. The stance, he supposed, was feminist. But no feminist he knew would have endorsed a single sentence. One blob argued for abortion and adoption with equal vigour. Another denounced sexism, then ruled men out of any job held by women. The sentences were very short; so were the words themselves. There was a peppering of exclamation marks. Scanning the page Patrick recognized it for what it was; a sustained self-advertisement and silly beyond belief.

He gave the paper back to Benn. 'It doesn't matter,' he said. 'I'm not interested in what she writes. It's the woman I'm in love with.' By saying the words he established the fact. It was like taking an oath. There was no going back on it.

His infatuation grew. He saw clearly, but through rose-coloured glasses. Cassandra was unique. Her faults were not to be excused, only accepted. One evening she told him that she had given the fiancé-in-waiting his marching orders.

'What did he say?'

'Nothing. I told him he was redundant.'

He kissed her then and, as always, thrilled to her instant response. Her bones seemed to melt and it was as if he was wrapped in a warm and shifting layer of cling-film. The heat was palpable. Her mouth was like an oven and her breasts moulded themselves to his ribs like loaves of bread. Not loaves, he corrected himself, but barm cakes, soft, white and chewy, the manna of his childhood.

The first time they slept together he asked her to marry him. It was early morning and his entire body ached deliciously after hours of making love. The duvet was rolled back and a small pool of sweat which had gathered in his sternum spilled icily over his belly as he turned towards her. 'Did you hear what I said?' he enquired.

'Perfectly.'

'Well, then?'

'I'm thinking.'

'Think aloud,' he said.

'It's a lovely idea.'

'Wonderful!'

'But there are things to discuss.'

'Now? Such as?'

'My career,' said Cassandra. 'It's important to me.'

Patrick nodded against the pillow. 'Of course it is. Onwards and upwards.'

'That's what the Admiral thinks.'

'Does he indeed.' Patrick propped himself up on one elbow and stared at her. First light was beginning to filter through the curtains and he could just distinguish her face. It was quite calm. Her hair was barely ruffled and her hands were folded neatly on her chest.

'The Admiral sees me as an investment,' she said. 'He wants to project me on TV, doing the same sort of column. On radio too. He says I could be really Big.'

'Big?' said Patrick, with a distaste he found hard to conceal.

'Big,' she repeated. 'There's nothing wrong in being big. Don't you think I'm up to it?'

He nodded cautiously. 'It depends what you want. Do you want to be Big?' The word clung to the roof of his mouth like a toffee coated in fluff. It did not properly belong to writing, he thought. There was something tacky about it. It was part of the language of PR men or film producers trying to drum up finance. 'It's more important to be good,' he said. 'Unless you're professional, unless you earn your reputation there's no point in being big. You can be a big nothing. There's nothing easier. The Admiral's a colossal shit. That's big. But what's the point of it?'

'He's been sweet to me,' said Cassandra.

'Naturally,' said Patrick. 'You're an investment.'

There was a long silence, broken only by the sounds of early traffic. Cars droned down the wet street. A motor cycle snarled distantly. He looked at her more closely and saw tears striping her face. 'I only meant you should get your priorities right,' he said. 'I didn't mean to upset you. I'm sorry.'

'You hate what I do.'

'Of course I don't,' he lied.

'You expect me to fail.'

'Certainly not.'

'I want to be good,' said Cassandra. 'I don't want to be trivial. But I need help.'

'There'll be plenty of that.'

'From you,' she said. 'I can't do it without you.'

Later he marvelled at the precision of her timing. It was like a perfect drop-shot or the moment in a ballet when the dancer hung in mid-air as the orchestra drew breath. He could not fail to respond. It almost called for applause, but instead he gathered her in his arms and drove between her thighs as if he was aiming for some point, marked with a cross on the inside of her skull. Everything yielded. He was surrounded by flesh. He felt the urge to invade and the impulse to protect. The blood roared in his ears and he lapped her wet cheeks, drinking the salt and tasting the sweetness beneath it. 'I'll help all I can,' he promised.

They were married a month later. The wedding was held at a registry office in Chelsea and there was a reception afterwards at the Meridiana. The Admiral was not present, but he sent his regrets and a wedding gift in the shape of a large, chromium-plated wine bin, embossed with a chain and anchor and containing six magnums of champagne. 'Whatever you're about to say,' Cassandra warned him, 'don't say it's vulgar.'

Patrick noted the vintage. 'Certainly not,' he said.

Some people danced on the tables. One of them was Bill

Pascoe, a man Patrick had known years before when he was a successful television producer, but contact between them was broken when Pascoe was struck by evangelical lightning while filming a rally at the Albert Hall and, born again, his career went into a decline. 'Has he still got God?' he asked.

'I doubt it,' said Cassandra. 'He's working for the Admiral.'

'As what?'

'He's going to produce me.'

'Doing what?'

'You know,' said Cassandra. 'He's going to coach me for TV. How to speak. How to project.'

'I know what you mean,' said Patrick. 'How to be Big.'

It was an exchange he thought of daily at the *Arbiter* office. Pascoe's magic had worked and Cassandra loomed large on TV panels and talk shows. Sometimes he dreamed of her as a Talking Head, disembodied, but endlessly and vehemently spouting opinion which gushed like rain-water from a gargoyle. Life-sized portraits of Cassandra flanked *The Arbiter*'s reception desk. When he first saw them Patrick's back went into spasm. Since then he had learned to walk past the blow-ups with his eyes closed.

It was a necessary precaution. His back was a constant problem and he treated it with respect. A specialist had told him, and X-rays confirmed the diagnosis, that two discs in his lower vertebrae showed signs of degeneration. 'Like brake pads that are wearing out,' he explained, as though expecting Patrick to take comfort from the homely analogy. But Patrick was not reassured. He took care in bending. All sports, except swimming, were out of the question and sex could be a painful experience. With Cassandra he had been prepared to take the risk. But now, with the shopping list in mind, it was yet another hazard to consider. He viewed potential partners like a boxer sizing up an opponent. How did she weigh in? Was she instantly aggressive or a counter-puncher? How many rounds would she go before the final bell?

It was not the stuff of romance, he thought. Nor was the drill he was compelled to practise to guard against the sudden locking of his spine. He slept on a hard mattress. He took care

43

to lift no heavy weights. He chose chairs with the minimum of padding. Six months earlier the specialist had prescribed hydro-therapy and this was his morning to join the class at the hospital.

Traffic was light as he drove through south London and he found a parking place without difficulty. He counted five taxis in the car park, one more than the previous week. Taxi drivers, he had been told, were more prone to back trouble than any other social group. It was why they were so evil-tempered, he supposed.

The changing room smelled of Lysol and in one corner he discovered a jock-strap, stained at the crotch and ripped at the seams. It was extraordinary what people left behind. Once he had found a packed lunch and a prayer book. No one had ever claimed them. The abandoned lunch he could understand, but the prayer book still kept him awake at night. Mysterious sounds boomed through the closed door, as though somewhere nearby engines were being assembled or torn apart. It was like being in an aircraft factory or a submarine pen. He stepped into a pair of trunks and headed for the pool.

A thin layer of steam hung over the surface. In the shallow end stood Nurse Pavey, whose costume shone with team and proficiency badges. She had short, blonde hair and thighs with which, thought Patrick, she could have strangled a shark. Bobbing around her, the water up to their chins, were a dozen or more members of the class. The taxi drivers formed their own team. There was also a dressmaker from Kingston, Jamaica, named Dolly Priest, whose skin was the colour of wholemeal toast, and a furrier named Drummond. They were all regulars. On the side of the pool several old ladies sat in wheelchairs. One by one they were helped into a crane with a bucket seat and ladled gently into the water.

'Someone help Mrs Fleming,' said Nurse Pavey and Patrick did as he was asked. Mrs Fleming floated into his arms and he towed her to the middle of the pool. Her costume was patterned with red roses and she wore a pair of blue plastic water wings.

'Thanks very much, dear,' she said. 'We're going to break the record today.'

'Across the Channel and back?'

'All the way,' she said. 'Your money's safe on me.'

It was like being back at school, he thought. But there were important differences. They were there, as Nurse Pavey reminded them, to work. Shoulder-deep, they stood with their arms outstretched and rotated their bodies, first to the left, then to the right. The exercise changed and he hooked his feet under the rail at the side of the pool while he paddled with his hands. It was restful, but it was also boring. He closed his eyes and let his mind drift. Lately he had been reading Lonely Hearts advertisements. Just for a laugh, he told himself, but some of the entries had a forlorn poetry which was hard to forget: HEDONIST WITH MONEY TO BURN REQUIRES INCENDIARY BLONDE; AFRICAN QUEEN, TIRED OF CRUISING, WANTS TO DROP ANCHOR; SOLITARY BUNNY GIRL OFFERS KEY TO HUTCH. The competition was fierce, he thought. The world was full of lonely people.

He had tried to find out what sort of response the advertisements attracted. 'Why?' asked Felix Benn. 'Are you thinking of putting one in?'

'Don't be absurd.'

'You could do worse,' said Benn. 'From what I hear it's like a knocking shop. Chap I knew wound up with two sisters. Right goers, the pair of them. First one, then the other.'

'They took turns?'

'Both at once,' said Benn. 'He was absolutely knackered.'

And serve him right, thought Patrick. His own approach, if he decided to make it, would be cautious, with suitable provisos. It should sound inviting, but restrained. He ran through several drafts and imagined the final version on the page:

DIVORCED, METROPOLITAN MALE, PERSONABLE 43, SEEKS UNATTACHED FEMALE FOR EMOTIONAL ADVENTURE. COMPANIONSHIP AND CONVERSATION GUARANTEED. CUDDLES BY MUTUAL AGREEMENT.

He was not happy with the final sentence, but the point had to be made. He was not looking for a platonic friendship. In a civilized way he was laying his cards on the table. The tone was light-hearted, but sincere. He had not lied about his age and it was not too much of an exaggeration to call himself personable. It was a neutral sort of word, but it implied self-confidence, a man-of-the-world assurance, which fell decently short of swagger. He drew breath and stared up through six inches of water. He unhooked his toes and surfaced. The entire class was watching him.

'Thought we'd lost you then,' said Mrs Fleming.

'Anything good down there?' asked Dolly Priest.

He followed her gaze and hitched up his trunks. His belly hung over the buckle and he sucked it in. He thought of Dolly reading his advertisement and hastily revised it. He needed to lose at least a stone before he could call himself personable.

'What I don't understand is why you're still moping,' said Joan Trimble. 'After all, it was never an idyll. You should simply resolve to do better.'

Patrick accepted another glass of whisky and nodded silently. His sister meant well, but her understanding of the situation was short on a few points. It did not involve her, but she was older than him by two years and her seniority, she felt, gave her the right to offer advice, regardless of the facts. She lived with her husband Richard in a bungalow at Epsom. Patrick remembered it from his childhood as a market town with distinctly raffish associations. It was not just its tradition of racing. Once, it had been a spa, visited by King Charles and Nell Gwynn and something of its raffish past still lingered in the saloon bars and snugs where purple-faced men bought drinks for smart ladies with sharp accents.

Nell was a tart, Joan informed him. The town had come a long way since then and its past was best forgotten. It was the principle on which she ran her life. Bury or burn; hoarding memories was a waste of time. She was tall and thin, with a high, certain voice and a way of cocking her head when she delivered judgement, as if daring the listener to disagree.

Richard was a psychiatrist, a short, secretive man with a flushed face and a strap of black hair which hugged his skull like a Band-Aid. In conversation he kept his voice low and his face averted. It was as though he was awaiting an invitation to reveal his true expression, his uncensored thoughts. That would be his flowering, his coming out of the professional closet. But the moment was forever deferred. Richard expressed himself in smiles and hints and silences. He had the reputation of being a deep thinker.

'Hand the nuts round,' ordered Joan. 'And see to the drinks. People here are dying of thirst.'

Sometimes, thought Patrick, his sister behaved as though the southern counties were in the grip of famine or drought, an emergency of which only she was aware. He circulated the nuts and stood by the decanters. There were three other guests: Molly and John Frobisher, who published medical text books, and Pauline Treat, whose husband had died the previous year. The Frobishers had driven her down from London, but Patrick was expected to drive her back.

'You're almost neighbours,' said Joan, shortly before they arrived. 'I knew you wouldn't mind.'

'You're not matchmaking, are you?'

'What if I am. There are times when you need a good push.'

He decided not to tell her about the shopping list. Most likely Joan would approve of his initiative, but not his requirements. He offered Pauline Treat the dish of nuts, but she shook her head. Her dead husband had been a colleague of Richard's, and Pauline, he now remembered, had conducted art classes in the hospital where they both worked. She had long, fair hair parted in the centre and her teeth were slightly rabbity.

'I've told him to stop moping,' said Joan. 'None of us are getting any younger. Including Patrick.'

'Do you put up with this?' asked Pauline.

He refilled her glass with sherry. 'Big sisters think they know best.'

'It's always the way,' said John Frobisher. 'When are we going to eat?'

He was a bluff, cheerful man whose grey, double-breasted suit swooped down over a bulging waistline. The last time they met he had suggested to Patrick that he wrote a book about his

47

back troubles. 'Great demand for it,' he said. 'Could have a best-seller there.'

'We need a happy ending.'

'Make it happen,' said Frobisher. 'Nothing to stop you if the spirit is willing.'

The man was a fool, thought Patrick, but he meant well. In fact, he realized, since he and Cassandra had parted, the well-wishers in his life had multiplied like amoebae dividing under a microscope. They surrounded him in genial clusters, urging him to make a fresh start, telling him to have a nice day. They believed in good intentions and simple solutions. By failing to respond he felt he was letting them down.

'Dinner will be in five minutes,' said Joan. 'Does anyone want to wash their hands.'

'Actually,' said Frobisher. 'I could do with a pee.'

His wife slapped his wrist. 'Language!'

It was a game they played: jolly John and reproving Molly. Perhaps their marriage was made in heaven, thought Patrick, but he did not want to borrow the blueprint.

They ate in the kitchen, a long, low room which led out to the garden. At one time the house had been a forge and heavy beams spanned the ceiling. In the gathering dusk a blur of midges hung over the bird bath and a doleful Triton dispensed water from a plastic conch. As they drank their soup Pauline's teeth chimed against the spoon. It was something, supposed Patrick, which happened all the time. He tried to imagine what it would be like to kiss her and realized that he was staring too closely.

'I was admiring your necklace,' he said.

'New, isn't it?' said Joan.

'Newish.' She fingered the rope of blue beads and held them out for inspection.

'Very handsome,' said Patrick. He would have to start giving presents again, he thought. It was one of the customs of courtship which he would have to re-learn. At forty-three, he was an old dog picking up on old tricks. Someone like Pauline could remind him of what was required.

Richard carved the duck and circulated the plates. 'One of our own,' he said.

'Your own what?'

'Duck,' said Joan. 'He died for the honour of the company.'

'Hand-reared,' said Richard. 'We know everything he ate, from first to last.'

Patrick studied the slices of breast that lay before him. 'And when was that? The last hearty meal, I mean.'

'Yesterday. He had a very good life.'

'I can imagine.'

'Did he have a name?' asked Pauline. 'Did he come when you called?'

Richard shook his head. 'They're not pets,' he said severely. 'We don't think of them as individuals. That wouldn't be right. They're food for the table. We treat them well and we kill them humanely.' He laid down the carving knife and fork as though he was shipping oars. God had spoken, thought Patrick. He wondered if all psychiatrists were so insufferably wise. The previous month Richard had asked if he had considered entering group therapy.

'What on earth for?'

'Joan says you're depressed. It might help.'

'Absolutely not.' In his imagination a home movie unreeled, busy with jump cuts, interrupted by hands jammed over the lens, in which a group of intense and unhappy people argued with each other about the meaning of life. He did not know whether the vision was true, but it was not the therapy he had in mind.

'Where exactly do you live?' he asked Pauline.

'Pimlico. Just behind the Tate.'

'I told you,' said Joan. 'She's almost a neighbour.' Their eyes met across the table and she winked, so broadly, thought Patrick, that it was like a clap of hands. He reached for the wine, then changed his mind. He was driving Pauline home and he needed a clear head.

It was a fine night and the roads were empty. Inside the car he smelled her perfume and the roses ('the last of summer') which Joan had cut just before they left. 'They were kind to me when my husband died,' she told him.

'They've been kind to me since Cassandra walked out.' The service had been returned, he thought. He waited for the game to proceed.

Neither of them spoke for several minutes until Patrick

swerved to avoid a cat which trotted in front of them, its eyes blazing green in the headlights. 'Are you still on your own?' asked Pauline.

'So far,' he said. 'I live in hope.'

They crossed the river and turned down a street of houses whose white-painted doors were mirrored in the carriage lights mounted on either side. 'On the corner,' she said. 'The one with the light on upstairs.'

'Anti-burglar?'

'The man I live with,' said Pauline. 'He's a doctor at Guy's.'

Patrick counted to three. 'I see,' he said. He applied the brakes but kept the motor running. 'Joan didn't tell me about him.'

'Joan doesn't know. It has nothing to do with her.'

'Or me.' He got out of the car and opened her door.

'I'm really sorry,' she said.

'There's nothing to be sorry about.'

'A couple of months ago it might have been different,' said Pauline. She leaned forward and kissed him. 'Don't give up,' she said. 'Things are bound to get better.'

'Of course they are.'

She paused at the door. 'Would you like to come in?'

'I think not.' He took the key from her hand and turned it in the lock. The breath of the house welled out to meet them and Patrick identified tobacco smoke, the ghost of coffee, floor polish and the tang of embrocation. They were all clues to a life in which he was to have no part. He felt a keen regret as she kissed him again, more briefly than before, and closed the door behind her.

He was inside his own flat ten minutes later. Above him he heard the clatter of Amos Bennet's typewriter, but he decided against paying him a visit. Bennet always quizzed him on his evening's activities. He did not look forward to describing how he had been turned down by a caring woman.

five

The menu in the hotel restaurant was not fit for breakfast reading, Patrick decided. At 7.30 in the morning he did not wish to be reminded of Korean cuisine, an anthology, so far as he could see, of a thousand ways in which to prepare offal. He scanned the list and shuddered. 'Squashed meat fried on a spit.' 'Fried pig ankles.' 'Rolled pig head.' None of them would do. He passed over 'Flavoured mad apple', and 'Fried tough duck', and arrived, with some relief, at 'Omelette with egg'. The tautology was unimportant, unless (his stomach heaved at the thought) the egg was another way of describing some vile animal spawn, whose origins defied translation. But it seemed unlikely. This was where visitors to the capital began their day. It was in everyone's interest that they were allowed to make a good beginning.

Already the restaurant was half full and most of the diners, he noticed, were men. There was a German table to his left, a French party to his right. The previous day Mr Lee had pointed out a Japanese delegation and a group from Iraq. 'Very important people,' he said. 'Good customers.'

'What are they buying?'

Mr Lee shrugged gently. 'They admire our weaponry.'

Patrick maintained a poker face. He remembered reading somewhere that every Scud missile launched in the Gulf had been made in North Korea. It was not his concern. The French peddled Exocets. The British sold tanks. Whatever the consequences, business was business. What amazed him was that it could be conducted here, where decisions were endlessly deferred, where deals were forever pending. He wondered what strings the Admiral had pulled to guarantee delivery of his newsprint. There was no doubt that he would have enjoyed the haggling. He was at home with war-lords.

Jack Blazer had promised to be at the hotel by nine. There was time enough, thought Patrick, for him to discuss the day's programme with Lottie before he arrived. It appeared that they were in Blazer's hands, while he, presumably, was acting on the orders of Mr Kim. Lottie was impatient to go to work. But nothing here was straightforward. There were rules to be observed, even by the Admiral's bimbo. Patrick braced himself to lay down the law.

Heads turned as she entered the restaurant. She was wearing an outfit similar to the one she had worn the day before, but this morning the stretch pants were scarlet, the sweater was white and the boots were studded with rhinestones. At a rodeo in Texas she would have passed unnoticed. On a grey day in Pyongyang she set the room alight.

'God,' she said, 'I'm starving.'

Patrick passed her the menu. 'I'm having the omelette.'

She nodded and he breathed in flowers and citrus, the fragrance of toilet water. 'And bacon,' she said. 'And sausages. And toast and marmalade.'

'They're not listed.'

'They'll have them,' said Lottie. 'They always do.'

He marvelled at her confidence. She was like the first explorer setting foot in Africa or Cathay, positive that the natives spoke English. He waited for her to be corrected, but the message was received and understood.

The waitress, slab-faced and sullen when he had tried to attract her attention, smiled and scribbled on her pad. 'Tea? Coffee?'

'Coffee,' said Lottie. 'Decaff if you have it.'

'The same for me,' said Patrick.

The waitress ignored him and pointed to Lottie's boots. 'Pretty,' she said.

Lottie extended one leg as if she was executing a high kick. 'Neiman Marcus. Bargain basement.'

'She won't understand,' said Patrick.

Both women stared him down and he shook out his table napkin and spread it on his lap. He knew instantly that he had said the wrong thing.

'What's to understand?' said Lottie. 'She likes the boots. That's simple enough.'

'She could never afford them.'

Lottie sighed. 'That's not the point. She liked to look.'

'She's not the only one.'

All around them diners were staring. Lottie waved to them and pointed her toe at the ceiling. One of the Germans waved back. The Japanese delegation bowed. It was cabaret time, thought Patrick, and they were the floor show.

'Don't be so miserable,' said Lottie. 'People want to be cheered up. Don't you want to be cheered up?'

'We've got a job to do.'

'So?'

'This isn't how to do it.'

'Wrong.' She spread her hands and he noticed that she wore no rings. 'The better you make people feel, the more help you're likely to get. Act like you expect people to go along with you and they probably will. Look at old Kim. He let me take the wedding picture.'

'That's what we have to discuss,' said Patrick. 'You're pushing too hard.' The room, he noticed, was beginning to subside. People were no longer staring, but there was a new note to their conversations, a lighter strain, as though a tenor had joined in the harmony. It was the sound of pleasure, he decided, or excitement, or anticipation. They were wondering what she was likely to do next.

'What we have to do is win their confidence,' he said. 'You can't go around snapping at will. We have to show them we're not trying to snoop.'

'Aren't we? Not just a little bit?'

'Certainly not,' said Patrick. 'That's not why we're here. The panda's the priority. Anything else is a bonus. We have to fit in with the arrangements.'

He heard his own words as if a tape was being played

back to him and he felt a rush of self-disgust. How pathetic he sounded. He could guess what she was thinking. The old fart had spoken. 'I don't mean you have to shut up shop,' he said. 'Just show willing.'

She nodded slowly. 'Buy the package. Let them hand us everything on a plate. Is that how you operate?'

'Of course it isn't.'

'That's not what I'm paid to do.'

'Really?' he said. 'And what, precisely, *are* you paid to do?'

'Photograph what's there,' said Lottie. 'Look for the story.'

'The panda's the story.'

'Part of the story. The biggest part, if you like. But there's this and this.' She pointed to the rhinestones on her boot and the waitresses ferrying plates between the tables. 'No one knows what it's like here. Nobody knows what people think. You can't tell me that's not interesting.'

'I didn't say that.'

'I heard what you said.'

He realized that his fists were clenched and he forced the fingers open like rusty springs. 'Lower your voice,' he said. 'Eat your breakfast.' It was absurd, he thought. He had not flown half way round the world to be instructed on the niceties of his job by someone half his age. Correction: nearly half his age. It was not the role he had imagined for himself or for Lottie. Bimbos did not sound off on journalistic principles. Senior columnists did not take reprimands lightly. No doubt she knew about his fading reputation. The glory days of Lamb's Tales were long gone. But he was still the leader of the delegation. Mr Lee had said so. He was still in charge.

Lottie sliced into her omelette and he envied her appetite. She drenched her bacon in ketchup and swabbed it around the plate. 'Rough night, was it?'

'Not good.'

'I can sleep on a clothes-line,' she said. 'Instant oblivion.'

'Lucky you.' They were mending fences and he was tempted to tell her about the dream. But it was too raw, too personal, too revealing. As always, it had been about Cassandra, starring in that favourite of all re-runs, The Worst Fuck in the World. He had learned to abbreviate the title. In his memory it was now catalogued simply as 'WF', like the initials on a pre-select button. Punching it by mistake was all too easy. He pushed his plate away. His throat felt as though it had been scraped raw.

'Do you take sleepers?' she asked.

'Do I take what?'

'Sleepers. Tranquillizers. Something to put you down.'

'Certainly not.' His doctor had prescribed a course of anti-depressants, but while they had helped him to sleep, they had also intensified the dreams, giving each one the definition of a new print with the images freshly minted, a movie groomed for infinity. 'They give me a hangover,' he said. 'I've never been good with pills.'

Sunlight lanced through the east-facing window and fell like a sash of gold across Lottie's breast. She looked like a winner, he thought, Miss Integrity, teamed for a short season with Mr Glum. He tried to smile and imagined that the muscles of his face actually creaked. 'I get better as the day wears on,' he told her.

'Let's hope so.'

It was well meant, he supposed, but it could have been said a little less brusquely. He saw Jack Blazer and Mr Lee approaching their table and prepared to order more coffee. Lottie jumped up to greet them and he changed his mind. As leader of the delegation he had been granted a certain status, but in the business of winning friends and influencing people he had everything to learn.

They drove to a warehouse on the outskirts of the city, speeding through streets on which there was little traffic and few people. 'Where is everyone?' asked Lottie.

Mr Lee bared his teeth in the first major smile of the day. 'At home. At work.'

'But isn't this the rush hour?'

'No rush hour here. No traffic problem.'

'Never?'

'Not since city was rebuilt. Everything taken care of.' He indicated rank after rank of cinder-grey tower blocks.

'Americans bombed city flat. Everything made new. No congestion. Plenty of room.'

Between the tower blocks and public buildings, crested with copper and clad in marble, Patrick glimpsed avenues and plazas, wonderfully clean and filled with nothing but sunlight. Most of them contained a statue. The pose varied; so, occasionally, did the uniform. But they were all of the same man. The face was plump, with butter-smooth jowls. A bracelet of fat bulged over the collar of the jacket. Patrick stared into the stone eyes of the Great Leader and hastily looked away. It was like being in ancient Rome, he thought, but a Rome in which the gods, celebrated on every street corner, had renounced their variety and now came out of a common mould. Their divinity was still intact, but somehow it had been homogenized.

They were no longer separate deities, responsible for the management of wars and music and medicine. Their offices had been amalgamated, their assets stripped. All prayers were addressed to the same being. All praise was due to the same benefactor.

'It's like the song says,' said Jack Blazer. 'Somebody loves me.' He hummed a few bars and drummed his fingers on Lottie's knee.

'How many are there?' Patrick asked.

'Who knows?' Blazer let his hand lie still like a dog taking its rest. 'Statues are a growth industry in these parts. They sprout up overnight. Ask Mr Lee. He's very keen on statues.'

Mr Lee nodded briskly. 'How the people say thank you. Mark of respect.'

Blazer hummed the melody again. 'See what I mean?'

In a square by the river they saw children playing handball. There were four of them, zipped into quilted jump suits, clumsy as moon-walkers as they chased the ball. 'Can we stop for a minute,' said Lottie.

'One minute only,' said Mr Lee. 'No pictures.' He tapped the driver on his shoulder and the car slid to a halt.

Lottie scrambled out and stood quite still. She was like a bird-watcher, thought Patrick, careful not to make any sudden movement which would alarm her quarry. Her camera was slung about her neck, but she kept her hands in her pockets. The ball bounced at her feet and she threw it back. 'Catch,' she said. The children froze in their tracks and the ball rolled past them. Lottie clapped her hands. 'Throw it to me,' she said. She jumped up and down and the rhinestones on her boots caught the sunlight. One of the children ran after the ball and held on to it. 'To me,' said Lottie, but the tableau remained in place. She reached into her pocket and took out a picture book. When she flipped the pages with her thumb the pictures moved. A cockerel danced with a duck, a bear shinned up and down a pole. 'Come and see,' she said.

Mr Lee reached for the door handle, but Blazer shook his head. 'Give her a chance.'

The children inched forward and the picture show went on. Four rapt faces peered over Lottie's shoulder and Patrick smiled to himself. It was a pleasure to watch a professional at work. He felt a surge of confidence, all the more pleasurable because it was unexpected. The bimbo knew her job: how to establish contact, how to advance a photo opportunity. What was more, she had taken his advice. She was not pushing too hard. Even Mr Lee had relaxed. He opened the car door and crooked his index finger. 'Time to go,' he said.

She came obediently and squashed herself between Blazer and Patrick. 'Room for a little one.'

'Not too little,' said Blazer, squeezing her knee. 'Just enough to go round.' He was wearing a fur hat and, beneath it, the hair boiled from his ears like candy floss. Her flesh dimpled beneath his fingers, but she did not pull away. Did this happen all the time? Patrick wondered. Was this what was meant by sexual harassment? He edged into the corner to make more room and as she turned to wave through the rear window she fell into his lap. His head was jammed between her breasts and he heard her stomach gurgle as she heaved herself upright.

'Sorry,' she said.

'Lucky old you,' said Blazer. 'That's how I met that girl in Catterick. Sharing a taxi with some mates and we had to dodge a bread van. She was with some other bloke, but she wound up with me.' He patted his hat into shape and wedged it over his ears. 'Seize the opportunity. That's what I always say.' He turned to Lottie. 'How about you?'

'That's what I say too.'

The warehouse was painted ochre and black and, belatedly, Patrick saw that the pattern of blobs and amoebic swirls which streaked the walls was intended as camouflage. The building was surrounded by a steel fence, hung with high voltage signs. Armed sentries manned the gate and four watch towers, spindly as garden furniture, complete with searchlights and more guards, marked the perimeter. In front of the fence there was a ditch crammed with razor wire. The Admiral would have approved, he thought. It was just like home.

Mr Lee ducked out of the car. 'I have to show passes,' he said.

They watched him enter the guard room and Patrick prepared himself for a long wait. 'Is this a high security place?' he asked Blazer.

'Not very.'

'Why all the bits and pieces?'

Blazer twirled a sprig of nose hair between his finger and thumb. 'If you think you're going to be invaded you take precautions,' he said. 'It's only natural. Then it becomes a habit. It's like paranoia. Sometimes it makes sense, sometimes not. But why take a chance? There's good stuff in there – blankets, uniforms, electrical gear. They want to keep it safe.'

'Who from?' asked Lottie.

'Anyone who wants it.' He wiped his hands on a clean, white handkerchief. 'Everyone.'

'Looters?'

'Criminal elements I think they're called. Don't bring it up with old Lee. He'd have a fit.'

They watched him emerge from the guard room and beckon them forward. He was more than an interpreter, Patrick realized, and he wondered why it had taken him so long to hit on the truth.

'He's a minder,' he said. He surprised himself. He had not meant to speak, but the words had tumbled out as though they had been pressed against a door which had burst open.

'The penny dropped,' said Blazer.

'Eventually.'

'Don't let it get you down.' He grinned widely and let Mr Lee back into the car. 'Are we all set then? All Sir Garnet?'

'Sir Garnet?' Mr Lee looked wildly from face to face.

'Sir Garnet Wolseley,' said Patrick. 'Victorian soldier sent to relieve General Gordon at the siege of Khartoum. It means that everything's under control.' Except that Gordon was dead by the time the relief column had arrived.

Mr Lee fished a notebook from his pocket and flattened it on his lap. 'Repeat please.' He wrote down names as the car jogged over the checkpoint.

'How did you know that?' asked Lottie.

'I must have read it somewhere.'

'I'm impressed.'

'Thank you.' It had come to something, thought Patrick, when he could only win points for his recall of trivia. 'I think I saw it on a matchbox,' he said.

They drove into the warehouse and the doors rolled shut behind them. There were several floors, all brightly lit and crevassed by service lifts, with catwalks linking section to section. Cameras craned over every aisle and there were television screens on each wall. On the nearest one Patrick saw himself standing in miniature. When he raised his hand the black and white image returned his salute. There was a strong smell of wool and leather and although in the recesses of the building he was aware of figures lifting bales and stacking trolleys, there was no sound. It was like being inside a huge box stuffed with fabric. The insulation was total. Even their voices were absorbed.

'I've got a little list,' said Blazer. 'Everything from knickers to willy warmers. We don't want you catching cold.' He led them to a table on which there were three separate piles of clothing. 'One for each of you,' he said. 'Madam at the end. Check them out while I read off the items. Try them for size if you like. Cubicles behind you.' He brandished a clipboard and clicked his ball-point. 'Right you are,' he said. 'Underwear, personnel, for the use of.'

The quality, thought Patrick, was surprising, from silk long-johns to shirts of fine merino. There were ski-suits, zippered from neck to crotch; gloves within gloves; a balaclava which encased him like a tea cosy. Everything seemed to fit. He had never enjoyed choosing clothes. Cassandra's insistence that he should be measured for a new suit had provoked one of their first quarrels. But this made shopping easy. For the first time since he had arrived he felt a throb of confidence. If everything was going to be so straightforward his worries were needless. It was, he recognized, the full PR treatment; the facility trip, with every perk provided. Unlikely as it seemed, he was back in the old routine. Instead of a film company picking up the tab, it was a government that was doing the necessary. Instead of a publisher, or a promoter, or a fashion house planning the day's events, the timetable was devised by Jack Blazer.

Freebies, he told himself, were the same the world over. They were nothing to be ashamed of. Veterans of Fleet Street – redundant now and forgotten with their by-lines – had told him of a time when free-loading was forbidden by any paper of repute. Beaverbrook, in particular, had made it a house rule that all tickets, all meals were to be paid for. The reporter, or rather the paper that employed him, was responsible for his own bills. It must have been a golden age, thought Patrick, measuring a fur-collared greatcoat against his chest. Its heroes mourned its passing.

'Now we choose boots,' announced Jack Blazer. 'Boots can't be hurried. Boots are what you die in. You've got to get them right.'

His own, Patrick observed, were dazzling. This warehouse, he supposed, was where the fifty thousand pairs seized from the British army were stored. In fact, if the kit with which they had been issued was anything to go by, several nations – or the armies of several nations – were represented here. The shirts were American, the ski-suits German and the long-johns French. The greatcoats were unmistakably Chinese. On their way through Beijing he had seen them being worn by a party of Chinese army officers at the airport. They were just the thing to keep out the chill of a Korean winter. He could see why looters would find them desirable.

'What we look for in a boot is support,' intoned Blazer. 'Support for the ankle, support for the foot and support for the toes. And we need to think about the toes. We don't want the poor little buggers squashed. We have to give them room to breathe.' He pointed an accusing finger at Mr Lee who was still wearing the shoes he had worn to meet them from the plane. They looked in even worse shape than they had done then. The toe-cap of one was cockled; the instep of the other was torn.

'Those little dogs that you have in there are talking to me,' said Blazer. 'And what they are saying is that they're in pain. How can you treat me like this? What have we done to deserve it?' He sprang to attention, turned smartly to the right and marched six steps before coming to an explosive halt. 'Left turn!' he bawled and obeyed his own command. 'You couldn't do that,' he said. 'Your dogs couldn't stand the strain. God knows what they'd do on a proper march.' He stood himself at ease and rocked on his heels. 'Good boots are the start of good soldiering. You take a tip from me. Look after your dogs and they'll look after you.'

Lottie put up her hand. 'Where does the marching come in?'

'A figure of speech,' said Blazer. 'Not so much of your left-right, left-right, but plenty of your up hill, down dale. More work for the old pins than you're used to.' He rubbed his hands together as though trying to ignite a spark. 'I thought you were looking forward to it. Plenty of fresh air. Lots of exercise.'

'We can't wait,' said Patrick. 'What about the boots?'

Blazer offered them a selection. An entire table-top was covered with footwear of every style and size. It was hard to imagine how it had been assembled. Some of it was military, some was high fashion. It was as though several museums and boutiques had been plundered and the contents flung together.

He rejected jackboots and boots worn by paratroopers ('They come too far up the calf'). He coaxed Lottie away from Italian boots made of soft kid and Dutch boots with squared-off toes. He allowed Mr Lee to lust briefly over a pair of Chelsea boots – elastic-sided, the colour of nutmeg – before producing what Patrick knew he had meant them to wear from the start. 'Fell boots,' he said. 'Light on the feet. Perfect for the terrain.' The soles were ridged. The ankles were padded. The laces hooked snugly over metal tags. 'Take my word for it,' said Jack Blazer. 'These are the beauties you're looking for. These are the dog's best friend.'

'So why don't you wear them?' asked Lottie.

Blazer studied his toe-caps. 'Too old to change.'

It was not true, thought Patrick. It was not age or even habit which kept Blazer faithful to his army issue. It was the memories they evoked. Boots, he had declared, are what you die in. No doubt it was British army bullshit, but it reminded Blazer who he was and what he had been.

The fell boots, though, were all that he had promised. He tied the laces and felt the mountains melt. The kitting-out was complete.

'Are we all fit?' asked Mr Lee.

'Are we what?'

'Fit? Present and correct. Is that the expression?'

'Indeed it is,' said Blazer. 'And what else?' He lifted one finger as if teaching a dog to beg.

'All Sir Garnet,' said Mr Lee.

'Good boy,' said Blazer and patted his head.

It was after lunch that Lottie went missing. 'I'm beat,' she said. 'I'm going to take a nap.' She yawned extravagantly and stretched her arms as if she was trying to haul something down from the ceiling.

Blazer sucked his teeth. 'Good idea. You toddle off. We'll give you a shout later.'

Since leaving the warehouse he had said very little. He was like an actor, thought Patrick, resting between performances. Kitting them out was an act which he had clearly enjoyed, but this was the interval. It was the time to ask questions. 'I've got some duty-free in my room,' he said. 'How about it?'

They climbed the staircase, taking care to avoid the hand-rail. Forewarned was forearmed, but the shock when he inserted his key in the door was no less severe for his having expected it. What happened to people with dodgy hearts? he wondered. Was the risk covered by his insurance policy?

The television set was turned on and in cloudy monochrome the Great Leader plodded across the building site. When he turned his back to the camera the fat seeped over his collar. 'I meant to tell young Lottie about that,' said Blazer. 'They've got a rule here. No pictures taken from behind. They don't think it's polite.'

'Including the statues?'

'Especially the statues. There are places designated where you can take pictures. The best angles and all that.' He watched Patrick pour whisky into his glass. 'It's just their way. They've got this thing about bad propaganda. It's hard to explain.'

'Like a lot of other things,' said Patrick. 'Why are the streets so empty? It's like a ghost town.'

They were alone in the room. Mr Lee was away making phone calls. Blazer dipped his nose into his glass and stared through the window at the square below. Two men with secateurs trimmed the cherry trees. A lorry drove by, its exhaust gasping. 'The fact is,' he said, 'not many people actually live here. No old folks. No cripples. It's a sort of show place. When they want the streets dressed they wheel in as many as they need. You should have been here on His Nibs' birthday. They filled the stadium. They had banners and flags. Parties everywhere. They went on for days. And it wasn't cheap. They reckon it cost around five hundred million.'

'Pounds?'

'Pounds,' said Blazer. 'Then there was the quilt.' He screwed up his eyes as if he was doing sums in his head. 'Stuffed with down from the necks of seven hundred thousand sparrows. Killed for the occasion. Just to say Happy Birthday.' He drained his glass and held it out for a refill. 'You heard none of this from me. Private information. Not to be repeated.'

'I'm supposed to report what I see.'

'Pull the other one,' said Blazer. 'Just you wait till we get out of town. You'll see all you want to then. You don't want to worry about all this bollocks. It's not important.'

On the television screen the Great Leader had been replaced by the snow-capped mountain. 'Mount Paekdu,' said Blazer, sitting down heavily in front of the set. 'It's where he had his HQ when he was fighting the Japs. It's a brand name now. They use it for soda water.' He pointed to the bottle in Patrick's hand. 'No competition. Everybody drinks it.'

'Do you get the news here?'

'Such as?'

'World news. What's happening in Russia. Tiananmen Square. Who won the Oscars.'

'Oscars?' said Blazer. 'Who gives a toss about Oscars? It was Rita Hayworth in my day. Whatever happened to her?'

'She died.'

'And Humphrey Bogart.'

'Him too.'

The TV film completed its loop and began again. 'We get headlines,' said Blazer. 'What was it they used to say? All the news that's fit to print. What you might call the authorized version. There's one radio station, one wavelength. People are told what they need to know. I pick up a bit extra, but it doesn't seem important. Everything's happening a long way away. It doesn't make a lot of difference.'

'What about the opposition?'

Blazer shook his head slowly. The hair in his ears, Patrick observed, did not bend when it made contact with the upholstery, but dug into it like twin picks. 'There is no opposition,' he said. 'There's the government and there are people locked up.'

'In prison?'

'In camps.' He spread his hands and the whisky splashed in his lap. 'Look,' he said, 'it's not like the good old UK. It's like wartime. There's no room for debate. They've got a bloody great plan to carry out and if you don't like it, you're the enemy.' He smoothed the spilt drink into the nap of his trousers. 'It's how they get things done. It's the system.'

'And you approve?'

Blazer threw back his head and laughed. It was a sound without humour, only a boundless contempt for the naivety of the question. 'I live here,' he said. 'I'm in for life.'

'I see.'

Blazer heaved himself to his feet. 'I doubt it. But it doesn't matter. I don't have to prove anything. I don't have to explain. You're just passing through. You need to stay here for a month or two before you pass judgement. You might have second thoughts.'

'Perhaps.'

The Great Leader was with the surgeons again. They watched him standing, grave and attentive, by the bedside. There was a cut-away of a hand holding a scalpel, an anaesthetist dispensing gas and air. It was like the average soap, thought Patrick. The good guys were bound to win; the patient would survive. The Great Leader had given his word and there was no one to argue. He felt exhausted as though the entire weight of the country was on his back. It was not his business. As Blazer had told him, he was just passing through.

Mr Lee returned five minutes later. 'Business done,' he said. 'Time for conference.' He unzipped his brief-case and took out a sheaf of papers. 'Itinerary for tomorrow. Much to do, plenty to see.'

'I'll get Lottie,' said Patrick. 'She'll want to ask you about pictures.'

There was no reply when he knocked on her door and when he opened it the room was empty. The bed was undisturbed; no one had lain there that afternoon. Boxes of film were stacked on the dressing table. The camera case lay open and empty by the foot of the bed. He felt a tremor of apprehension. The pit of his stomach seemed to fall away, as though someone had cut along a dotted line. He looked in the bathroom. There was a bottle of moisturizer and several tampons on the edge of the bath. The floor was dusted with talc, and, pointing in all directions like the instructions from a book on ballroom dancing, he saw the prints of Lottie's bare feet. It was like the scene of a crime, he thought. Only the body was missing.

He ran downstairs but she was not in the lobby or the lounge. In the restaurant the tables were being laid for dinner. The waitresses looked at him blankly when he asked if they had seen her. 'Blonde lady,' he said, raking his fingers through his hair. 'Lady wearing boot,' he said, pointing to his own brogues.

'Not here,' said one of them at last, and he backed out, his face locked in a sheepish grin.

Blazer and Mr Lee were waiting for him by the reception desk. 'She's been nicked,' said Blazer.

'She's what?' He did not want to believe what he knew to be true.

'Arrested. For taking unauthorized pictures. Snapping away as if she was on Brighton pier.'

'Very bad,' said Mr Lee. 'Bad for everyone.' He appeared to be on the verge of tears. He had bitten his bottom lip and, as he spoke, he dabbed at the blood with a dirty handkerchief. 'Mr Kim was informed. He is very angry. We have to report to him now.'

'Where?'

'Down at the nick,' said Blazer. 'Where people get locked up.'

six

It was at a house party at Beechers that Patrick first met Lottie. Beechers was the Admiral's country home, a hundred-acre estate in Surrey where the cooking was dreadful and old newsreels, most of them featuring the Admiral in his boxing prime, were shown after dinner. It was either that or game shows, to which the Admiral was addicted. There was one called Yo Ho Ho which he had bought on a visit to Tokyo, in which the host was dressed as a pirate and competitors wearing boiler suits walked the plank in pursuit of prizes. If they gave a wrong answer to questions they were tipped into a tank full of live eels which they had to catch and stuff into their boiler suits. Two or more eels won them bonus points. No eels at all meant eating a penalty meal of raw fish. It was people's TV, said the Admiral. The previous week it had been number one in the ratings.

Dominic Downey delivered the invitation in person. 'Just the usual thrash,' he said. 'He wants you to get to know the girl.'

Patrick did not try to disguise his gloom. 'I suppose there'll be dancing.'

'Naturally.'

The dancing was performed to records played with thorn needles on a wind-up gramophone, which the Admiral claimed

67

had a better tone than any of the latest equipment. On previous occasions it had been Patrick's duty to partner the Admiral's wife – Nora, as she told him to call her – in the waltz and the slow foxtrot. She was stout, nimble and tireless. By the end of the evening Patrick was exhausted.

At Christmas they had also danced the tango. Mrs Nelson wore a dress strung with bugle beads and a tiara which perched on her brindled hair like the grille of a small sports car. The tune was Jealousy and she had sung the words in his ear as they swooped over the parquet. 'You can't imagine how it takes me back,' she confided when they paused for breath.

'Was the Admiral keen on dancing?'

'Keen as mustard. He was light on his feet in the old days.'

Nothing had changed, thought Patrick. The Admiral was still fleet of foot, but he now expected others to do his dancing for him. He also expected his guests to be punctual. Patrick was summoned for three o'clock, but as he drove through the iron gates, embossed with anchors and capstans, he saw that he was more than an hour late.

Rain had been falling since first light, drenching the tennis courts, diluting the chlorine in the outdoor pool and shattering the last roses of an uncertain summer. It was going to be a ghastly weekend, he thought. The weather would keep them indoors. There would be no escape.

'He's been asking for you,' said Downey. 'You're to go straight up.'

Harry Miller, the Admiral's valet, let him into the suite marked Trafalgar and pointed him to the bedroom. 'Through there,' he said. 'In the bog.'

The Admiral sat on a lavatory, moulded in the shape of a dolphin. The seat conformed to his personal contours and it was electrically heated. There was a telephone within easy reach; a television set was mounted on the opposite wall. At times of extreme displeasure this was where the Admiral held court. To Patrick's certain knowledge he had fired two editors while so enthroned. The intention was not merely to add insult to injury. Irritation quickened the Admiral's bowels and he was not a man to let opportunity go to waste.

'So you got here,' he said.

'It was the traffic,' said Patrick.

'It's always the bloody traffic. Start sooner.'

Patrick bowed his head and remained silent. He remembered his mother's advice: 'Least said, soonest mended.' She would never have imagined it being applied to the present circumstances.

'I want you to be nice to Lottie,' said the Admiral. 'They tell me she's bright. Full of ideas.'

Patrick hummed non-committally. He dreaded photographers with ideas. Usually it meant persuading the subject to strike a pose which was completely lunatic; juggling, perhaps, with a bowl of custard or squatting, stripped to the waist, on a fishmonger's slab. From the research he had already carried out he knew that she had photographed the Admiral squinting shrewdly through a telescope. Clearly, she knew the theme to pursue. A little flattery went a long way with the Admiral; a lot of it made preferment certain.

'Who are the other guests?' he asked.

'Some people from the city. Lady Larkin. Cassandra.'

He groaned before he knew he was about to do so. 'I see.'

'Is that a problem?'

Patrick shook his head. It was months since they had met. He had no idea how he would react. 'Does she know that I'll be here?'

'I may have mentioned it.' It was clearly of no importance. They were aboard the Admiral's ship and they were both members of the crew. Each would do his or her duty. It was a condition of service. 'Has Miller run my bath?' he demanded.

'I don't think so.'

'Do it.' He dismissed Patrick with a wave of his hand.

In the bathroom he released a silent scream. How, he wondered, could one man possess so many loathsome qualities. The Admiral was coarse, devious and tyrannical and, without doubt, he always had been. But while some people mellowed with the onset of power, the Admiral had never seen the need. Money gave him the licence to be himself. The real man was rarely on public display; Downey and his staff made sure of that. But on his own ground the beast ran free.

He turned on the taps and water gushed into the sunken

bath. There was a pillow at either end and in a rack designed as a mini-harbour the Admiral's fleet of toy boats jogged at anchor. In the past when, legally or not, he had been in the oil business, this was where routes and sailings had been planned. Out of sight the lavatory flushed and the Admiral emerged, shedding his robe as he did so.

He tested the temperature with his toe and paddled down the short flight of steps into the water. 'There's one more thing,' he said.

'What's that?'

'Keep Lady Larkin off the gin.'

It was easier said than done. Lady Larkin was a veteran guest, whose objective was to drink as much as she could in the shortest possible time. She did not become drunk, but her knee joints suddenly gave way – sometimes when she was in the middle of a sentence – lowering her to the ground like a collapsed deck chair. It had a disconcerting effect on whoever she was addressing, although Lady Larkin was not in the least put out.

'I'm quite comfortable,' she assured Patrick the first time he saw it happen. 'Carry on with whatever you're doing. Don't worry about me.'

She had been a famous beauty in her youth, a heroine of picture postcards and a confidante of kings. One of the Admiral's newsreels showed her on safari in Kenya, dead lions dumped around her like hearth-rugs, while men with rifles toasted her from hip-flasks. Her husband was dead. She complained loudly and often that she was broke and that her contemporaries were decrepit. 'All of them have lost their marbles,' she said. 'I keep company with the marble-less.' The Admiral held her in awe. She was his direct line to a past he could not buy.

At dinner Patrick sat at her right. It was supposed to be a strategic position from where he was meant to control the amount of drink that went into her glass. It was an impossible assignment, made worse by the fact that Cassandra was sitting opposite.

'You're looking well,' he said.

It was an understatement. She looked ravishing. Her hair framed her face like a cloche. She had painted her lips with something silvery beneath the rouge and her eyes glistened. She seemed to emit light and his heart laboured in his chest as she switched on to full beam.

'Thank you,' she said. 'I feel terrific.'

Meaning, supposed Patrick, that now he was out of the picture, life had resumed its upward swing and prospects were boundless. He would not, he resolved, ask her what was happening career-wise. Her column had been expanded to fill two pages and the TV series was about to be launched. She was already Big and about to become Bigger. The Admiral's investment was paying off.

'You look tired,' said Cassandra. Her tone was solicitous, but he recognized the come-on. What he was supposed to do now was confess to disappointment and loss; the natural consequences of her going.

'Too many late nights,' he said. 'You know how it is.'

'I can imagine.'

I'm sure you bloody well can, he thought savagely. 'I'm off on a jaunt,' he said. 'Foreign parts.'

'Somewhere nice?'

'Somewhere different. North Korea.'

She nodded sympathetically as if he had announced a bereavement. 'I wouldn't want to go there.' She shuddered inside her dress, a shift hung with black and silver tassels, and he was punished with a sudden vision of her flesh. He remembered its look and its texture and yearned to touch it. Involuntarily, he leaned across the table, greedy for the scent that he knew was being funnelled from the neckline.

She denied him by sitting back in her chair. 'I've just met the girl you're going with,' she said. 'Down there, wearing blue.'

He saw someone plump and blonde and impossibly young. 'Pretty gel,' said Lady Larkin and he nodded agreement.

The group from the city sat on Cassandra's side of the table. One was Australian. The others, he thought, were probably Indian. 'Khan,' said the man sitting beside Cassandra. 'Ashram Securities.'

'Before the war,' said Lady Larkin 'we had Indian servants.

Rather light-fingered, I'm afraid. And we had to watch out for the ayah. She used to put opium beneath her finger-nails for the babies to suck.'

Cassandra frowned politely. 'As a sedative?'

'And how!' said Lady Larkin. 'Out like a light, poor dears. My husband was quite upset. Un-British, he called it.'

'Neither was it Indian,' said Mr Khan primly. 'We abhor such customs.'

Lady Larkin affected not to hear. 'Lovely food, though,' she said. 'All those delicious curries. Baby makers we used to call them.' She bowed her grey head and speared a piece of pheasant with her fork.

One of the snags of being seated next to Lady Larkin, thought Patrick, was that you were blamed for her clangers. It was guilt by association. Not that she meant to be rude, but she had never found it necessary to be polite. Cassandra, on the other hand, was direct because someone had once told her that confrontation was an interviewing technique which beautiful women could use to their advantage. Few people had the nerve to tell her to piss off.

He watched her engage Mr Khan's wife in conversation. She spoke with great deliberation, as though she was addressing someone deaf. 'How do women in your country feel about sexual equality?' she asked.

'Sex?' said Mrs Khan.

'Sexual equality. With men? With your husband?'

Mrs Khan's red lips parted in a glossy smile. 'Sex very good,' she said.

'And equality?'

'Very good also.' Her hands were plump and supple and her rings flashed red and yellow in the candle-light. She made Patrick think of rooms walled with marble, in which caged birds sang and princes fondled their favourites. Cassandra was wasting her time. It was not only that Mrs Khan spoke practically no English. The questions themselves were irrelevant. On the page, he supposed, she would re-invent the dialogue. It was already in her head. She had a fund of such fiction. It was why she believed implicitly that she knew what women thought, what they wanted. No one would ever be able to persuade her that she was simply reading her own mind. He imagined the print-out unfurling in an enormous scroll. There was enough copy there for a thousand columns, an infinity of TV programmes. Yob culture was being served, he thought. Cassandra was not only its counsellor, but its icon.

The table was cleared and more wine was poured. Lady Larkin rinsed hers between her teeth. 'Something under my plate,' she said loudly.

Patrick looked the other way. It was, at least, better than the last time when she had actually taken her teeth out and sluiced them in her glass. It was all to do with confidence, he thought, with being not merely indifferent to what other people thought, but oblivious to their opinions. Lady Larkin was so old that she had become an antique. She was cherished now for her rarity.

They ate lemon sorbet and sherry trifle ringed round with palings of ratafia. It was food which would have gone down well at a children's party. The Admiral, he noticed, had an individual serving of spotted dick, the suet studded with currants and heavy with grease. It reminded him, he said, of his days in the navy – a fact which had appeared in several profiles. It was a mark of favour to be offered a taste from the Admiral's plate. An MP who had refused had seen his support in the paper dwindle to nothing.

He beckoned with his spoon to the girl in blue and she crouched at his side and opened her mouth. Patrick felt his throat constrict in sympathy. The Admiral dabbed her lips with his napkin and waved her back to her seat. She swallowed hard and, as she did so, saw that Patrick was watching. She pulled back her chair, out of his eye-line.

After dinner came the newsreels, screened on a vast TV screen encased in gilt at the far end of the living room. The length of the programme varied. The running time was usually an hour, but it could be extended to two or even three hours if the Admiral was in reminiscent mood or wanted to remind guests of his place in history.

The problem was how to stay awake but, with Lady Larkin in tow, Patrick had no difficulty. She had commandeered a bottle of gin and a large goblet filled with cracked ice. As the lights dimmed she tilted the bottle. 'Just a little eye-opener,' she murmured.

'Can I find you a smaller glass?'

'The one I have is splendid.'

She sipped stealthily, then tilted the bottle again.

'Could I get you some tonic?'

'Never touch it.'

At least, he thought, they were already sitting down. If her legs went no one would know. Her fist thumped his knee and she cawed with laughter. 'Just look at David,' she said.

On screen a young man wearing plus fours shook hands with a Red Indian chief. His expression was deeply serious as if he was offering a peace treaty or a cure for piles. It was evidently a solemn occasion. 'The day after that we all went off to Manitoba,' said Lady Larkin. 'On our own private train. I taught him how to Charleston.'

'You were actually there?'

Lady Larkin waved her goblet. 'There,' she said, 'next to the one with the braids. 'God, he smelled awful. Bear grease, or something.'

It was one way to study history, thought Patrick, like watching a re-run of the battle of Waterloo with Wellington on call to explain the strategy. She nudged him with her sharp little elbow. 'I knew him too.'

He looked up to see a bearded man with flyaway eyebrows emerge from a garden hut and start to harangue the camera. 'He was vegetarian,' said Lady Larkin. 'Nut cutlets and spring water. And he knew the answer to everything.'

'Very handy.'

'Inexpressibly tedious. Except for his postcards.'

'Did he send them to you?'

'Dozens. He knew I'd tell everyone what he said. Gossips have their uses.' She jerked her head in the direction of Cassandra. 'Not her. She'd never pass on the jokes. She's not interested in what other people think. I know it's supposed to be her business, but it's all pretend.' She raised her glass as the sage slammed the door of his garden hut. 'We have to pass the jokes around,' she said. 'It's how we pay our way.'

The newsreel changed and Downey cleared his throat

to call the class to order. There was a fanfare from fifty years ago and Stoker Nelson stepped through the ropes at the Albert Hall. Patrick squirmed in his seat. He had lost count how many times he had seen the fight, but it was not without interest. This was where the image was born. The contest was abbreviated, of course. Rounds one and two flashed by in less than a minute, but the third round was shown in its entirety. The two men were evenly matched. Harry Miller was perhaps an inch taller than the Admiral, with a longer reach. But the Admiral held the centre of the ring, forcing Miller to work round him, wasting energy as he circled the canvas. There was a flurry of punches and Patrick craned forward for a closer view.

The Admiral's left fist sunk into Miller's stomach and his right delivered a perfect uppercut. Miller lay prone as the referee counted him out and the Admiral danced a jig of victory, his hands clasped above his head.

'Bravo!' called Nora and kissed the Admiral's cheek.

'Wonderful,' said Cassandra, kneeling beside the champion.

The group from the city clapped their hands and Lady Larkin raised her goblet. 'What did you think of that?' Patrick asked her.

'What I always think of it.'

'What's that?'

She lowered one eyelid in a wink so brief that he could have imagined it. 'The quickness of the hand,' she said.

He saw what she meant. The camera angle was obscure and the print as sallow as old newsprint. But from where he sat there was no mistaking it. The old one-two had won the fight. But the Admiral's left hand had definitely been low.

His bedroom was one of those allotted to other ranks. There was a bunk bed and drugget on the floor. The only picture was an engraving of Lady Hamilton; the only reading matter, a biography of the Admiral, composed by a hack whose pension had been at risk at the time of writing it. At least, thought Patrick, it was one job which he had been spared.

Somewhere in the house the Admiral was conferring

with the men from the city. Deals were being discussed which, sooner or later, would affect his future and the future of everyone else who sailed on the good ship *Arbiter*. His opinion had not been sought. He was there to take orders, to fire the cannon and climb the rigging. His bones ached from the labours of the day.

There had been dancing, as he had expected, followed by party games including Hunt the Slipper and Sardines. They were played to please Nora, who believed all her guests to be children at heart. Explaining the rules to Mrs Khan was left to Dominic Downey, whose salary, Patrick imagined, was immense. Seeing him earn it was one of the few pleasures he could salvage from the weekend.

Patrick had tried to nobble him between frolics. 'No one's briefed me about this panda,' he complained.

'What do you need to know?'

'Everything. How to handle it. How to feed it. How to wipe its arse.' He ticked the list off on his fingers. 'It's worth a fortune. What do I do if it catches cold?'

'There'll be vets standing by. Everything's arranged.'

'So what am I supposed to do?'

'Follow instructions,' said Downey. 'See it into its box. See it on to the plane. Write a perfectly lovely story and make sure that there are even lovelier pictures. It's quite straightforward.'

'When are we going to run the piece?'

'Pieces,' said Downey. 'A nice little series. When we're home and dry. We keep quiet until then.' He put his finger to his lips. 'Absolutely schtumm. Not a word to anyone.' As master of the revels he was wearing a matelot's hat, blue and white, with a red pom-pom. It was not his fault that he looked a complete prat, thought Patrick, but he could summon up no sympathy.

'I'll have to discuss it with the editor,' he said.

'Why?'

'He runs the paper.'

'Don't be absurd,' said Downey. 'He does as he's told.'

And, of course, it was true. The editor of *The Arbiter* was a thin and anxious Glaswegian named Dunbar. He had held the job for three months, a month longer than his predecessor.

He was keen and capable but, above all, he was obedient. The master plan was spelled out by the Admiral. Dunbar would follow it to the letter.

Downey blew the referee's whistle that hung about his neck. 'Now we're going to play Murder,' he said.

In other circumstances, thought Patrick, it might have been an opportunity worth exploiting. When he was twelve years old he had played the game with slightly older cousins. His first sexual encounter had been on that night, crammed inside a wardrobe with a girl named Peggy. It was she who had made the first move, clamping his hand over her small breasts, unzipping his fly and releasing his penis which she seized, far too tightly, jerking it up and down until to his surprise and embarrassment, it spurted the juice which proved his coming of age. Sandwiched between a Harris tweed jacket and sheepskin overcoat, he nearly fainted. She held him up and wiped him dry. Neither of them spoke. It was her gentleness that he recalled now. He was unlikely to find anyone like her in the Admiral's house.

While Downey assembled his cast of murderer and murderees he slipped out of the room and up the back stairs. No one would seek him out. The party was winding down. He climbed into bed and tested the springs. At home he slept on a mattress that was like a board, but this was not only firm but lumpy. He kneeled down and pummelled it with his fists. His knuckles stung, but the corrugations remained in place. There was a knock on the door and he paused in mid-assault. 'Come in.'

It was the girl in blue. She put her head round the door and smiled. 'Lottie Moffat,' she said. 'I'm supposed to say hello.'

'Hello,' said Patrick.

'Is this a bad time?'

'Not at all.' He tried to envisage how he looked. Was his hair combed? Did his pyjamas fit? Was any vital part hanging loose?

'There's not been a chance all evening,' she said.

He reached for his dressing gown and put it on. 'It's always like that down here. It's what you call over-organized.'

'That ghastly pudding,' she said. 'I thought I was going to be sick.'

'I could see.'

'Nobody warned me.'

'It means that he likes you,' said Patrick. 'Or so I'm told.' He wondered if he should put on his glasses. Normally he wore them only for work, but they gave his face a certain dignity. He slid them on to his nose and instantly felt better dressed.

'Have they decided when we're off?' she asked.

'Not yet.'

'When do you reckon?'

'Soon,' he said. 'It's just a matter of getting the visas.'

'Are you excited?'

'Am I what?' Her innocence surprised him and, against all his expectations, he did not want to disappoint her. 'It could be interesting,' he said. 'I suppose they've told you it's all hush-hush.'

'Absolutely!' She clasped her hands as though the secret was within her grasp. 'Mr Downey made me promise. I won't tell a soul.'

'Right you are then.'

'Should I swot up on pandas?'

'If you like.'

'Somebody should.'

'Somebody will,' said Patrick. 'That's my job. Don't worry about it.'

She drew a deep breath and smiled radiantly. 'That's all right, then. I'll let you get some sleep.' She reached for the door knob, then paused, as though seeing the room for the first time. 'It's a bit of a dump, isn't it?'

'It is, rather.'

'Mine's better than this.'

'It would be.' He felt as though he had been caught out, his true status revealed. 'Beauty before age,' he said. 'Make the most of it.'

He opened the door and stood aside to let her pass. As he did so he saw Cassandra at the far end of the corridor. She smiled severely and wagged her finger. There was nothing to be said. The sighting, he supposed, would be reported to the Admiral, not as a major incident, but in passing, to demonstrate that Cassandra was all-seeing and that he was lecherous and unreliable as she had always intimated.

'Nighty-night,' said Lottie and kissed him on the cheek.

Cassandra saw that too, he realized. He closed the door and took off his glasses. What he needed was not twenty-twenty vision, but a sensor of some kind which warned him of hazards invisible to the naked eye. Lady Hamilton ogled him from the wall. His face, where Lottie had kissed him, was on fire.

He was not allowed to escape until mid-morning. As he had expected, the Admiral knew of Lottie's visit the night before. 'I thought I told you,' he said. 'No funny business with that girl.'

'We were just talking. Nothing happened.'

'It was under my roof. I'm responsible.'

'Ask her yourself,' said Patrick. 'I didn't invite her in. She came to see me.' His back felt as though he had lain on cobbles. Pain made him reckless. The Admiral was still in bed, the duvet piled with newspapers. He looked well-rested, ready for the first raw meat of the day. Interrogating Patrick was no more than an appetizer, but it was better than nothing.

'I've been reading your column,' he said. 'It's piss-poor.'

'I'm sorry you think so.'

The Admiral spread the page in front of him and jabbed it with his thick finger. 'Look at this,' he said. 'What's this about game shows? What do you mean, they sanctify greed?' He spat out the phrase as though it was tainted.

'It's just one show,' said Patrick. 'I wasn't generalizing.'

'And this. What do you mean, "presumptuous royals"? What's that all about?'

It was an item concerning a station-master in Derbyshire who had been ticked off for failing to halt a celebrity train in precise alignment with a strip of red carpet on the platform. Someone in high places had complained. 'I felt they were coming on a bit strong,' said Patrick. 'Why make a fuss about it? What does it matter?'

'Getting it right matters.' The Admiral rolled the paper

into a ball and threw it across the room. 'There's nothing presumptuous about keeping up standards. And who the hell are you to decide? Who are you to say what's proper?'

Patrick shrugged. 'It was just an opinion.'

'It was a stupid opinion.'

As tantrums went, it was a minor one, but there was no doubt that the Admiral was peeved. Something had got up his nose, Patrick decided. Or rather, something in the column had got up the nose of someone else on whose good-will the Admiral depended.

'They could always write in,' he said.

'Who could?'

'People who don't like my opinions.'

'I don't like your opinions,' said the Admiral. 'That's quite sufficient.'

It was the moment to resign, thought Patrick, but lately the moments had been coming thick and fast. There was not only his position to consider, there was also the job market, the papers which had already gone to the wall, the possibility that he might never again write a column which bore his name. He postponed his departure, yet again.

'And another thing,' said the Admiral while he hesitated. 'I don't like the title. What does Lamb's Tales mean?'

Patrick debated how full an explanation he should volunteer. 'It's a pun,' he said. 'It's my name and there's that part of the animal. And there's a literary reference.'

The Admiral stared at him without blinking. 'There was a writer called Charles Lamb,' he continued. 'He wrote a book called *Lamb's Tales*.'

'So it's not original.'

'He's been dead a long time,' said Patrick. 'He wouldn't mind.'

The Admiral shook his head. 'We don't want second-hand stuff. We'll give it a rest for a while. You'll be away for a week or so. When you're back we'll think again.' He pressed the bell by his bedside. 'Tell Miller you're going. There'll be one less for lunch.'

The Admiral was right about the column, Patrick admitted

to himself as he drove back to London. He was producing feeble stuff and he was not surprised that he had been put on hold. There had been a time, not long ago, when he had been read and quoted by everyone. Perhaps he was losing his grip. Did he still know what interested readers of *The Arbiter*? Did he still have the common touch?

At Hammersmith he made a detour to call on Brian Seeley. Until he resigned two years earlier he had been Curator of Mammals at London Zoo where, in a pure spirit of subversion, he had given Patrick some of his best stories. He now ran a diet research unit for a firm manufacturing dog food. Television companies employed him to advise on films about wildlife. He was the very man, thought Patrick, to tell him about pandas.

'To be honest,' he said, 'I've never cared for them. Difficult to handle. Practically no sex drive. Not all they're cracked up to be.'

'But cuddly.'

'Don't you believe it,' said Seeley. 'Bad tempered buggers. I wouldn't go near one.'

His office was divided in two. On one side was his desk; on the other, behind a wall of plate glass, was what he described as his private theatre. Each month he filled it with a new act. There had been golden marmosets, small cats and once, Patrick recalled, a pack of desert foxes. It was armchair research, claimed Seeley, and it was also therapeutic. This month it housed a family of acouchis. They had long noses and twittered like birds.

'South American rodents,' he said. 'Related to the guinea pig. More interesting than pandas.'

'Pandas are rarer.'

'That's true. There are only about a thousand left. Fewer every year. Their habitat's going and they don't breed fast enough.'

Patrick experienced a surge of fellow feeling. It was true of all endangered species. 'I'm going to collect one,' he said. 'The Admiral's done a deal. He's going to be a benefactor.'

'How did he manage that?'

Patrick supplied the details. Given the complexities of the Admiral's business arrangements, it all sounded fairly straightforward. 'They're keeping it under wraps,' he said. 'Nothing's being announced till we get back.'

'Why's that?'

'It's our story,' he said. *The Arbiter* wants an exclusive. If there's a cock-up they don't want anyone else telling tales.'

Behind the plate glass the acouchis played tag, hurtling along freeways, skipping over artistically arranged driftwood.

A female stopped in her tracks and hoisted her tail. Her mate read the signal and, without hesitation, mounted her. The coupling was over in seconds. The chase went on. In a way, thought Patrick, it was enviable. There were no white nights for acouchis, no time wasted in anguishing over past mistakes.

'What puzzles me,' said Seeley, 'is where it's coming from.'

'What do you mean?'

'The panda.' He pointed to a world atlas, pinned to one wall. 'As far as I know, they're pretty exclusive. The Chinese say they've got the world population in just three provinces. There've been no other sightings. Nothing official.'

'Does every sighting get reported?'

'Of course not.'

'No one's explored North Korea for years. Half a century almost. No one's been let in. Nothing's been let out. They could have mammoths there for all we know. Why not the odd panda?'

'No reason,' said Seeley. 'The habitat's right. Plenty of mountains. Forest and bamboo. Not many people.' He tapped his teeth with a pencil. 'They could travel, I suppose. Anything can go walkabout. Anything's possible.'

He was still not convinced, thought Patrick. But they were the opinions of a man who did not like pandas. He looked at the map and drew comfort from its empty spaces. There were thousands of square miles without towns, without villages; vast vacant lots on which no sign of habitation was inscribed. Here, he told himself, there could quite possibly be dragons, but he did not propose to seek them out. He would settle for a bulky, black and white mammal, resembling a bear, which feasted on bamboo and had a perilously low sex drive.

seven

There was no way of telling what intensity of sex drive the exhibit before them had once enjoyed. It reared on its hind legs, embracing a plastic tree trunk, its button eyes encircled by black rosettes, its teeth bared in a sorry grin.

'Giant panda,' announced Mr Lee enthusiastically. 'Shot by Great Leader. Presented to students for their edification.' He pointed to a plaque which told the tale. 'Prize specimen. Male. One metre tall. Weight, one hundred kilograms.'

Seeley would be interested, thought Patrick, although there was no indication where the beast had been killed. Wherever it had lived it was a trophy now, for home consumption. There were no wildlife defenders here to cry foul.

Crouching beside him Lottie took pictures, and behind her Mr Kim toyed with an unlit cigarette. For a chain smoker, Patrick decided, it must be pure hell. Museums were places of deprivation where addicts were brought to be punished. The no-smoking rule applied to everyone; even the top brass had to conform. It was small consolation, but he savoured it to the last drop. There would not be many other opportunities.

It was an hour since they had arrived at the police barracks. Blazer had not been optimistic. 'They don't like it,' he said. 'Unauthorized photography puts you right on the shit list. And she's been warned.'

Mr Lee was even gloomier. 'Bad girl to break rules,' he said. 'Trouble for everyone.' In the overheated car his body odour was overwhelming. It was the smell of fear, Patrick realized. He would be held responsible. He was scared to death.

Their first sight of the barracks did nothing to raise their spirits. Iron gates clanged behind them. They were hustled through a front office, quartered by desks and filing cabinets; down a long corridor which reeked of disinfectant; across a courtyard and into a bungalow, ringed by azaleas. Their petals had been browned by frost. They looked like cemetery flowers.

Two guards, one in front and one behind, steered them into a vestibule. There were no chairs; the walls were blank. It was like a cell, thought Patrick, or rather the ante-room to a cell where appalling things could happen. He tried to damp down his imagination and yearned for the passport which he had surrendered at the hotel. Without it, he was stripped of his identity. He remembered the appeals for unknown political prisoners, most of which he had ignored. He gave to famine relief, to the victims of earthquake and flood. But the plight of those others, held without trial or explanation had been too remote. He would know better next time.

Mr Lee's teeth chattered, like keys loosely held, and Patrick patted his skinny back. 'Cheer up,' he said, 'it's not the end of the world.' He had never sounded less confident.

It was then that he heard the laughter, loud and un-restrained, and he knew that it was Lottie, in full cry. The door swung open and he saw her, perched on the edge of a settee, the rhinestones winking on her boots, and Mr Kim joining in the joke. He registered an extraordinary blend of emotions; relief for a start, followed by surprise, exasperation and pure rage. He wanted to shake her, to slap her face, to stop the guffaws which flushed her cheeks and made her breasts bounce. 'Where did you go?' he demanded. 'You had us scared to death.'

She leaned back and wiped her eyes. 'There was no need. I was perfectly okay.' She pointed across the room. 'Mr Kim took care of me.'

'Safe in my hands,' said Mr Kim. He extended them, palms upward, to demonstrate his reliability.

'But the police phoned the hotel. They said you were very angry.'

'Angry?'

He spoke rapidly to Mr Lee, whose jitters seemed to have abated. He nodded several times in what was clearly his interpreter mode. 'Mr Kim says that he was not angry, merely concerned. He was contacted by the police and made himself available. The matter is now resolved.'

It was instructive, thought Patrick, how Mr Kim's English came and went. He dummied up when it suited him. His explanations were given extra weight when they were delivered second-hand. 'Resolved how?'

'I told him about the problem,' said Lottie.

'Which problem?'

'You know.' She frowned heavily, telling him that he was being obtuse. 'How I needed to take pictures. Without someone standing over me. He hadn't realized I'd been having difficulties.'

'But I explained . . .'

'You didn't make it clear,' she said. 'I told him what I wanted and he understood.'

Somewhere along the line the message had been scrambled; he had not been given the necessary code. The leader of the delegation had been by-passed. Bimbo tactics, he thought savagely, had won the day. He had a sudden, stomach-churning vision of Lottie gulping down a portion of the Admiral's pudding. Like most photographers, like all women, she would do whatever was called for to get her way. 'You seemed to be getting on well,' he said. 'Sharing a joke with friends . . .'

'I was telling him about the Admiral's party,' said Lottie. 'About how you looked after old ladies. Mr Kim thinks you're very gallant.'

'Is that what he said?'

'More or less.' She stood up and dusted her lap. 'Anyway, we've got the all clear. We're going to see a panda.'

There was no argument; he could not complain. But as they trailed through the museum, pausing at a platoon of terracotta soldiers; guardians of a seventh century tomb; loitering in front of a fresco, endorsed as fine art by the Great Leader himself, he realized that Mr Kim was giving them, not what Lottie wanted, but what he had decided it was politic for her to have. She was the Admiral's favourite; it was sensible to make concessions. Patrick was simply the foreman of the job in hand. There had to be sweeteners to ensure that the operation ran smoothly. The solution was to keep everyone busy, to lay on a programme which filled every waking hour.

Driving from the barracks he told them what was planned. It sounded more like a state visit than a chance to meet the people. First they would visit the university, then a school for acrobats.

'I'd like to visit someone's home,' said Lottie.

'Possibly,' said Mr Kim.

'How about Mr Lee? I'm sure he wouldn't mind.'

'We will discuss it further,' said Mr Kim.

It was good to know that he must be dying for a smoke, thought Patrick, as another acre of museum confronted them. He took bets with himself on how long he could hold out. Showing them the panda, he decided, had been a miscalculation, something which Mr Kim had latched on to on the spur of the moment and which, when he weighed it on the scales of good and bad propaganda, he would regret.

He caught Mr Lee's elbow between his finger and thumb. 'Ask Mr Kim if the beast was dangerous.'

'Which beast?'

'The one back there. The one the Great Leader shot.'

The question was relayed and Mr Kim fiddled with the buttons on his coat before replying. 'He was not present,' said Mr Lee. 'But he has no doubt it was collected in the interests of science.'

Patrick nodded. It was the old, familiar argument, always advanced as a rare species became rarer. 'We'll make that plain then,' he said. 'When we publish the photograph.'

He heard Jack Blazer suck in his breath and stood transfixed as Mr Kim gave him his full attention. He studied Patrick as if calculating his body weight and what drop would be sufficient to break his neck. It was an unnerving experience, made more so by its professionalism. There was no hostility, no loss of control. It was a look which practice had made perfect and he wondered how many people Mr Kim had regarded in that way. What was more important, how many had lived to tell the tale?

It was dark by the time they left the museum, but the day was not done. Mr Kim had been busy on their behalf. There were sights to see, people to meet. 'We are to attend a concert at the Children's Palace,' announced Mr Lee. 'Very amusing, very instructive.'

And very long, thought Patrick, two hours later. He had a deep aversion to performing children; talented tots had driven him from many West End musicals. But this evening there was no escape. Already he had sat through a marching display and recitals by a pianist, an accordionist and a violin trio. He had watched dancers and jugglers who spun plates and batons and he had endured two loud and, to him, indistinguishable tunes performed by a brass band. Now they were on to the comedy routines.

Four small girls wearing coloured sashes capered in front of a dummy wearing the uniform of an American army colonel. They brandished toy rifles and made fierce faces. Mr Lee sniggered in his ear. 'Watch now,' he said. 'Favourite item for audience.'

'What's it called?'

Mr Lee pointed to the programme. 'Let's Tear Limbs Off American Imperialists.'

'I see.' He read the lettering on the sashes. The girls repre-sented Cuba, Vietnam, the Palestine Liberation Organization and the Korean People's Army. They took aim and fired their guns and the dummy disintegrated. First the arms flew off, then the legs, and then the head.

Mr Lee applauded wildly. All around them people were cheering. It was just possible, thought Patrick, that they were proud parents. But it was unlikely. There were too many of them. Their enthusiasm was not spontaneous, but rehearsed. They were responding not to bad jokes, but good propaganda. Mr Kim would have approved, but he was not there to see it. He was backstage with Lottie, smoking his head off without a doubt, topping up on the nicotine which the time spent in the museum had denied him.

'How much longer?' he asked.

'One hour. An hour and a half.'

'Can't we leave?'

'Not polite. Mr Kim has arranged reception.'

He bloody would, thought Patrick, reminding himself that Jack Blazer had managed to duck out of it. 'Seen it all before. Have fun,' he said as the car swept him homewards. By now he would have eaten dinner and be on to the first of several nightcaps. But he could hardly be blamed for taking evasive action. Anyone in his right mind would do the same.

Another group of infants took the stage ('Removing American bomb from railway line as express train approaches,' explained Mr Lee), and he tried to imagine the life of an old expatriate, north of the 38th parallel. It was not a pretty picture. For Blazer, he supposed, it was like pitching camp on an ice floe, becalmed on a sea whose temperature rose dramatically every day. The world outside was warming up, but still the thermometer told lies. Official policy was to deny the changing climate, even as the ice melted. It was a risky place to be; there were no lifeboats, not even a raft. The show went on and Patrick rolled with the punches. Everyone had to live with history, he thought. It was hard to decide whether a comic-strip version was any worse than the other kind.

At least Lottie seemed happy. 'Lovely kids,' she told him as she wound on another roll of film. The performance was over at last, but she was still eager for action.

'Haven't you got enough?'

'Be prepared,' she said. 'Girl Guide's motto.'

He envied her stamina. If the going was good she could probably give Mr Kim a run for his money. If his plan was to waste her enthusiasm on make-do stories, he was unlikely to succeed. He wondered what her shooting ratio could be. If only one in twenty of the photographs she took was worth printing, she would probably be content. It was a prodigal use of film, but amateurs and professionals had different expectations. Lottie, he had already noticed, shot from the hip. She made great play of setting up formal groups, refining the pose and experimenting with the Polaroid. The print was there to see in embryo, to be admired or corrected. The sitters knew, or thought they knew, how they would appear.

But the quickness of the lens deceived the eye. Lottie was taking pictures while they drew breath or brushed out their navels. In the old days the technique had been called candid camera. But she had absorbed it seamlessly into an act that was all-singing, all-dancing, which was an entertainment in itself. It was a confidence trick, he thought, but no one was being short-changed. The product was the final test. If the picture was true, whether or not it was the one which had been rehearsed, that was what counted.

He helped her to pack her camera bag. Each roll of exposed film was carefully labelled. The dancers were there and so was the brass band. There was a panda roll and a railway roll. Already he thought, there was a week's work for the dark room.

'So many photographs,' said Mr Kim.

'So much to photograph,' said Patrick.

The English, he noted, was operational again which would suggest no immediate crisis was pending. He prayed that the reception would be brief. To be at the sharp end of hospitality required a strong constitution. The kitting out, the trek round the museum and the concert had exhausted him, besides which, there was something in the air – like dust, too fine to filter out – which abraded the lungs and made breathing itself hard work. Perhaps it was the monotony of the place, the tunnel vision which planted the Great Leader at the end of every perspective. After a while fatigue became a defence mechanism. The body did peculiar things. He remembered how, when his back first started playing up, he had visited an acupuncturist. As the needles went in the pain had miraculously ebbed away.

'It doesn't hurt any more,' he exclaimed.

The acupuncturist gave the needles another twirl. 'Natural anaesthetic,' he said. 'The spinal cord releases lecithin. You get it in plants. Remember your Beatrix Potter. Lettuces are so soporific.'

The relief was short-lived. But the effect was still amazing. Perhaps the same process, or one of its variations, was taking place now. While Lottie sparkled, he would sleep-walk through the rest of the evening. He shook the first cluster of hands and switched himself on to automatic.

It was too soon. Mr Kim waited until he had downed his first glass of ginseng and then unleashed his killer punch. 'After the reception,' he said, 'I have arranged a visit to the Great Leader's birthplace.' He shook his head as Patrick tried to frame his objections. 'It will be a moving experience,' he said.

The birthplace was a thatched hut in a park overlooking the city. It was a fine night, bright with stars. Below them the river curved like a hoop of steel and a boat moved slowly downstream. Dimly, they could see towers and a grid of streets, but there were few lights, no sound of traffic.

The staff, Patrick realized, had been put on stand-by. There was a man wearing a blue tunic and a woman in a severely-cut costume. Her shoes had the squat heels which Cassandra had once called lavatory-pan. Both their faces were set in expressions of extreme piety, as though they had been freeze-dried at the moment of seeing a vision. There was no doubt what the vision was. This was where the Great Leader had first drawn breath. They were standing on holy ground.

'The museum is closed,' said Mr Kim. 'But if you wish . . .' His voice trailed away suggestively.

'No thank you,' said Patrick. 'I mean, I don't want to put them to any trouble.'

He was nagged by a memory that he could not yet place. There was not much to see. The hut had three rooms. The floors were swept clean, the walls were painted white. There were cooking pots by the fire, a brass-bound chest and, in one corner, a desk. The woman pointed out initials scratched on the desk top. 'Carved by the Great Leader,' said Mr Kim. His fingers traced the indentations. It was as though he was touching the stigmata.

He allowed Mr Lee to take up the tale. This was where the Great Leader's grandfather had laid plans to blow up an American battleship in 1886. This was where his father had organized resistance against American missionaries. This was where his mother had turned gun-runner against the Japanese invaders. This was the cradle of the revolution.

Against one wall there was a collection of farm implements.

There were several rakes, a plough, a loom and a pile of sleeping mats. It had clearly been a spartan childhood. Next door there was an ox-stall and, above it, the tiny room in which the Great Leader had slept. His stone figure stood beside one of his father and as he studied their polished faces, Patrick felt his memory leap like a trout. What they were being subjected to, he realized, was a skilled piece of god-bothering of which any Bible class would have been proud. The details had been rejigged. There were no wise men, no star in the east. But as Mr Lee chattered on, parcelling chapter and verse, he ticked off the parallels between one story and the other, the childhood persecution, the escape to China, the return to his native land, the maxims which were prophecies.

One was engraved in gold on the wall beside him. 'Landlords and capitalists who are oppressing the working people should be known in the world . . . When we get rid of them all people can be happy.' The Great Leader had uttered the words when he was twelve, Mr Lee assured him, which suggested that, like the performers they had seen earlier, he had been a talented tot, possible divine.

He watched Lottie set up her camera. She was using a tripod, which meant serious work ahead. 'What's to photograph?' he asked.

'Something symbolic.'

He thought, with a nostalgia that surprised him, of the picture desk at The Arbiter. 'They won't want anything like that.'

'I want it.'

There was no sense in arguing. The sooner Lottie completed her business, the sooner they could leave. He had learned long ago not to enter into discussion with photographers. They acted on instinct, not logic. Besides which, he was beginning to revise his opinion. Lottie appeared to know what she was doing. He had never before encountered a bimbo with brains. She was an opportunist who grabbed whatever chance came by, but what was impressive was the savvy with which she exploited the possibilities. It was unlikely, as she had first assumed, that Mr Kim was a sweetie. He had rarely met anyone less deserving of the description. But some part of him, at least, was human. By asking favours, by keeping on about them to the point of embarrassment, she had managed to make herself his dependant. It was a working relationship. The absurd itinerary was a handout, no more tasty than the Admiral's pudding. But by gulping it down she was already putting herself in line for better things. The panda at the museum had been an unexpected bonus. The next titbit, or the one after that, might be even more tasty.

Patrick inhaled the frosty air and stared into the darkness. The red tip of a cigarette hovered beside him. 'The name of the river,' said Mr Kim, 'is the Daedong. There is an island in the centre of the stream. All our vegetables are grown there.'

'Very convenient.'

'There is also an orphanage for children whose parents were revolutionary heroes.'

Patrick prayed silently that he was not going to propose paying it a visit. 'We have orphanages too,' he said.

Seconds passed and Mr Kim did not reply. He extinguished one cigarette and lit another and when he spoke his tone was pitched somewhere between compassion and contempt. 'I remember England,' he said. 'The state is not concerned. What you have are charities.'

The bar at the hotel was still open when they returned. It was not a festive place. The kind of muzak that reminded Patrick of travelling in lifts filtered from a mini-forest dividing one part of the room from another and embedded in the greenery was a stone basin in which goldfish lolled. The surface of the water was powdered with prawn crackers, offered in the hope of stirring the fish into life. They showed no interest. The crackers dissolved slowly into soup. A group of salesmen sat at a table playing poker. One of their colleagues perched on a stool, chatting up the barmaid.

He looked up with relief as Patrick joined him. 'Frobisher,' he said, offering his hand. 'Textiles from Leeds. What are you trying to sell the buggers?'

'Nothing.' Patrick introduced himself and ordered a beer.

'You're the one with the blonde. Very tasty. Where's she got to?'

'In her room. She'll be down in a minute.'

'Thank Christ for that. There's not a woman here knows you're alive.' He jerked his head towards the barmaid. 'I've been telling her all night that I love her. Not a ripple. They're a funny lot here. They just don't want to know. You might as well be talking to yourself.'

'I can imagine.' The barmaid was quite pretty, he thought, but her mind was clearly on higher things.

'You can't even find a tart,' said Frobisher. 'Bloody Whitehouse City. All you can do is tie a knot in it. I've been here for a week and there's not been a sniff.' He waved to the barmaid and kissed the air. 'Look at her,' he said. 'Not a flicker. And you can't push your luck. I had a mate here last year who came on a bit strong and they hauled him off for an AIDS test. Bloody needles stuck in his arm. Mind your manners, they told him. They don't mess about, these lads.'

'What happened to the girl?'

'Someone said she was packed off to a labour camp.' He settled himself more firmly on the stool, rotating his buttocks as if screwing himself into place. 'Best not to ask too many questions.'

They were joined at the bar by the poker school. Patrick was introduced to Morgan of plastics and Lumsden of metal alloys. Both came from Manchester. Both enquired after Lottie.

'We saw you at breakfast,' said Morgan. 'Very tasty that girl you had with you.'

'Mr Frobisher said the same thing.'

'He's going round the bend,' said Morgan. 'Seven days without nookie and he's foaming at the mouth. We don't know what to do with him. God knows what he'll be like if we're here much longer.'

'God forbid,' said Lumsden. He bought them all another beer. 'Get it down you,' he ordered when Patrick took a tentative sip. 'I thought it was mother's milk to you lot. It's about the only thing worth buying here.'

'What about ginseng?'

'What about it?' demanded Morgan. 'Have you tried the one with the snake in the bottle?' He shuddered extravagantly. 'We ought to get danger money.'

They were all readers of *The Arbiter*, members of that large but fickle audience which made up the circulation figures. They were not as he had imagined them.

His own readers, he had always supposed, were people like himself; vaguely liberal, supporters of the arts and causes deemed to be good. He had never envisaged an exact mirror image. But he had nothing in common with the group at the bar.

Except, he thought guiltily, his pursuit of women. Frobisher's quest sounded remarkably like his own. He decided to edge the subject from the agenda, but it was not easily done.

'They don't drink much,' said Lumsden.

'Who doesn't?'

'The women here,' he said impatiently. 'There's none of what you might call social intercourse.'

'No bloody intercourse whatever,' said Frobisher. He tossed another serving of prawn crackers into the fish basin. 'They think we want to corrupt them. Bloody cheek. It's not their minds I'm after.' He leaned on one elbow and looked moodily up into Patrick's face. 'I suppose you're writing one of those articles about East-West relations. About barriers coming down.'

'Possibly.' He must not mention the panda, he reminded himself. When they read the story in the paper they would remember him as a man of discretion.

'It's going to take years,' said Morgan. 'Centuries maybe.'

'But you're here doing business. That's a start.'

'Keeping an eye on us, are you,' said Frobisher. It was a statement rather than a question and no answer was required. 'I'll tell you what we're doing,' he went on. 'Showing the bloody flag, that's what. With much bloody effort and to no purpose whatever.' He waved his free hand, dismissing the empty chairs, the fish tank and the piped muzak. 'One whole week and I've not sold a bloody thing. This is supposed to be the market of the future, but nothing's happening.' He leaned forward and breathed beer in Patrick's face. 'You should put that in your paper. Right between the tits on page three. Someone might see it then.'

There was a rattle of applause and it was evident that

Frobisher had made the speech before. Morgan patted the top of his sweaty head. 'He gets a bit hot and bothered,' he said. 'But that's not how it works. The truth is we don't know what they really want to buy. We're just fishing. So while they make up their minds we do a bit of business between ourselves. Just to keep in practice, like.' He drew diagrams on the bar top in spilt beer. 'Say you've got some fruit juice,' he said. 'You trade that for a consignment of cotton from the Somalis and you trade *that* for a load of shirts from France. If you're very lucky you trade *them* for some lemons from Lebanon and then you might have a deal. If the Koreans snap it up you get a letter of credit drawn on a Swiss bank and you can bugger off home.' He dabbed his lips with a handkerchief. 'If you've got no lemons you sit and wait.'

The muzak coughed and died and Patrick heard his name on the speaker. 'Overseas telephone call for Mr Lamb,' said the announcement. 'Please report to the reception desk.'

He had booked a call to Dominic Downey the day before, but the lines had been constantly engaged. This, he had no doubt, was an enquiry as to why he was bothering them at all. He pressed his ear to the receiver and recognized Downey's voice through a peppering of static. 'Hello, hello. Is everything all right?'

'There's been a development,' he said. 'We're not just collecting the panda. We have to catch it first.'

'Don't be ridiculous.'

'Believe me,' said Patrick. 'We're joining an expedition. God knows how long it will take.'

'How long do you suppose?'

'I've no idea. Weeks, I should think. Did anyone warn the Admiral?'

'He's said nothing to me.'

'You'd better tell him then. He may want to call it off.'

'Why should he want to do that? You're on the spot. Just get on with it.'

It was so easy for Downey, he thought; easier still for the Admiral. Gods issued edicts and expected them to be obeyed. If anything went wrong, thunderbolts were dispatched. There were no mitigating circumstances. Any excuse, valid or not, was regarded as an obstacle to the divine will. Any cockup was sacrilege.

'You have to remember,' he said, 'I'm not an expert.'

Downey sighed across deserts and oceans, a long way for irritation to travel. 'We've already discussed this. I assume they have experts of their own.'

'I'm sure they do.'

'Then make use of them. Show some initiative.' He paused for several seconds and, in the distance, Patrick heard music. It was like the echo of a civilization, achingly out of reach. He felt faint with longing for his own country. 'Is there anything else?' asked Downey.

'You could warn people we might be delayed. Lottie has a family. They'll want to know.'

'Very well. He imagined him jotting the memo on his lizard-skin pad. 'And what about you? Is there anyone I should inform?'

Patrick thought hard. 'No one,' he said.

The line went dead before he could say goodbye and as he put the phone down he saw Lottie coming towards him down the staircase. She had changed into a blouse and skirt, a transformation which would please the boys in the bar, he thought.

'Someone's been messing about with my camera bag,' she said.

'How do you know?'

'I've just checked the exposed rolls,' said Lottie. 'The panda film's gone.'

eight

Amos Bennet rang the doorbell at nine a.m. precisely. 'Time for safari,' he said.

It was Bennet's term for any domestic expedition, as if by making it sound exotic he could add thrills to a visit to the launderette or shopping for groceries. Patrick checked his wallet and selected a carrier bag. He was not thrifty by nature, but one cupboard of the kitchen dresser was crammed with bags which he could not bring himself to throw away. He had brought them with him when he moved in. Originally they had contained clothes bought by Cassandra. Latterly they had held books, a frying pan and an alarm clock: the tools of bachelordom. The lettering on their sides – Liberty, Aquascutum, Burberry – reminded him of other days. He found them as nostalgic as a Beatles record.

Amos tapped his watch. 'We should be making tracks. They'll be all over us.'

Bennet planned his trips to the supermarket as meticulously as he would a military exercise. Timing, he said, was of the essence. Although the store opened its doors at 8.30, business was slack for the first hour. But then 'on the very dot' as Amos reminded him, there was a rush of customers which turned shopping into a brawl. It was as though a cattle chute had been slotted into each entrance. Women with trolleys, women with baskets, women with no weapons but their bare hands stormed down the aisles and grabbed what they wanted. The first time he saw them coming Patrick had fled. It was not worth risking his life for a jar of mayonnaise.

'We're going in your jalopy?'

'I suppose so.'

Amos was a non-driver. It was not a disadvantage, he argued. 'London's full of cars. Plenty of people to give you a lift, only too pleased.' Being a passenger did not inhibit him from criticizing others who used the road. 'Look at that stupid woman,' he exclaimed, as Patrick turned on to Battersea Bridge, fractionally behind a red MG. 'No signals, no indication.' He leaned out of the window as they drew abreast. 'Go home madam,' he roared. 'Go home before you kill someone.'

The driver of the other car raised two fingers. She had short streaked hair and wore dark glasses. 'Don't shout,' said Patrick, 'it's very distracting.'

'You saw what she did.'

'Of course I saw. I almost hit her.'

'You should report her,' said Amos. 'People like that should be locked up.'

Patrick reduced speed and the MG shot ahead. 'She's getting away,' complained Amos.

'I want her to get away.'

'Did you take her number?'

'Of course not. I'm driving.'

'I'll take it then.' He fumbled for his ball-point, but he was too late. 'Did you get a good look?' he said. 'Dirty little scrubber.' He sat back, his mouth crimped in disapproval. 'Imagine the state of her underwear.'

'Her underwear?' He tried and failed to make the connection.

'If she wears any, that is.'

'I hadn't given it much thought.'

'I suppose not. It doesn't bear thinking about.'

The preoccupations which Amos sometimes revealed were disconcerting, thought Patrick. It was like admiring a classical facade and realizing that behind it voyeurs and tyrants were secretly at work. When they looked out of the windows it was either to gloat or complain. Amos, he knew, had received a visitor the night before. Waking early he had heard the street door open and close, followed by the tap of heels on the pavement. He resolved not to mention it. Sexual success for Amos was usually followed by a lecture on his own dismal performance. He did not have long to wait.

'I spent a very therapeutic evening,' said Amos.

'Good for you.'

'Very necessary. Keeps the glands working. Shunts the old blood round the system.'

He could have been describing physical jerks, thought Patrick, or some operation in a railway siding. No doubt it was one of his nice little arrangements, entered into without affection or even desire. They were not alike. They were not driven by the same demons. Amos was troubled by an itch, while he was plagued by an ache. His own compulsion, he thought as the lorry behind him flashed its headlights, urging him into the fast lane, was the harder to explain. Cassandra had dealt him a blow which, although it was not mortal, showed no sign of healing. In the paper that morning an item in Open Heart had caught his eye. 'Men in the bedroom,' he read with a prickle of apprehension, 'are an alien species. The laws which rule their desires have little to do with the law of the land.' He put the paper down. There was no need to read on. This was Cassandra's sermon on rape and he knew it by heart. She had already given it several trial runs, but this was the definitive version – inspired, he could only assume – by seeing him at Beechers. He wondered if Lottie read the column and, more importantly, if she identified him as the villain in Cassandra's lightly-veiled memoir. If she did see him as Mr Bad it could seriously affect their working together.

He flinched as the lorry swung out behind him and clattered past in a cloud of exhaust fumes. 'For God's sake,' said Amos. 'Didn't you see him flashing?'

'I saw him.'

'You should pay more attention. It's what I was saying. You have to keep the glands working. Open up. Invigorate the system.'

He had cued himself in. He described how he had spent the evening in detail. As Patrick had supposed, it was a nice little arrangement, one which left him with pink cheeks and a clear conscience. 'I'm amazed you didn't hear us,' he said. 'We gave the old bed springs a good seeing to.'

'How did you meet her?'

'She came to interview me,' said Amos. 'Something about sex in the middle years.'

'So you gave her a demonstration.'

'You could say that.'

It was a pity that he already had, thought Patrick. Amos had a way of filing his anecdotes under convenient headings and he had supplied a handy reference. He wished, not for the first time, that Amos did not look quite so fit. It came, he would say, from practising what he preached and while it was easy to disapprove of the process, the working model was in wonderful shape.

He saw a parking meter, miraculously free, but as he indicated that he was about to turn, the red MG shot into the vacant space. He stalled on the crest of the road. Horns yelped at his tail and he fumbled with the ignition. It was five minutes before they were again driving down Kings Road and ten minutes more before he had found somewhere to park.

'You will note that I am saying absolutely nothing,' said Amos.

He stood at the kerb, waiting for Patrick to lock the car door. In profile he looked like the photograph on his book jackets, although it had been taken many years earlier. It was a reasonably famous face, made familiar not only by bookshop displays, but also by his regular appearances on TV. At the start of his public life Amos had specialized in looking rude. It did nothing to discourage the punters, he said. People smiled at him in the street and seemed grateful when he did not actually spit in their eyes. Sometimes they spoke to him, reciting the list of his books that they owned and he nodded gravely, acknowledging their good taste. Occasionally, he gave autographs.

It was happening again, Patrick thought, as a middle-aged couple, both wearing green loden coats, paused on the pavement, and engaged him in conversation. The man was clutching a book and Amos took it from him and flipped open the cover. He scrawled his name on the fly-leaf and handed it back. The reaction was not what he had expected. The couple stared at the inscription and voices were raised. Two of them were in German, and squinting at the book, which was now being waved in Bennet's face, Patrick saw that it was a street directory. Amos brushed them aside and strode in the direction of the supermarket.

Patrick hurried after him. 'What was that all about?'

'Bloody foreigners. Can't even speak the language.'

'What did they want?'

'Directions for somewhere or other. Hopeless people. Complete waste of time.'

His face was slightly pinker than it had been when he was proclaiming his state of health and he was breathing heavily. A mistake had been made. Why was it so deeply satisfying, Patrick wondered, that it had been made by Amos Bennet.

He had not told Amos about the Lonely Hearts letters; he was not sure that he could tell anyone. In his cubicle at *The Arbiter* he took a handful from his brief-case and spread them on the desk. Some of them he already knew by heart.

Dear Personable 43

I am unattached and in search of emotional adventure. I think emotion is the most powerful force in life. We are what we feel. I am a mature lady, considered by many to be attractive, as well as good company. I enclose a photograph. The dog I am holding passed away last year. Perhaps you would return it to me in due course. The photograph I mean, not the dog. I enjoy conversation, ballroom dancing and good books. I am genuinely affectionate.

Hi there!

Your ad really hit the spot. I value frankness above all and sense that we have a lot in common. Cuddles by mutual agreement could be the first giant step for mankind. Womankind too! I am mad about Italian food and late-night movies. Preferably on video with a remote control!

> Dear Horny Old 43
>   I can read your mind. Ring this number and find
> out if you can handle a real woman.

Where did they spring from? he asked himself. How could
his discreetly worded advertisement have produced such a
response? There were thirty letters, some of them abusive,
some with photographs, some evasive, but most of them
disconcertingly direct. He was grateful for the anonymity of
the box number. There were several of his correspondents he
would not dare to meet face to face.

He thought of consulting Felix Bell. Indirectly, he had
endorsed the Lonely Hearts initiative, but it was unlikely
that he had further advice to offer. For Bell it was amusing,
but emphatically downmarket. In his circle, friends did things
with friends and no outside agency was required. Patrick
stirred the pile with one finger and took another random
sample.

> Dear Box 302
>   I am thirty-five years old, single and professionally em-
> ployed. I would be interested in meeting a fellow explorer.
> I attach my telephone number. You may call me between
> 11 a.m. and noon.
>   Judith Wales.

It was certainly different, he thought. It was not coy, or
coarse, or desperate. It seemed to have been written by
someone, not unlike himself, who preferred to look the
ground over before waxing more enthusiastic. The tone
was cool, but not uninterested. Why would she write at
all if his invitation had not touched a chord. He looked
up and down the corridor and waited until two secretaries
had passed. Then he dialled the number. 'Is that Miss
Wales?'

'Speaking.'

'This is your fellow explorer.'

'I beg your pardon.'

'It's what you said in your letter. You answered my advertisement.'

He heard a comfortable easing of breath; a welcoming sound, he thought. 'So I did.'

'I liked what you had to say.'

'Thirty-five, single and professionally employed,' she said reminiscently. 'And who are you?'

He told her his name. 'I'm a writer.'

'Forty-three and personable.'

'I know it sounds absurd,' said Patrick, 'but it's not easy to describe yourself in twenty words.'

'You managed very well.'

'Thank you. Perhaps we could meet.'

'Where and when?'

He had the sensation of having stepped on an escalator that was travelling much faster than he had anticipated. It was not too late. He could put the phone down. But he pressed on. 'How about this evening?'

'Eight o'clock,' said Judith Wales. 'Bunting's Bar in Jermyn Street.'

'How will I recognize you?'

'Watch out for the cats,' she said.

It was the day that he visited his osteopath. His name was Bassett and his consulting rooms were in an office block behind Baker Street. He was a tall, dejected man who wore a thick gold watch on his wrist. Before he began his examination he always took it off and placed it on a chair beside the couch.

'A gift from a grateful patient,' he told Patrick. 'I made him walk again. Literally. Eighteen carat gold and jewels wherever you look. He couldn't thank me enough.'

'I'm grateful too.'

'I'm not surprised. You were in a pitiful state when you came to me. Bad posture. Wrong diet. Years of neglect.'

Mr Bassett could never be called an optimist, but he pursued hope like a terrier chasing a rat. His teeth rarely made contact, but he had no doubt that his quarry was there, somewhere in the dark, within an inch of being caught. Occasionally they were both rewarded by some slight shift in the joints, a movement of the vertebrae which caused Mr Bassett to hiss with excitement. Lately, though, there had been little progress. Each week Mr Bassett looked more solemn and his references to the watch became more pointed. It was not *his* fault, he was saying. He had performed miracles in the past. But his subjects then had been more responsive, perhaps more deserving and certainly more rich. Patrick failed on all counts.

When the receptionist showed him in he thought he had entered the wrong room. Mr Bassett was not alone. With him was a girl in a white coat, with a deeply-tanned face and dark hair cut in a fringe. 'May I introduce Miss Flynn,' said Mr Bassett. 'She's joining the practice.'

They shook hands and Patrick tried to match her firm grip. 'Are you taking me on?'

'If that's all right with you.'

'Absolutely. No objections.'

Mr Bassett gave her his case file. 'Very stubborn, this one. If he'd come sooner we'd stand a better chance now.'

'I came when it all started,' said Patrick.

Mr Bassett shook his head. 'That's what you believe. But you ignored the symptoms. Most people do.'

It was Mr Bassett's fail-safe, thought Patrick. He had always wanted to introduce him to his brother-in-law. Mr Bassett and Richard had much in common, including a nodding acquaintance with God. 'Look at the dates,' he said. 'I've been coming here for years.'

'Not soon enough.'

'You never said so before.'

'Why depress the patient,' said Mr Bassett. 'In your case depression is a factor that weighs heavily. We don't want to add to the weight.'

He showed the X-rays to Miss Flynn, sighing audibly as he did so. Patrick sat down and studied his finger-nails. Pictures of bones reminded him of his mortality. He was aware of the skull beneath the skin and it occurred to him, painfully and without warning, that this skeleton was the vehicle in which he was travelling to what he had described in his advertisement as 'an emotional adventure'. He wondered if it was roadworthy.

Miss Flynn waved him behind the screen. 'Would you undress please.' She put the X-rays back in the file and washed her hands. 'We're starting from scratch,' she said.

He heard Mr Bassett close the door behind him and stepped out of his trousers. His underpants were all right, he thought; they were clean on that morning. His stomach sagged over the waistband and he sucked it in hopefully before letting it slide. He was not fat, he told himself. His mother had always described him as 'pleasantly plump', but that was years ago. He had usually been able to find ready-made suits to fit him, but his measurements were on the move. Instead of sweaters marked M, he was more comfortable in those labelled XL. Half an inch had gone on to his neckband. Old jackets were tight under the arms and, running upstairs, he found himself short of breath.

'Would you step on the scales,' said Miss Flynn.

He did so and willed the inches away. 'I tend to put it on in the autumn.'

'So I see.'

She measured his height and ran her finger down his spine. Her finger tips were cool against his skin and he shivered pleasurably. It was as if she was reading him in Braille. His secret life, such as it was, lay open to her touch. 'I suppose some backs are more interesting than others,' he said.

'I suppose they are.'

'Someone suggested I wrote a book about mine.'

'Indeed?'

'Not just mine. About backs in general. He said it could be a best-seller.'

He was showing off, he realized, but it was excusable. Nakedness induced either humiliation or bravado and he felt the need to impress this woman to whom he had been newly introduced and whose knowledge of him, so far, relied on Mr Bassett's assessment.

She looked him up and down, back and front. 'Your left shoulder,' she said, 'is higher than your right. Half an inch I'd say.'

'Is it really.' It was like learning that he was deformed. How could he have not noticed?

'It's not that unusual,' said Miss Flynn. 'It may simply be the result of bad working habits. We can change those.' She motioned him on to the couch and switched on the overhead lamp. 'We'll start with some heat to relax the spine. Then comes the laying-on of hands.'

'That sounds promising.'

'Wait and see.'

He was not disappointed. Lying face downwards, his cheek cushioned by a towel, the lamp hot on his back, he let his mind drift. Talcum powder fell like soft, dry rain and breathing its bathroom scent he daydreamed of childhood. Relationships were simple then, he thought, even with women. Especially with women. Because they were in control there were no arguments. It was when the child became a man that he became an enemy.

Her hand spanned his back and began a circular massage. 'How does it feel?'

'Delicious.'

Her finger probed more insistently and he felt her breath baste the back of his neck. It came from immaculate lungs, he told himself. He imagined them expanding and contracting, the machinery in perfect order, the breasts rising and falling beneath the white coat and he realized that, in all innocence, his body was responding to the treatment. He had an erection which threatened to hoist him from the couch. He raised himself on one elbow to relieve the strain and the massage stopped.

'Is anything wrong?'

'Just a twinge.'

'Let me see if I can find it.' The hands descended again and he thought desperately of trains and multiplication tables. He thought of Cassandra and of his coming journey and, temporarily, he felt himself shrink. 'I've just remembered an appointment,' he said. 'I really have to go.'

'I've almost finished.'

She pressed him down on to the table and the erection sprang back, as rampant as before. There had been times, he thought, when he would have welcomed such a speedy return to form. It would be reassuring to know that it could be relied on when he met the explorer from Lonely Hearts. But not now. Her thumbs eased his vertebrae apart, nudging them into alignment, and he recalled the X-ray photographs whose shadowy text he could not bear to read. There was a word meaning boneyard, he reminded himself. Ossuary. From the Latin. It had a suitably gloomy sound, but it was no help. The hands withdrew and he remained where he was.

'All done,' said Miss Flynn.

'In a minute.' He turned on the table so that he was facing away from her, but he was still several paces away from the screen where he had left his clothes. He slid his feet on to the floor, his hands cupped in front of him as though he was fielding a catch driven from the rear. It was a ridiculous posture.

'Are you having difficulty?' enquired Miss Flynn.

Patrick hobbled forward a foot or two, then dropped his hands. As you can see.'

Miss Flynn regarded him impassively. 'If it will help I'll leave the room while you dress. But I can assure you, it's happened before and it will happen again. I'm not in the least offended. It's quite natural. You mustn't be embarrassed.'

'But I am,' said Patrick, feeling himself wilt as he spoke. The collapse was almost as upsetting as the erection itself.

'Don't be.' She wrote something in her notebook. 'Forget it ever happened.'

He dressed behind the screen – a pointless formality in the circumstances – and wondered if the incident was now part of his case history. It was no use telling him to forget it had happened. It had never happened with Mr Bassett.

It was after eight when he found Bunting's Bar. He had allowed himself plenty of time to park, but the West End was crowded and he wound up half a mile away outside the Atheneum. From there it was a brisk walk, and he arrived sweating slightly and out of breath.

The bar was only half full. In the farthest corner, with a clear view of the door, sat a woman with cropped red hair. Her face was pale, with a red slash of a mouth and two Siamese cats were sprawled on her lap. He walked up to her table and, without thinking, he bowed.

'You look like the waiter,' she said.

'How do you mean?'

'Bowing like that.'

'I'll try again,' he said. 'Are you Miss Wales?'

'Judith,' she said. 'And you must be Patrick.'

He nodded, more eagerly than he had meant to. 'I'm late.'

'Not very. Sit down.'

He had the feeling that she was on familiar ground and that he was being interviewed. 'It was the parking,' he said. 'I couldn't find anywhere near.'

'I take taxis.'

'Very wise.' He offered his finger and both cats rammed their faces against it. 'I like cats,' he said. 'I had one, but it ran away. I think it's gone wild.'

She stroked their flat heads. 'This is Charlie,' she said, 'and this is Rupert. I take them everywhere.'

He saw that they wore collars and leads of plaited red leather. 'Just like a dog.'

'Nothing like a dog,' she said. 'There are cat people and there are dog people. They're quite different. I like cats because they're discreet. They have perfect manners.'

He was reminded of his duty. 'Would you like a drink?'

'I was drinking white wine,' she said. 'This is a wine bar. Do you mind?'

'Not at all.'

They shared a bottle of Chardonnay while around them the bar filled up. Were there many replies to your advertisement?' she asked.

'Quite a few.'

'Funny ones?'

He hesitated. 'Some of the photographs were a bit off.' There had been one of a girl standing knee-deep in a stream, looking back at the photographer through her splayed legs. She was naked and on the back of it she had written: 'Nature in the raw'. He decided not to mention it.

'I've never sent a photograph,' she said.

He choked on his wine. 'Have you done this before?'

'Once or twice. It's a way of meeting people. It cuts the corners.'

'This is my first time,' said Patrick. He felt as though he was confessing to a lack of moral fibre, a deficiency which might lose him a job or a promotion. The cats squirmed against his hand and he scratched behind their ears. 'They're very friendly,' he said.

'They sleep with me.'

'So did mine.'

She smiled over the rim of her glass. 'That's one thing we have in common.'

They had dinner at an Italian restaurant in Queensway. He fed scampi to the cats and allowed them to lick his fingers. 'They like you,' she said.

'That's just cupboard love.'

'Doesn't that strike you as a peculiar expression?'

He thought about it. 'I suppose it means pretending affection for something you want. Out of the cupboard.'

'I've never done that.'

'Bully for you,' said Patrick.

Conversation was not exactly sticky, but topics were restricted. They shared no friends and no joint enthusiasms had so far emerged. She read books, but had no favourite authors. She went to see films, but only as a way of passing time. The theatre, she said, was boring. She did not go to galleries. 'Tell me about your job,' he pleaded.

'You don't want to hear about that.'

'Yes I do.'

'I run an agency,' she said. 'Model girls.'

'You mean fashion.'

'A bit of that, but we specialize. Centrefolds, page three and screamers.'

'Screamers?'

'Girls who scream,' she said patiently. 'On paperback covers. The ones who are going to get their throats cut. Or shot. Or raped.' She rolled her eyes and flopped back in her chair. 'Victims,' she said. 'You must have seen them.'

It was a Lamb's Tale, thought Patrick. His fingers itched for his notebook. 'You mean there are girls who specialize in doing that?'

'Of course there are. It's practically an art form. Some of them have quite a following.'

'I can imagine. You must choose them very carefully.'

'It's instinct,' she said. 'And imagination. I can usually spot a good screamer. I know what people want.'

Her flat was in Holland Park. There was a lime tree outside the house and beneath it the pavement was still gummy from the nectar which had fallen during the summer. The cats nibbled at their paws and Patrick picked them up. 'I'm on the first floor,' she said.

He followed her up the stairs and into a living room. The furniture was all white and cushions were scattered on the floor. A vase of chrysanthemums stood on a circular glass table and beside a television set there was an assortment of bottles on an antique tray.

She put her hands on her hips and looked around. 'Here we are then.'

He remembered the last time he had seen someone home. 'Do you share with anyone?'

She shook her head. 'I'm all alone.'

Patrick stroked the back of the settee. 'Charming,' he said. 'And it's been a delightful evening. I'm glad you came.'

'Would you like a drink?'

'A brandy perhaps.'

'You can bring it into the bedroom,' she said.

He was not sure that he had heard correctly. She spoke with no inflection and her face gave away nothing. 'What did you say?'

She opened a door to her right and crooked a finger. 'This way.'

The escalator had speeded up again. Nothing had prepared him for the instant invitation. He peered over her shoulder. There was a large double bed with a pink duvet and, beside it, a lamp with a dull green shade. The walls and the ceiling seemed to be covered with the same fabric and when he looked closer he saw that they were carpeted. 'It's for the cats,' she said. 'They like their fun and games too.'

He still hesitated and she sighed gently. 'Don't worry. There's nothing nasty in the woodshed.'

'I should hope not.'

'There's no need to sound smug. How about you?'

'There's nothing wrong with me,' he said stiffly.

She kicked off her shoes. 'It depends what you mean. How long have you been divorced?'

'Not long.'

'And it's on your mind.'

'Not especially.'

'Something is. I don't get many refusals.'

'I'm not refusing,' said Patrick. 'I'm just a bit . . .' He groped for the right word.

'Shocked?'

'Surprised,' he said. 'We only met this evening.'

She sat on the edge of the bed and turned back the duvet. Behind her on the wall he saw the framed photograph of a woman wearing a short black slip. The strap had fallen from one shoulder and she was drawing back in apparent horror from a shadow that streaked the floor. Her mouth was wide open and she appeared to be screaming.

He pointed to it in sudden recognition. 'That's you.'

'In happier days.' She spread her arms and beckoned him closer. 'Let's take a look at you.'

He advanced until their knees were touching and stood motionless as she pulled down the zip of his trousers. He was afraid to look, but felt her hands sliding the underpants over his hips and lifting his penis between finger and thumb. He was being inspected, he thought, tested for fitness and quality. He had been to markets where meat underwent the same scrutiny. If it passed muster it was awarded a purple stamp. His foreskin was unfurled like the finger of a glove and he felt it growing taut, melting into flesh as his erection returned. Her touch was even more clinical than Miss Flynn, but his reaction was spectacular. 'Very presentable,' she said. 'Now get the brandy. And bring one for me.'

He was gorged with blood, rooted to the spot. 'I'm not sure that I can walk.'

'Crawl then. You can have the bathroom in five minutes.'

The cats rubbed against his legs, weaving between his feet as he made his way back to the drinks tray. Cats were discreet, he reminded himself. They were witnesses who would never be called to testify. He wondered what they had seen, what guests had been made welcome by Judith Wales. He remembered what she had said at the wine bar. It was a way of meeting people. It cut the corners. He had lied when he told her that he was not shocked, but the shock was already dissolving like an unimportant bruise

111

which would leave no reminder of what had caused it. What happened here was secret. It was a meeting between equals, by consent and in camera.

'The bathroom's free,' she called and he took the drinks through, averting his eyes as he passed the bed. He did not want to look; not yet. He washed himself and left his clothes piled on a laundry basket. When he returned, the door to the living room was closed and the cats were pacing between the dressing table and a chest of drawers. Judith Wales lay with the duvet up to her chin and he peeled it back, fold upon fold, as though he was putting away a flag.

She watched him with wide eyes, breathing through her mouth and panting slightly. 'What are you going to do to me?'

'What do you want me to do?'

She stretched her arms above her head and he saw that there were scarves knotted around the bed posts. 'Tie me up. Not too tightly.' She shivered as though she was racked by a fever and her breasts trembled. The nipples were bright with rouge and there was more of it, tracing the folds of her labia, blurred on the shaven mound.

He stroked her cheek and she jerked her head away. 'Not that.'

'Sorry.' There was clearly a procedure to follow, but he felt it was impolite to ask what it was. He tethered her wrists and saw her strain against the silk. 'Not too tight?'

She gritted her teeth and groaned. Out of the corner of one eye he saw the photograph on the wall. They were both role-playing, but fiction had succumbed to real life. Now they were actually doing it. The freeze frame had become a live performance.

He stroked the inside of one thigh, but she clamped her knees together. 'On the table.'

He saw what she meant. Neatly arrayed beneath the lamp, there was a selection of condoms. Some of them were flavoured. Some were ribbed. One packet showed a protuberance like a coxcomb. The sheer variety was distracting. He made his choice and stripped away the foil, but she shook her head again. 'Give it to me. In my mouth.'

He placed it on her tongue, like a tablet or a communion

wafer, and knelt over her. It was confusing, he thought. The surgeon being operated on by the patient. Her lips held him securely and he felt himself being caparisoned within a robing room whose walls were wet and muscular, where there was a single servant, deft and experienced. When he leaned back the condom was in place. The one he had chosen, for no good reason, except that it was the nearest to hand, was green. The packet said that it was lime-flavoured. It looked, he thought, as though he had strapped on an iced lolly.

Her thighs parted and she arched her pelvis. 'Fuck me,' said Judith Wales.

He entered her easily and she rose to meet him, rearing from the mattress, almost pitching him to the floor. Her legs thrashed from side to side and the scarves bit into her wrists. He withdrew to hover on the edge of penetration and as he lunged forward again, something landed on his back, digging in its claws as he wrenched his shoulders, trying to dislodge it. The pain was lacerating, but she locked her legs about his waist, holding him captive. Her teeth were bared in a fierce grin. He felt that he was fighting for his life. 'Don't stop,' she ordered. 'Don't you dare stop.'

One cat was followed by another. He saw them bound from the bed, on to the carpeted wall and from there to the ceiling, where they hung for a moment before dropping down again. They were playing a familiar game and he had been made part of it. His back was their launching pad. It must be bleeding, he thought, but as he turned to inspect the damage Judith Wales began to scream. At first it was like a sob at the back of her throat, rising in pitch and intensity, tearing away his inhibitions until he was screaming too. Someone will hear us, he thought, but then as he came, ejaculating in fear and ecstasy, he saw the carpeting and knew that they were safe. The Screamer had taken precautions. The room was soundproof.

'You can untie me now,' she said.

He did as he was told and awaited further instructions. They lay side by side, not speaking. He peeled off the condom and knotted the open end. When the lavatory was flushed it would sail out to sea, lime green on the morning tide. He stroked her back but she did not respond. They had not made love; they had met in battle. He had no complaints, nor did he have any illusions. The shopping list had been his idea, but Judith Wales had been the shopper.

nine

The black and white birds jaunted across the runway and perched on top of the control tower. 'Magpie,' said Patrick.

'Mockpie,' said Mr Lee.

It was not a word which he had encountered on the Linguaphone records and he was having trouble with the pronunciation. Two hours had passed since they had arrived at the airfield, but practice had not yet made perfect. 'It's an English species,' said Patrick. 'Very common at home.'

'Common here too.'

The plane was late and they were running out of things to say. They had admired each other's outfits, but the compliments had reached a dead end. The ski-suits had been replaced (at Mr Kim's suggestion, he suspected) by olive-green fatigues, lined with acrylic fleece, and in the pale morning sunshine Patrick felt uncomfortably warm. The weather was fine and the skies were clear. 'An excellent forecast,' Mr Kim had announced when he told them they were off, but time was not on their side. Unless the plane arrived soon there would be another postponement. Patrick stamped his feet. The fell boots reminded him of mountains to climb, rivers to cross. It promised to be a hard slog, but he could not contemplate another delay. It was like dressing up for a party, only to learn that it had been cancelled. He was eager to be gone.

A cancellation would tax even Mr Kim's ingenuity, he thought. In the past twenty-four hours he had laid on visits to the Acrobats' Theatre, where a magician conjured bales of cotton from an empty chest, followed by a banner reading 'Let Us Improve the Quality of Our Cloth', and the Fine Arts Museum, where squads of apprentices toiled on vast canvases, showing the Great Leader about his business of visiting steel workers, founding universities and giving on-the-spot advice to chicken farmers. 'On-the-spot' was a nice touch. It sounded a note of informality, but at the same time, implied that he could turn up anywhere, unannounced, ubiquitous and all-knowing. The master painter concentrated on the Great Leader's hands and face. The apprentices filled in the rest. It was not an equal division of labour. Effort was applied where it was most likely to be noticed.

He had nerved himself to mention the missing film, blaming no one, letting the facts speak for themselves. It had not gone down well.

'We have no thieves here,' said Mr Kim. 'It must have been mislaid.'

'It was in my bag,' said Lottie. 'I put it there myself.'

'How can you be sure? There was so much equipment.'

'I wrote on the label. You saw me do it.'

'So many labels. So many rolls of film.' He sighed reproachfully. 'We will make a search. Perhaps we will find it.'

But they had not found it, and Patrick assumed that it was now part of a dossier, already fat with details of Lottie's truancy, unguarded scraps of conversation and, for all that he knew, the information that he snored while he slept. Everything came in useful. Without doubt, it would also contain a record of his visit to the hospital. It was not an important item, but in days to come Mr Kim could turn to it for comic relief.

It had not been planned. As they were leaving the Fine Arts Museum, flinching from an icy wind which whipped the entrance as they took extended leave of the director, his back had gone into spasm. There was no warning. He was gripped by tongs of fire which bent him double, restricting his view of the world to the granite steps and Mr Lee's cockled shoes. He groped for support and saw the shoes point in his direction.

116

'What is wrong?'

'My back,' he gasped. 'It happens sometimes.'

He was led down the steps and slotted into the car. 'What can we do?' asked Lottie.

He lay breathless on the rear seat. The slightest movement sent flames leaping from the base of his spine to the nape of his neck. He could see them, red and black, like the breath of dragons. 'Just give me a moment. It'll pass.'

She bent over him, bringing their faces level.

'Does it really hurt?'

'Of course it bloody hurts.'

'You should see a doctor.'

'What doctor?'

'We'll find one.'

He heard her in rapid conversation with Mr Lee, then she slid on to the seat beside him. 'We're taking you to the hospital,' she said. 'They must have back people there.'

There was nothing he could do. He tried to brace himself as the car took them on a mystery tour, speeding through unseen streets, swerving round invisible corners, and coming to rest at a destination which he could only imagine. He imagined himself as the yolk in an egg, immensely fragile, suspended in a shell which the slightest jolt would fracture. Her hair brushed his face. 'Don't move,' she said. 'They're going to carry you in.'

'Don't go away.'

'I won't.'

He was loaded on to a trolley and wheeled through swing doors. He saw green-painted walls and a dingy ceiling. More doors opened and closed. He saw an instrument tray and a semi-circle of white jackets. There was a powerful smell of disinfectant. Hands reached down and he was turned on to his stomach.

His coat was peeled away and his shirt unbuttoned. His skin pimpled in the sudden chill. 'Please describe your symptoms,' said Mr Lee.

It took a long time. There was so much ground to cover. He told them about the hydro-therapy and the osteopath. He listed the last three attacks. Someone took his blood pressure; his respiration was checked. The white coats withdrew and he heard them muttering across the room. 'What are they going to do?'

'Something to relieve you.'

His trousers were pulled down to his knees and he felt the sting of alcohol on his right buttock. There was the stab of a needle and a moment of pure agony, as if acid had been flushed into his veins. 'The doctor wishes me to warn you that the injection will cause great pain,' said Mr Lee.

He was entirely correct, thought Patrick, and only a few seconds too late. He was panting as though he had run too fast and too far. But, almost immediately, he felt his back unlocking, the fiery tongs being folded away. He stretched himself experimentally and found that he could move.

'Did it work?' asked Lottie.

'I think so.'

'You had us all scared.'

'I'm sorry about that.' He turned away as he hitched up his trousers. 'Sorry about the strip-tease. Beyond my control.'

The doctors were watching him as if he was likely to fall down. He took three or four steps and they clapped their hands. 'Thank you,' said Patrick. 'Thank you very much.'

As always, when the pain retreated, he felt a fraud. Had it really been as bad as he had imagined? Pain had no memory. He could only recall what he had done, not the sensation which had induced the behaviour. If only the recollection of other discomforts was as short-lived; but humiliation lingered, so did loss. There was no analgesic powerful enough to send them packing. He massaged his still-tender buttock. 'Strong stuff,' he said.

A day later he could still feel where the needle had gone in. But now, he thought, it was not the only pain in the arse. The wait was becoming intolerable. Outside the reception shack he saw Lottie and Jack Blazer checking their baggage, piled high on loading trolleys. There were tents and sleeping bags, ground sheets and shovels, cases of rations and cooking pots. The quantities were ominous. There was enough food to keep them going for weeks.

Mr Kim was inside the shack making telephone calls. The

previous afternoon he had been waiting for them when they returned from the hospital. 'I was distressed to hear of your misfortune,' he said.

Patrick put on a brave face. 'Your doctors were wonderful.'

'I'm glad to hear it. You are recovered now?'

'Oh yes,' he said. 'Perfectly fit.'

'Quite certain?'

'Absolutely.'

'Excellent,' said Mr Kim. 'The expedition begins tomorrow.' He waited until the excitement subsided. 'And for Miss Lottie,' he said, 'we have another surprise. We have arranged a visit to Mr Lee's apartment.'

The probability, thought Patrick, was that Mr Lee was surprised too. But his double take was well concealed. If Mr Kim had made the arrangements, his part in the proceedings was to fall in line. There were always contingency plans and it was the job of minders to be adaptable. He had shown no great capacity for thinking on his feet. But taking orders came naturally. 'It will be an honour to welcome you,' he said.

The apartment was on the sixth floor and there was no lift. Patrick hauled himself up the concrete staircase and stroked his bruised thigh. On the fourth floor Jack Blazer caught up with him. 'How are you doing?'

'I'll get there.'

'Take your time. It won't go away.'

The rest of the party was well ahead, but the smell of Lottie's perfume and Mr Kim's cigarette smoke trailed behind them to mingle with an all-pervading reek of cabbage. Jack Blazer sniffed loudly. 'It hasn't changed much.'

'Since when?'

'Since I lived here.'

'When was that?'

'Years ago. This was the first block they put up after peace broke out.'

'What was it like?'

'What do you think it was like? I was on my jack. Just one room, twelve by twelve. And I was one of the lucky ones.'

'Luckier now.'

'You make your own luck,' said Blazer. 'Fitting in, that's

119

how it's done.' He savoured the tang of cabbage that swirled around them. 'It's the staple diet,' he said. 'That and rice. Boiled, braised, stir-fried. It's why they fart so much. You've probably noticed.'

Inside Mr Lee's apartment the smell was even more intense, but the picture that was presented was one of domestic bliss. Mr Lee's wife and their two daughters stood in line beside the television set. The sound was off, but in tireless mime the Great Leader went through his routine. The sequence was unaltered. First the construction workers, then the harvesters, then the hospital. It had all been shot years ago, thought Patrick. The man giving his advice to the workers was still young. He was overweight, the lard was already building up beneath his collar. But the face was unlined, the gestures vigorous. Mr Lee's family had grown up with the image. Did it ever occur to them that the figure on screen was now eighty years old? It was like falling in love with a movie star – Monroe, perhaps, or Dietrich – and feeding the infatuation with repeats. He forced himself to look away. The film was habit-forming and, like all junk, it created addicts. Repetition was the secret of all propaganda, good or bad. This show would run and run.

The Lee daughters shook hands and curtsied. They wore their hair in pigtails, tied with red ribbon. Their dresses were cotton prints, their shoes black and shiny. Lottie gave each of them a small box of chocolates. They looked hopefully at Mr Kim, hesitating until he nodded his approval. Mrs Lee accepted a slightly bigger box and murmured to her husband.

'She asks if you will take tea.'

'That would be lovely,' said Lottie. She looked around her and beamed with satisfaction. 'Isn't this cosy!'

It was one way of putting it, thought Patrick, but there were others. The apartment had three rooms. There was a kitchen, a bedroom and a living room. There was a table and four chairs. A single light-bulb with a coolie-hat shade hung from the centre of the ceiling. What appeared to be a roll of futons was stacked in one corner. On top of the TV set was a blue vase containing a spray of artificial flowers. Above the table hung a brightly coloured portrait of the Great Leader.

Mr Kim followed his gaze. 'It is not compulsory to hang the portrait,' he said. 'They do it out of love.'

'Out of love,' echoed Mr Lee fervently.

Patrick tried to guess the dimensions of the room they were in. It seemed very small. Even the ceiling was low. When he took an incautious step his head banged against the lampshade. 'How much space do you have?' he asked.

'All together?'

'All together.'

'Total of one hundred fifty square metres,' said Mr Lee. 'Sufficient for family of four.'

Mr Kim held his cigarette at arm's length and Mrs Lee sprang forward with a saucer before the ash detached itself. 'The quality of life . . .' he began, but then his English appeared to fail him. He addressed himself to Mr Lee, whose face took on an owlish solemnity. He could have been drunk or simply stunned by the importance of what he was being told.

'In the words of the Great Leader,' he intoned, 'the quality of life is enhanced by its limitations. Difficulties inspire even greater effort.'

Patrick willed the wax to rise in his ears. For most of his working life he had been a connoisseur of claptrap. But here was a specimen which took the biscuit. He stared hard at Mr Kim, inviting him to crack a smile. In vain. Mr Kim's gaze remained fixed on the portrait of the Great Leader. If there were games to be played, this was not one of them.

The tea came in shallow green bowls without handles. 'Sit, sit,' Mr Lee urged them, dusting the chairs and pulling them away from the table. He and his wife remained standing, their children arranged neatly in front of them, as if they were being treated to some rare spectator sport. Probably, thought Patrick, it was the first time they had played host to anyone. He burned his lips on the bowl and smiled through his tears.

'I thought we'd do a family group,' said Lottie. 'Quite formal beside the portrait. Then we might have Mrs Lee in the kitchen. And maybe putting the children to bed.'

Mr Kim raised his eyebrows. 'Is that necessary?'

'Not essential. It's just another situation. A change of scene.'

'But they are wearing their best dresses. It is in your honour.'

'That's wonderful,' said Lottie. 'I appreciate it. But I thought we'd try something a little more relaxed.'

'I think not,' said Mr Kim. 'There would be no point.'

Lottie peered into her light meter as if it contained a crib advising her how she should pursue the argument. 'I want to show that all families have things in common. That all children are alike.'

'But they are not alike,' said Mr Kim. 'Their environment is different. So is their education. So is their political awareness.' He spread his hands and shrugged. 'You saw them at the Children's Palace. You saw their performance.'

Indeed we did, thought Patrick. There was no hope of winning the debate. 'Do the family group,' he said. Lottie looked mutinous, but he squeezed her arm until she winced. 'Just do it.'

The chances were, he reassured himself, that of all the possibilities, it was the one most likely to succeed. The limitations of the pose could be an advantage. Arranging people like objects put them centre stage where they expected to perform and unconsciously, if not unselfconsciously, they projected something of themselves. Sometimes it seemed to shine from them like spokes of light, a radiance which declared who and what they were. It was an odd quality, rarely to be found in an official likeness. Public people were photographed too often. After a while their essence leaked away. Their image became as dull as a rubber stamp.

'My Mum had an old Kodak,' said Jack Blazer, whispering as if he was in a theatre. 'One of those you fold up like a concertina. We thought it was magic. She used to take our pictures on our birthdays to show how we'd grown.' He sighed reminiscently. 'She never wanted to be photographed herself. Said she looked stupid.'

'I don't suppose she did.'

'Course not. She was a cracker.'

'Is she still alive?'

Blazer shook his head. 'She passed away just after they put me in the cage. It was five years before they told me. Nobody bothered.'

'I don't suppose they could get in touch.'

'They could if they'd wanted to.' He blew his nose and wiped it tenderly. 'I still get narked when I think about it.'

They watched Lottie go to work. She ignored Mr Lee and his wife, concentrating instead on the children, smoothing their pigtails, straightening the pleats in their dresses, buffing up their shoes until the toecaps dazzled like anthracite. She knelt in front of them, inching them into position. 'Hold hands,' she told them, and they linked their fingers, clinging to each other as if they were practising kerb drill. It was like a shot from a television commercial, sentimental and sweetly incongruous in the drab room.

'Should we smile?' enquired Mr Lee.

'If you like.' She ducked forward and tweaked a ribbon into place.

'Important to know.'

She did not reply, but stared into the viewfinder. It was as though she was meditating, waiting for an image to form. The silence lengthened. Mr Kim cleared his throat. There were voices on the landing. A door opened and closed. The girls scuffed their toes on the rush matting and stared up at their mother. She did not speak, but her hands crept down and cradled their faces. Mr Lee stroked their hair fondly, protectively, and Lottie pressed the button.

It was a pose, Patrick realized, which she could never have suggested, let alone rehearsed. The family had come together, uniting in the presence of strangers. It was the picture she had planned and he felt a rush of pride, as sudden as it was unexpected.

'Are you happy?' he asked her as they drove back to the hotel.

'More or less.'

'You got what you wanted?'

'Some of it.'

'I thought you did brilliantly.'

'Don't sound so surprised.'

'I'm not,' he said. 'Not at all. I was impressed. I just wanted you to know.'

They had left Mr Lee at his apartment and a second car had taken Jack Blazer home. Mr Kim described the schedule for the following day. They were to rendezvous at eight; the plane would take off two hours later. 'I should speak to London,' said Patrick. 'They'll want to know what's happening.'

Mr Kim nodded in the darkness. 'They will be informed.'

'I should tell them myself.'

'If it can be arranged.' He wound down the window and his cigarette cart-wheeled into the night. 'We are in touch with London. They will be told of developments.'

'But they may have questions.'

'We can tell them what they need to know.'

'You don't know what they'll ask.'

'We have all the necessary information.'

It was like trying to talk to a machine, thought Patrick. For every initiative offered there was a stock response, not rude or hostile, but dispensed automatically like a tablet, foil wrapped, according to prescription. What was just as unsettling, when he considered it, was the assumption that London – which meant the unspeakable duo of Dominic Downey and the Admiral – was content with the way things were. Matters were proceeding on the basis of need to know. Mr Kim had used the very words. What it meant, he supposed, was that the details of the operation were considered too unimportant to alert London if they were altered or that events were dictated by a master plan in which he and Lottie were players too insignificant to be briefed on the grand strategy. Neither alternative did much to boost his confidence.

'You should arrive at your destination tomorrow afternoon,' said Mr Kim. 'You will be met by an army detail and driven to your base camp.' He lit another cigarette and stretched his long legs. 'To my great regret I shall not be with you. Jack Blazer will lead the expedition. He enjoys – how does he put it? – getting down to the nitty-gritty.'

'A bit of this and a bit of that,' said Lottie.

'I beg your pardon?'

'He says that too.'

'Ah, yes.' Mr Kim's cigarette traced the nodding of his head. 'Jack Blazer says many things. Hard to follow at times.'

'You seem to manage,' said Patrick. 'In fact, I've been admiring your English. Amazing how it comes back.'

'It comes and it goes.'

'I'll bet you never needed Linguaphone lessons,' said Lottie.

The cigarette wagged slowly from side to side. 'Life is a better teacher,' said Mr Kim.

He accompanied them into the hotel lobby where several members of staff positioned themselves like gun-dogs, quivering under the threat of orders. He ignored them, just as he ignored the salesmen trooping from the restaurant into the bar. 'Aye, aye,' said Mr Morgan draining an imaginary glass, but Patrick shook his head. It had been a demanding day and he was not in the mood for another instalment in the saga of British businessmen abroad.

'Very wise,' said Mr Kim. 'You should have an early night. Plenty of sleep. Ready to make a good start.' He took Lottie's hand and kissed it lightly. 'Remember the words of our Great Leader,' he told her. 'Difficulties inspire greater effort.' He turned on his heel before either of them could reply, but his expression hung in the air like the ghost of the Cheshire Cat. He was not mistaken, thought Patrick, as the street door hissed open and closed. He had said it with a smile.

At the airfield no one was smiling. The sky was blue and empty. The magpies flew sorties over the reception shack, but there was no other activity. 'That bloody plane,' said Jack Blazer. 'I'll have their guts for garters.'

Like Patrick, he wore a suit of olive-green fatigues and pinned over his heart the Great Leader scowled from a small plastic badge. It was an indication of rank, he explained. 'Everyone has to wear one. It shows you're in charge.'

'What do they call you?'

'"Sir",' said Blazer. 'That's good enough.'

For a British army deserter still on the run, thought Patrick, it was very good indeed. 'What's the latest news?'

'The plane's on the way. Kim's been giving them a bollocking. It's always the same. One lot tells you one thing, the other lot tells you something different. They want to get themselves organized!' he said. 'There's too many chiefs and not enough Indians. Like every bloody army.'

Ten minutes later the plane touched down. It was not a military aircraft. It had propellers, which made it a period piece and there was something about it – a cobbling together of glass and aluminium, dented and smudged from nose to tail with Cyrillic script – which reminded Patrick of a greenhouse. The wings appeared to have been patched in several places.

'From our Russian friends,' said Mr Kim, coming up behind him. 'An Ilushyin 14. Most reliable, I am told.'

'It doesn't look it.'

'Newly serviced,' said Mr Kim. 'That was the reason for the delay.'

'You mean they were putting it back together.'

'Nothing so extreme.'

Across the weathered tarmac the plane taxied to a stop. People got out. The baggage trolleys went to meet it. 'Don't go by appearances,' said Jack Blazer. 'They don't bother making things look pretty, but they work all right.' He grinned broadly when Patrick still looked doubtful. 'Honestly,' he said. 'It won't fall apart. It's got years to go.'

No one else seemed to be apprehensive. Their baggage was stowed away. The plane was refuelled. At the last minute, as they drank their coffee and extinguished their cigarettes, the same troupe of greeters who had met them only a few days earlier arrived with bouquets of azalea and pine twigs. Mr Kim must have had them waiting in the wings, thought Patrick. It was almost an act of faith, but not quite. Would they have made an appearance if the plane had failed to show? He supposed not. Significantly, the bouquets were only half the size of those they had been given before.

Cold weather may have reduced the variety of flowers, but the entire operation had an air, which he had only just detected, of penny-pinching. Protocol was being observed, but on a budget. Everyone was going through the motions, but their hearts were not in it. As a veteran of press junkets, Patrick had learned to interpret the omens – the watered whisky, the leathery sandwiches, the stale peanuts – and the message he was now receiving told him to beware.

As they stepped outside he saw that the weather was on the change. The sun was still shining, but the wind had freshened and black clouds were rolling in from the north. 'It won't be much,' said Jack Blazer. 'Bit of snow most likely.'

'More where we're going, I suppose.'

'Just a touch.'

'But nothing to worry about.'

'Not a thing.' He paused in mid-stride and caught Patrick's arm. 'They fly through this sort of stuff all the time. There's no problem. On my life.'

'On your *life*?'

'That's what I said.'

And rather self-consciously, thought Patrick. He imagined a thesis: *The Effects of Exile on Idiom.* By the end of the expedition he would be well qualified to write it. But he now doubted whether Jack Blazer ever did or said what came naturally. He sounded spontaneous, but candour was not what had kept him alive and kicking for forty years in the Great Leader's republic. Other qualities had helped him to survive.

Mr Kim walked ahead, one hand resting on Lottie's shoulder. In the past few days, Patrick recalled, he had been doing more and more touching. It was not sexual, although it was only Lottie that he touched. Nor was it paternal; there was nothing fatherly about Mr Kim. Comradely was a better description, as though, in Lottie, he had found a playmate; someone he could challenge and tease, whose limits he was curious to discover.

He imagined a dialogue between Mr Kim and Jack Blazer on the nature of Western women. Where would they begin? Both of them relied on memory, refreshed by rumour. If they believed only a fraction of what they read, their prejudices would be rampant. But neither could have the remotest idea of how dramatically, how irreversibly women had changed in the past four decades. Jack Blazer's time at Catterick was history. So was Mr Kim's tour of duty as a Soho waiter. Lottie must be a revelation to them both. And not only to them. Patrick watched the sway of her buttocks beneath the green denim and, for the first time in days, felt cheerful.

He was the last on the plane. Mr Kim shook his hand and shouted in his ear. 'Your back,' he screamed. 'Take care.'

'Right you are.' Patrick gave a thumbs up and stepped back smartly as the door slammed shut.

The greeters waved their pine branches and Mr Kim hung on to his hat. The engine noise grew louder and the tarmac became a blur. He saw the magpies scatter and snow blot the window, then they were above the cloud and climbing into the blue.

'ETA sixteen hundred hours,' said Jack Blazer.

'What did you say?'

'We should be there around four o'clock.'

'Thank you,' said Patrick. 'It sounds better in English.'

Blazer looked wounded and twirled the hair that branched from his right ear. 'Military usage prevents confusion.'

'Not for me,' said Patrick. 'I'm hopeless with that twenty-four hour stuff. I forget where I am and have to start again.' It had always enraged Cassandra, he recalled, especially when his inefficiency meant that he failed to record a programme on which she was appearing. It had happened more than once. What it meant, she told him, was that he resented her TV exposure.

'You mean you think I'm jealous?'

'Precisely.'

'But I'm not. Being jealous means that you covet what someone else already has. I don't want to appear on the box. I don't want anything to do with it.'

'You would if you were asked.'

'I've been asked.'

'By that potty little programme on Tyne Tees.'

'It doesn't matter where it was. I didn't want to do it.'

'London would have been different.'

'No it wouldn't,' he said. 'I've always told them no.'

And so he had. But, as always, the truth was many-sided. It was true that he distrusted television and its ability to manufacture so-called personalities. But what the camera did to him was much more damaging. It was hard to recognize the person he saw on the monitor; fat, shifty and pompous, a face for whom the off switch was invented. Not only his vanity was outraged; his sense of identity was shaken to its foundations.

He had never admitted as much to Cassandra. To have

done so would have been to present her with an even broader target when the shooting was resumed. But it was an image he found hard to forget. Was it his true self, he wondered. Was the unctuous, uneasy, untrustworthy creep appearing under his name the real Patrick Lamb? He had seen the apparition once and refused all invitations to give a repeat performance. Cassandra was wrong to suppose that he was jealous. His real fear was that one day he would be found out. He was perfectly sincere in questioning her ambitions to make it Big (even now the word made him want to spit), but there was no virtue in staying small. He heard himself groan. Moments of truth, like colic, gave him an actual pain.

'Are you okay?' asked Lottie.

'Nothing to worry about.'

'I heard you groan.'

'I do that sometimes,' said Patrick. 'Some people talk to themselves. I groan. It's a comment on the state of things.'

'At least we're on our way.'

'We are indeed,' he said. 'Into the wild blue yonder.' He looked out of the window and through a patch in the cloud saw railway lines and the dark smudge of a city. The map in Seeley's office had not been so explicit. Its very vagueness had given him hope and he did not want to lose sight of that. It was the accumulation of detail which sapped confidence. There was more and more, he decided, that he did not wish to know. Ignorance was not bliss, but it lent buoyancy, the means of floating over obstacles.

'How long d'you think we'll be?' she asked.

'As long as it takes. A few days I should imagine. They've probably got the panda pinned down already. There's been an advance party there for nearly a week. They sounded pretty positive.'

'Is that what Blazer says?'

'Blazer says they've found signs.'

'What sort of signs?'

'Tracks, scratches on tree trunks. They're very hopeful.'

'Terrific.' She rested her chin on her camera and looked at him through narrowed eyes. 'What do you think the odds are?'

'On finding it? Fifty-fifty perhaps.' In fact, he thought,

the odds should be significantly better than that. Blazer had sounded cheerful enough, but his optimism was perfunctory. He had told Patrick of the advance party's findings almost absent-mindedly as they waited outside Mr Lee's apartment and he had supplied further information only when asked.

The advance party comprised five men, he said. 'There's a vet and four squaddies who know the area. They've got a truck and a radio. When we get the panda they'll signal for a chopper to take it out.'

'Where will they take it?'

'Back to base. We fly it on from there.'

The ground below was changing. Towns were few and huge, unfenced fields bled away into forests and pasture. His eyes were heavy, but there were plans to be laid, strategies to be decided. Sleep was impossible, he thought, and slept before he had time to change his mind. He dreamed of falling and awoke as the plane touched down. There were two or three distinct bounces as the wheels met stones and pot-holes, then it rolled to a halt. The engines were switched off. Panels and rivets clicked and sighed like a house at night. Patrick felt his composure restored. He gathered his bags and made for the exit.

The sun had almost set but the landing strip extended like a jetty into grassland and ploughed fields. The air smelled of soil and smoke. It was very cold. 'Here they come,' said Jack Blazer, and a truck, its headlights blazing, drove down the approach road, parallel to the plane.

Blazer ran to meet it. Doors clashed open and shut. There was a brief but vehement burst of conversation and they saw him pick something up from the rear of the truck and turn towards them, holding it in his arms.

'Take a look at this,' he said.

'What is it?'

'Take a good look.'

He opened the neck of a black plastic bag and thrust it forward for inspection. Patrick lowered his head and sniffed tentatively, then more deliberately. 'Is this what I think it is?'

The hair in Jack Blazer's ears glowed in the dying of the light. 'Panda shit,' he said. 'The genuine article. We're in business.'

ten

Walking from the lift to his office Patrick passed three women in tears. They were not crying discreetly, as he remembered women used to cry, but loudly and disconsolately as if they were advertising grief. It was not an unusual sight at *The Arbiter*. Over the past year the unhappiness rate had soared. There was more to be anxious about. Tempers were shorter. Voices were frequently raised. Executives, even lowly ones, behaved like terrorists.

It was a fashion, thought Patrick, a kind of ruthlessness which was meant to indicate efficiency.

He could still hear the sounds of weeping when he sat at his desk. The cubicle had no door to close. Only the din from all sides ensured a partial privacy. Noise built in layers, one stratum burying another. When his telephone rang he counted to ten before picking it up. A gut feeling warned him that it was not a day for good news, but sometimes the bad news could be postponed.

'Lamb's Tales,' he said.

'Is that Patrick?'

'Uh, uh.' It was a woman's voice which he thought he recognized, but he hesitated before committing himself.

'Well, is it?'

'Possibly,' he said. 'Who wants him?'

There was a pause, then a long sigh. 'This is your fellow explorer.'

Oh God! he thought. 'Hello,' he said. 'And how are you?'

'Surprised,' she said. 'You left without saying goodbye.'

'You were asleep. I didn't want to wake you.'

'I'm awake now.'

He stared blindly out of the window. He had not expected her to call and he had no idea what to say. He had left the flat at first light. The cats were asleep at the foot of the bed and he had crept into the bathroom to dress. She lay on her back with the sheet down to her waist. There were still traces of rouge on her breasts, but it was like old graffiti. The message had been obliterated. She did not stir when he opened the door and when he closed it behind him he could hardly remember her face.

'I'm waiting for the verdict,' she said.

'The verdict?'

'How was it?' she asked. 'What every woman wants to know. On a scale of one to ten. Did we meet expectations?'

'Wonderful,' said Patrick fervently. 'Ten out of ten.'

'Honestly?'

'Absolutely. Quite fantastic.'

He heard himself laying on the superlatives as if he was filling in a ditch. It was a panic reaction. No one had ever asked him to rate their performance. Cassandra had always taken it for granted that she was beyond reproach and that it was her standard he had to meet. He wondered how he had scored on Judith Wales's clapometer.

'You were pretty fantastic yourself,' she said.

'Thank you.'

'I mean it. When are we having seconds?'

His heart thumped as if someone had struck him hard on the chest. 'I beg your pardon?'

'Don't be silly,' said Judith Wales. 'You heard what I said.'

And so, in all probability, had the switchboard, thought Patrick. It was a listening post where gossip was plucked from a thousand calls and recycled throughout the entire office.

He had to end the conversation and there was no polite way. 'I have to go,' he said. 'The editor wants me. I'll call you later.' He put the phone down and watched it nervously. If it rang again he would not answer.

What he needed was time to think. It was absurd to feel nervous. Judith Wales was not threatening, she was simply direct. She had kept her part of the bargain. She had even invited him back. But the speed of the transaction, the ease with which it moved from bottom gear to overdrive left him incredulous and uneasy.

It had been a wild night, but nothing had been left to chance. From start to finish events had followed a well-plotted scenario. If he closed his eyes he saw an action replay, as clinical as it was pornographic – the bound wrists, the tinted labia, the condom juggled on an agile tongue. Each image was like a text-book illustration designed to instruct as well as excite. And the stimulants had not only been visual. He remembered the scents of sweat and salt, the body's gravy. His response had been predictable, although he had not expected the violence with which he had reacted. But all that it meant was that the right buttons had been pressed. No sentiment had been involved. There had been no gentleness, no affection.

It had not been promised. In the jargon of *Arbiter* columnists, especially Cassandra who would have bored for England on the subject, his relationship with Judith Wales was performance-related. This time it had worked. The next time round – if there was a next time – the results could be humiliatingly different. He did not know whether he wanted to take the chance.

He was living in limbo. The date for the panda hunt had still to be decided and since the Admiral had put Lamb's Tales on hold he had no regular assignment. Theoretically, at least, he was available for other jobs. To avoid the worst of them one had to be creative. Patrick had come to an arrangement with the obituaries editor, and his in-tray was full. Already he had updated the lives of the Queen, a champion racehorse and a South London gangster too patriotic to emigrate to Spain, and he was looking forward to reassessing the career of Amos Bennet. He was not seeking revenge, but justice would be done.

'I quite enjoy it,' he told Felix Benn when they met for lunch. 'You can say what you like and the buggers can't sue.'

'What will you say about Amos?'

'That he was vain and arrogant and thought he was God's gift to women.'

'Does he still?'

'Implicitly. He could be right.'

Benn speared a grilled sardine and drenched it in lemon juice. 'I thought he was past all that.'

'Not a bit of it. I get all the details. How often and how long. He's an example to us all.'

'Not to me,' said Benn. 'It's too dodgy these days. It's an alphabet soup out there with AIDS and HIV. People are just dropping off their perches.'

'None of our lot. No one you've known. Personally, I mean.'

'Not yet,' said Benn. 'Give it time.'

Patrick felt a goose walk over his grave. In the warm restaurant he shivered. He had considered asking Benn's opinion about Judith Wales, but the moment had become inopportune. It was one thing to discuss Lonely Hearts and whether or not one could find a suitable partner by post and quite another to describe having already taken one to bed. In the light of the current conversation he could be thought to have jumped the gun.

'Mind you,' said Benn, 'natural causes are doing a pretty good job. How many was it last year?'

Patrick did his sums. 'Four altogether. Two strokes. One cirrhosis of the liver. One fall from a speeding bus.'

They reviewed the casualties.

'I'll come to yours if you'll come to mine,' said Patrick.

'Fair enough.' They shook hands across the table. 'Bring me up to date,' said Benn. 'What's happened to the column? Has it gone for good?'

There were no real secrets in the trade they practised. Word invariably got out, no matter how tight the security. But he was always reluctant to be the first to tell. 'It's just on ice for a while,' he said. 'I'm going on a trip.'

'Somewhere nice?'

'Hardly.' He gave him an edited version of what he was likely to be doing in Korea. He did not mention the panda.

'But what's it in aid of?'

'Business mostly. The Admiral's wheeling and dealing out there. He wants a little back-up. A couple of pieces to make him look good.'

'Really?' Benn looked disbelieving.

'He's buying newsprint. Very hush-hush. They're still fixing the price.'

'Anything I can write about?'

'Not yet,' said Patrick. 'Wait till I'm out of the way.' It was purely a courtesy that Benn had asked his permission. Once he had outlined the facts there was no copyright. But he could rely on Benn not to land him in it. Other sources would be invoked. The timing of the diary item would be carefully calculated. It was not only friendship that was at risk; revealing too much, too soon was unprofessional. For his own part it was like taking out insurance. Favours accepted meant favours to be returned. Leaking the occasional paragraph was like casting bread upon the waters. No one could guarantee that it would come back. But it was a sensible investment and sometimes the dividend was instant.

'If you're writing about Amos,' said Benn, 'you should ask him what it's like being a Senior Centrefold.'

'A what?'

'A pin-up. For *The Fogey*. I hear he's baring all.'

It was an appalling notion, but entirely possible, thought Patrick. *The Fogey* was a magazine for pensioners which in one ill-conceived swoop managed to be ageist, sexist and inconsequential. It published unfunny cartoons, dud jokes and comment on contemporary affairs. It was based in London but it seemed to reflect a parallel universe where values were distorted, resentments magnified and the young detested and feared. In theory it was pro-sex, although so far it had not shown a sex object appropriate for wrinklies. The Senior Centrefold sounded like a breakthrough.

'You've not actually seen the pictures.'

'Not yet,' said Benn. 'I live in hope. We have a fink in the dark room. We're paying good money.'

'And you've not spoken to Amos.'

'There's no point. I want the snaps in my hot little hand before we come out with it.'

'Why tell me? What am I supposed to do?'

135

'Nothing concrete comes to mind,' said Benn. 'I was just sharing information. If you're writing an obituary you need all the facts.'

'And I might pick up a few more which I could pass on to you.'

'There's that too,' agreed Benn.

They split the bill and left the restaurant. At mid-afternoon Soho was full of people like them – middle-aged, flushed with wine and expense account lunches. They ate and drank too much because someone else paid the bill. It was a tradition which had become a duty. If they shrank from it the economy would suffer.

Patrick saw Felix Benn into a taxi and glanced at his watch. In an hour's time he was due for a session of hydro-therapy. He wished that he had not ordered the cassata after the osso bucco, but it was too late for regrets. He already had far too much to be sorry about. He decided to walk to the hospital. Only recently he had read that, in terms of healthful exercise, a three-mile walk was the equivalent of a brisk bout of sexual intercourse. He could tell Nurse Pavey that he was well up on the week's average.

Dolly Priest was wearing a costume the colour of old gold. She looked better in white, thought Patrick, but the gold costume was cut high on the thigh so that, on either side, her groin was added to the total area of exposed flesh. It was not unattractive but it looked like an afterthought, a lecherous doodle on the sketch-pad which had somehow been incorporated in the design. It was not domestic wear. It was making a statement, but it seemed impolite to ask what it was.

She waved to him across the shallow end of the pool. 'Looking good.'

'So are you,' he said warmly.

He could not say the same for Nurse Pavey. Her skin was too pink, her hair too blonde, her thighs too muscular. She was not so much a woman as a manifesto, besides which she was excessively fit, built for combat rather than comfort. Patrick imagined holding her, his fingers skidding on the armatures of her flesh. He had known car seats like that, moulded from solid rubber, yielding to nothing less than a head-on collision. Kissing her would be an exercise in oral hygiene, a tour of perfectly-enamelled teeth, conducted by a disinfected tongue. He shook his head to rid himself of the thought. He was staring, he realized, and Nurse Pavey was staring back.

'Something going on between you two?' asked Dolly.

'Certainly not.'

'Big eyes, the both of you.'

'I was miles away,' said Patrick. 'I didn't even know where I was looking.'

Dolly chuckled and the gold of her costume shimmered like hot metal. 'Trouble on the way,' she said. 'Leaping before you look.'

He began to tell her how wrong she was, but Nurse Pavey's whistle cut across his explanation. It was the signal for everyone to stop talking. In the water, she said, it was the only way to get attention. But she blew it too loudly and too often for that to be the whole truth. In the new world order, thought Patrick, all commands would be given in whistlespeak. It was a language which excluded discussion and did away with dispute. Editorials in *The Arbiter* demonstrated how easily it could be transposed into print.

'Today,' said Nurse Pavey, 'we are going to be daffodils. Blowing in the breeze. Stretching our stalks from side to side.'

She waded into the pool and faced them, her arms level with the surface. 'Twist to the left,' she said. 'And to the right. Stretch, stretch, stretch, stretch.' The class swivelled obediently, not daffodils but men and women in varying degrees of pain. Patrick could not understand why it was thought helpful to pretend otherwise. He had never seen himself as any kind of flower, not even at infant school where they had been urged to curl themselves up in sleep like bulbs in winter. He was also unconvinced that the exercise was doing him good. What he felt mostly was embarrassed and uncomfortable.

Nurse Pavey blew her whistle. 'Mr Lamb, you're not swaying.'

'Yes, I am.'

'Not hard enough. Like this.' She wrenched her body from left to right, slapping the water with her breasts. 'Show your

137

body that you mean business,' she said. 'Build up a rhythm. Keep it going.'

Patrick did his best to obey, but he could not keep time. He had experienced the same difficulty when he was learning to dance. Off-beat and on-beat were meaningless terms. His partners hated him. He paused to draw breath and saw Dolly Priest thrashing the water to his right. Her sense of rhythm was perfect. She could hear the music in her head, he thought. Her eyes shone and her teeth dazzled. 'Join the party,' she called.

'I'm trying to.'

'Just follow me.'

He tried to mimic the thrust of her body, but the beat still eluded him. It was like stumbling in mid-air. There was no obstacle, nothing to fall over, but his feet left the bottom and he breathed in water.

Nurse Pavey hauled him upright. 'It's very simple,' she said. 'Five year olds can do it.'

'Good for them.'

'What we need to do is loosen up that back.' She put her hands on his hips and as she rotated him gently, turning him like a screw, their thighs bumped. She was as solid as he had imagined. 'Just relax,' she said and repeated the operation. Perhaps it was his fate to be manipulated by women, thought Patrick. It was not the destiny which he had mapped out for himself, but his forecasting was notoriously bad.

'It's feeling easier,' he said eventually.

'That's good.'

'I think I can do it myself now.'

'Very likely.'

Her hands remained where they were and he looked down, slightly surprised. He was three or four inches taller than Nurse Pavey and his nose was level with the parting in her hair. She tilted her head back and smiled. 'Give it a try then.'

He attempted the exercise, his arms held awkwardly above his head. 'I could do it better if you let go,' he said.

She still held on and their thighs bumped again. The length of her body grazed his and one hand slid inside his shorts. Patrick gasped. He felt himself being gripped firmly

138

and inquisitively and over Nurse Pavey's shoulder he saw Dolly Priest's broad grin. She had been right, he thought; something was going on. In a public bath surrounded by fellow patients, he was being groped by his therapist. He looked into Nurse Pavey's eyes – baby-blue surrounded by bloodshot whites – and wondered what was the most tactful response.

He was being paid a compliment, he supposed, but it was not one he had looked for. He had not guessed that he was any kind of favourite; rather the opposite. The sensation was not pleasant. His nervousness increased. 'Something's caught up,' he said. 'Down there.'

Nurse Pavey's grip did not slacken. 'I thought it might help.'

'Not now,' said Patrick. 'Not here.'

She squeezed harder. 'Where do you suggest?'

'Later. Somewhere else. You're hurting me.' His voice, he realized, was at least an octave higher than usual and he was standing on his toes.

Nurse Pavey patted his shoulder with her free hand. 'Keep going,' she said. 'Think of the back. Stretch, stretch, stretch, stretch.'

Each command was reinforced by a brief tug as if he was a dog on a lead, dawdling over his morning ablutions. People were staring, but it was painful to disobey. 'Why are you doing this?' he hissed. 'Let me go. Someone will see.'

Nurse Pavey jammed her face close to his. 'What will they see? That the joke's over?'

'What joke?' He winced as she held him fast.

'Whatever you and that black bitch were laughing at. Something about me.'

He remembered Dolly Priest's remark about big eyes. He had barely understood what she meant. How could he explain it now? 'I didn't,' he said. 'We weren't.' He tried vainly to disengage her hand.

'I don't like being laughed at,' she said. 'Not by anyone.'

He shook his head wildly. 'We weren't laughing. Not about you. Honestly.'

'Don't you ever,' she said.

He felt her fingers pinch tight, then fall free. He sobbed

with relief. 'No more jokes,' said Nurse Pavey. 'Concentrate on the back.' She turned a somersault in the water, presenting him with a view of her black-costumed buttocks. When she surfaced it was as though nothing extraordinary had happened. 'Everyone a bouncing ball,' she said. 'Bounce, bounce, bounce.'

Dolly Priest swam up behind him. 'What was that about?' He waved her away. 'I'll tell you later.'

He was numb where Nurse Pavey's fingers had gripped his flesh. Tomorrow there would be a bruise. If he complained (although he could not imagine who he could complain to) his humiliation would be compounded. It was no use insisting that it had all been a mistake. Even if he was believed, an apology would remind everyone how ineffectual he had been. He saw the tale passing into female folklore. Mothers would tell it to their daughters. Columnists would extend the mileage. Cassandra would present it as a parable of crime and punishment in which sexist attitudes got their comeuppance. The hairs on his neck stood on end.

It was better, he decided, to let it go, to say nothing, even to Dolly Priest. It was a friendship he would have liked to pursue. But it was time to escape, the sooner the better. The impulse was so strong that he heaved himself on to the side of the pool where he lay beached and bewildered, certain only that he should be somewhere else.

Nurse Pavey's whistle stilled the chatter. 'And where are you off to Mr Lamb? Is there an emergency?'

'That's right.'

'Is there really?' Her voice was tart with sarcasm. 'A matter of life and death, I suppose.'

'Yes.'

'Whose, may I ask?'

'Mine,' he said.

Amos Bennet poured him a large whisky. 'I'm not sure about this hydro-therapy lark,' he said. 'Is it doing you any good? You look shagged.'

'I may have overdone it,' said Patrick.

It was early evening and the street outside was filled

with the din of Londoners going home. Car engines raced, gears clashed, the occasional curse rose above the harmonies of traffic. Listening to it all from an upstairs room with the lamps lit and a drink in hand induced a mild euphoria. It was comforting to know that the turmoil was at a safe distance. Bad things were happening, but they were happening to someone else. And about time, thought Patrick. The day which was nearly done had brought him more than his share of upset. He had been allowed to make his escape from the hospital pool without name-calling. But he could imagine the speculation he had left behind. Any story which Nurse Pavey chose to tell stood a fair chance of being believed.

'Any interesting women there?' asked Amos.

'Too many.'

'Spoiled for choice?'

'I wouldn't say that.'

'Not up to it then?'

'Could be.'

The interrogation was proceeding along normal lines. The questions which Amos asked or rather let fall like pebbles on a beach, were not intended to give offence. Instead, they were a kind of revving up which flushed the system and primed it for conversation to come. What Amos wanted to talk about was himself. The adrenalin had almost reached the necessary level and he was ready to take off.

'You'll be seeing more of me soon,' he announced.

'Indeed?'

'More than usual, I mean. Maximum exposure you could say.'

Patrick suppressed a groan. Amos was being roguish and the preliminary strip-tease could not be avoided. 'It sounds intriguing,' he said.

Amos tapped his nose, then lowered it into his whisky glass. There were times – usually when he was most pleased with himself – when he behaved like a grand old character actor, a snuff-taker perhaps, given to pinching the bottoms of chamber-maids. Amos saw his entire life as an ongoing production. He was never off-stage.

'You've seen *The Fogey*?' he enquired.

'Now and again. I don't buy it.'

'Why not? It's very good.'

'It seems to know its readership,' said Patrick carefully. 'It knows about targetting.'

'It certainly does,' said Amos. 'On the button.'

'It's a bit silly sometimes.'

'What do you mean, silly? Not to the people it's addressing.'

'I suppose not.' He had a point, Patrick conceded. *The Fogey* fed suspicion with prejudice, rumour with gossip. Its readers were given what they wanted and so far the policy had paid off.

'D'you think one should appear in it?'

'Write for the magazine? Why not?'

'More than that,' said Amos. 'They've photographed me. Naked. I'm their first Senior Centrefold.'

Patrick did his best to look surprised. 'How original.'

'I'm glad you think so,' said Amos. 'It's a new concept. Anti-ageist. Every wrinkle honoured. No re-touching. What you see is what you get. I think it's quite a compliment.'

'They couldn't have picked a better man.'

'Do you really mean that?'

'Absolutely.'

'I'm glad,' said Amos. 'Your ex-wife thinks the same.'

Patrick counted to five before putting down his glass and wiping his lips. 'Cassandra?'

'She's putting me in her column. The editorial lot at *The Fogey* wanted to leak the story and they thought she'd do it best.'

'I can imagine.' He would have to warn Felix Benn that he had been pipped at the post. And he would have to do it soon. Cassandra was not one to hang around before leaping into print. 'When did this all happen?'

'Lunchtime today,' said Amos. 'She interviewed me here. She's quite different from what I'd imagined.'

'How's that?'

'Not as you described her. More sympathetic.'

'I'll bet,' said Patrick. Cassandra's interviewing style was much admired. He had heard it described as heavy petting and once, by a man who still bore the scars, as soul surgery. She came on as vulnerable, in need of support. The interviewee became her accomplice. He recalled an earlier conversation with Amos. 'She's deserted ship,' he had told him. 'Look for another hand.' But that was then and this was now. 'Did she mention me?' he asked.

'Just in passing.'

'How closely in passing?'

'She asked how you were.'

'And if I was seeing anyone.'

'Possibly.' Amos leaned forward in his chair. 'It's only natural that she should be interested. She's a compassionate woman.'

'I beg your pardon.' It was the dreaded 'C' word. He could not believe what he was hearing. It was as if someone had reached inside the Bennet skull and, swiftly and painlessly, rotated the brain so that foul was fair and vice versa.

'I should warn you,' said Amos. 'I shall be seeing her again.'

'I'm not surprised.'

'She says that I transcend time.'

'Terrific.' Now and again, thought Patrick, Cassandra surpassed herself. What was so impressive was that she did it without thinking. Instead, she obeyed her instinct, allowing herself to be led to some hot-spot of the mind where an entire shooting script awaited her. Dialogue flowed into her mouth like saliva. A print-out unrolled behind her eyes. Anyone could see that Amos was vain. But to be presented with the precise phrase – windy, flattering and phoney – which made him her captive was almost magical. He smiled to himself.

'What's funny?' demanded Amos.

'Everything.' He wondered, not for the first time, if the enchantment worked both ways and she too was deluded.

'I hope you'll be civil if you see her here.'

'Of course I will.'

'I've had to re-assess myself,' said Amos. 'She's made me aware of my responsibilities.'

'No more little arrangements?'

'I doubt it.'

Quite possibly, thought Patrick, he was witnessing the end of an era. Amos was just as he had described him to Felix Benn. In the age of the new and caring man he was a dinosaur. He was out of time and there was no reprieve, but it was sad to see him galloping towards extinction. He remembered the original purpose of the meeting. 'May I see the pictures?'

Amos spread them out on the table. As he had said, every wrinkle was honoured. There were more of them than he could have anticipated, especially about the neck and chest, but he wore them with distinction. The rest of him was in good shape. His belly was flat, his thighs were firm, his penis was large. As a novelist, Amos had a considerable following. As a Senior Centrefold, thought Patrick, he might add to his flock.

Back in his own flat he rang the office to see if there were any messages. Judith Wales had called twice. 'Very stroppy,' said the girl on the switchboard. 'Is she a friend of yours?'

'Hardly.'

'She wants to talk to you. She says its urgent.'

'Did she say what about?'

'She made me write it down,' said the girl. 'A matter of mutual concern. Does that make any sense?'

Patrick felt his heart go into free fall. He did not know what to answer. He did not dare to guess.

eleven

The crowing of a cockerel awoke Patrick before dawn. He lay on his back, his mouth gummy with sleep, and wondered where he was. The ceiling was the colour of parchment and as it rippled above him he heard the wind blow. He was in a tent, he realized, and he was zipped into a sleeping bag. There was another body several yards to his right and as a head with horns turned in his direction he recognized Jack Blazer and remembered that they were sharing quarters. Lottie was in the tent next door and Mr Lee was with the army vet. The privates were in a slightly bigger tent, but by the sound of it they had already started on the day's chores.

He heard water slopping into buckets and the crackle of a fire taking hold. 'Noisy buggers,' said Jack Blazer. 'They want us to know they're up.'

'It's not light yet.'

'Light enough. We have to be on the road by 0700 hours.'

'Seven o'clock,' said Patrick.

'Suit yourself.' Blazer unzipped his sleeping bag and stepped on to the bare earth. He sucked in his breath. 'Christ, it's cold. I'll just see if they've brewed up.' He put on his boots and a fleece-lined coat and went outside. The wind worried the tent flap until he returned, a steaming mug in each hand. 'The only way to start the day,' he said. 'A nice drop of *chai*.'

Patrick propped himself on one elbow and drank it down. It had been made with condensed milk and tasted of woodsmoke. 'Does Lottie get one?' he asked.

Blazer jerked his head. 'She's got one. She's been up for hours.'

'What's she doing?'

'Getting her gear together. Taking pictures.'

'What of?'

'Whatever's happening.' Blazer tucked a towel around his neck and looped a toilet bag over his arm. 'Off we go then. Shit, shave and shampoo. There's a nice little ablutions tent and a bog behind the bushes. No lock on the door. Whistle while you work.'

He watched Blazer duck through the tent flap and drew the zip up to his chin again. He must not go back to sleep but he was too comfortable to move for a while. Firelight sketched patterns on the canvas walls. He was surprised by how well he had slept; surprised too by his lack of apprehension. He looked forward to whatever the day held in store. Somewhere the Admiral and his cronies played with their bricks of empire, raising one edifice, demolishing another. But they were a world away. No fax could track him down. Once they had left camp only a radio would report on their movements and for most of the time there would be nothing worth reporting. He put his hands behind his head and breathed the air of freedom.

He heard a clamour of voices, people laughing, and he looked out of the tent. Four men in single file were parading round the fire. They seemed to be performing a dance, although there was no music and their steps were clumsy and unsynchronized. The first man in line held a cockerel in his arms. His hands were locked over its wings. Its feet were tied together and its head jerked nervously from side to side.

Jack Blazer pushed his way through the crowd and stood watching. The firelight bounced from his bald head and shone rosily in the thickets of his hair. He began to clap his hands, softly at first, then loudly and rhythmically, and the dance took on a new shape. Others joined in. They were villagers, Patrick realized, the farmers whose houses they had

146

passed on their way to camp the previous night. None of the windows were curtained and, from the back of the truck, he had seen their lives on display. On some walls a fork or a scythe hung like sculpture. There were family photographs, candles which picked out the contours of a shrine. No two houses were identical, but in every one of them a television set glowed in the corner. On each screen the Great Leader advised surgeons and builders and chicken farmers about their business.

Most likely the film had already begun its daily repeat, he thought. But its audience was held by an older ritual. He saw Lottie, ahead of the dancers, walking steadily backwards and firing her camera like a hand-gun. There was no sign of Mr Lee, but Jack Blazer beckoned him forward. 'You ought to see this,' he said. 'They're giving us a proper send-off.' His skin was shiny with shaving soap; his breath sweet with mouth-wash.

'What are they going to do?'

'They're wishing us good hunting.'

The dance came to a ragged end. The cockerel was raised like a totem above the heads of the crowd. Its beak gaped, but it made no sound. From the circle of firelight came a hand clasping a knife. It was disembodied, a weapon rooted in air. The blade ran red with reflected flames, then it was plunged three times into the cockerel's breast. Its head slumped to one side and a white membrane veiled its eyes. 'Now they'll burn the readies,' said Blazer.

A bag of bank-notes was emptied on to the fire. They flared briefly, white turning to black as the wind whisked up the ashes, drawing them into a spiral that dissolved in the brightening sky. Patrick saw them fall like feathers. 'Was it real?' he asked.

'Funny money,' said Blazer. 'What it signifies is good intentions. Spirits understand that. They don't need the real thing.' He put his arm round Lottie's waist as she backed into them. 'Happy now?'

She had wood ash on one cheek and her smile was radiant. 'Happier. If it goes on like this.'

'Why shouldn't it?' said Blazer. He wiped her face clean and patted her behind. 'Trust me.'

It was easy to say, thought Patrick, as he brushed his teeth in the ablutions tent. But his faith in Jack Blazer was firmer than it had been for days. It was action that did it. Too much thinking, too much speculation was bad for the nerves. Doing something positive was the cure. Even if it was not exactly positive and only a warm-up routine, it made a promise that there was no reason to break. Lottie had found something to photograph. Or rather, she had been given something to photograph which was well outside the guide-lines approved by Mr Kim. No one had tried to stop her. There had been no sign of Mr Lee.

'Where is he?' he asked Blazer when they met over breakfast.

'The captain took him on a little recce. I thought he should see the sights.'

'Such as?'

'The equipment we've got. The route we'll be taking. I wanted him to feel part of the action.' He sucked porridge from his spoon. 'Did you want him for something? He won't be long.'

Patrick deliberated. 'You got him out of the way. While they killed that cockerel. While Lottie got her pictures.'

'Why should I do that?'

'You tell me.'

'Cheered her up, didn't it?'

'You know it did.'

'There we are then. Nice girl, Lottie. Can't have her being disappointed.' He put down one mess tin and picked up another in which sausages lay blanketed in tomato sauce. 'Did you get some of these? Straight from the US of A. Next year's field rations. Maybe they've not made up their minds yet.'

'How did you get them?'

'Ways and means. They're just samples.'

'Have you tried them on the locals?'

Blazer grinned wolfishly and shook his head. 'No. We're in with a rough lot here. They've only just stopped chucking rocks.'

'At each other?'

'Certainly at each other. It was a game they used to play.

Village combat. One lot on one side of a ravine, the others on the other. They'd all line up. Someone'd wave a flag and they'd set to.'

'All at once?'

'No, no.' Blazer shook his head as if he was dealing with a dunce. 'There's always rules. They took turns. Very particular about that. You could duck, but you couldn't dodge. And the rocks had to be the right size. Nothing bigger than half a brick.'

'Did anyone get killed?'

'Not often.' Blazer looked through the open door of the tent. 'There's not a lot for them to do out here. They have to make their own amusements.'

The fire was dying down. To one side of it the cook was propping up his pans to dry. To the east the sky was bright red, flecked with gold. They were surrounded by fields which ran into scrubland. Then there were trees, their upper branches clad in mist. And, behind them, mountains. Patrick glanced at his watch. 'Time to make a move.'

They sat on benches in the back of the truck. There was a canvas roof which Blazer tied back and grips attached to the uprights for them to hang on to. 'Gets a bit bumpy in a while,' he said.

Lottie sat by the tail-board. Her jump-suit was zipped up to the neck and her hair was tucked under her cap. Patrick thought she was asleep, until he saw her lips move. She was singing to herself. When they slowed down momentarily he caught snatches of her song. 'Onward Christian soldiers, marching as to war.' While they were travelling the rush of wind made conversation impossible. He braced himself against the side of the truck and watched the world bounce by. The pine trees were giving way to rhododendron, shrub-like at first, but then becoming tall and straggly. To their right the ground fell away steeply and he caught glimpses of a river foaming over rocks, gnawing at banks of shingle. With each mile the country grew wilder, the road rougher. There were ruts to avoid, ribs of stone which suddenly emerged from the carcase of the track. When they hit one of them a pile of equipment shook loose from its tethers and rolled across the floor of the truck.

Blazer had delivered a lecture on it all the previous night, striding around the camp-fire as they stooped over their mess-tins. 'We've got some local help,' he told them. 'People who really know the old *bei-shung*. Of course, we've got our own anaesthetized darts and so on – but they've got years of experience. Centuries of it. And we're going to put it to work.'

He showed them a shoot of bamboo. 'This is what pandas eat. But not all the time. They like a little lamb chop now and then. For years everyone thought they were vegetarian, green as green. But they kill sheep and when the locals set traps they bait them with a bit of boiled mutton. Very fond of that is the old *bei-shung*.'

He showed them nooses and knots. 'Basic stuff for your woodcraft badge. What they do is put a wire noose at the end of a sapling and hide it in a pitfall, just big enough for the panda's foot. When he steps into it he slips a peg which releases the noose and, bingo, the sapling springs up, panda attached.' He shook his head, goring the dark with his twists of fire-reddened hair. 'In answer to the question you were about to ask: no, the panda is not injured. And it's not the method we favour. But, just in case someone gets lucky, we have these articles to keep him in order.' He held up a pair of iron tongs, three or four feet long. They looked like implements of the Inquisition, tools of torturers and bear baiters.

'What you must never do,' continued Blazer, 'is think of *bei-shung* as cuddly. It's one of those words we never use. You don't go up and stroke him. He's got a hell of a bite and a bloody bad temper. And with us on his trail it's likely to get worse. You've got to watch out. We don't want to hurt him. But we don't want to get hurt either.'

'You've handled one before?' said Lottie.

'More than one.'

'Where was that?'

'In transit, in zoos.' Blazer hesitated, as though loath to reveal secrets. 'I went to Beijing for a while. They breed pandas there. The idea was to get some experience. And I was here a couple of years back. You'll get some great pictures. Believe me.'

She blew him a kiss across the camp-fire and Patrick felt a

spurt of jealousy. It was soon dispelled. It was absurd to envy Jack Blazer. Besides being a deserter from the British army he was also the regime's odd-job man, a fixer who would turn his hand to whatever task he was told to perform. His scruples had long been abandoned. What he preached was practicality and what he practised was endurance. Patrick watched him amble round the fire, his nose and his ears skewered by bright hair, and he caught himself smiling. Blazer was a rogue, but he was an ally too.

The wind whipped Patrick's face and he bent down to squint at his watch. They had been driving for more than an hour and, if Blazer's calculations were correct, they would be meeting up soon with the advance party of villagers. There were six of them, all with dogs. They had been following tracks near where the droppings had been found for two days. There was no doubt, said Blazer, that they would have news.

The truck slowed down as they approached a clearing and stopped by a man waiting at the roadside. He wore a scuffed leather cap with ear-flaps and a torn sheepskin coat. The legs of his trousers were bound with twine and his boots were caked with mud. He raised a rifle over his head and Patrick felt a stir of excitement. Until now he had not seen himself as one of the hunters, but something had changed his perception. Perhaps it was dressing for the part, as if his quasi-military outfit – cap, jump-suit and fell-boots – entitled him to feel soldierly, one of a team.

The same thing, he suspected, had happened to Mr Lee. Blazer had joked about making him feel part of the action. But the joke had come true. Mr Lee might be a city boy, but now he was braced for an outdoor adventure. With a length of cord in his hands, he sat with his legs crossed, practising knots. Patrick watched him make a running noose and draw it snugly about his wrist. He tugged the cord and his fingers spread wide. He was catching a panda.

Blazer's door swung open and he spoke to the man with the rifle. There was some pointing and pantomime (fingers aimed at the ground, then at the tree-tops), followed by broad smiles. 'Everybody out,' said Blazer. '*Bei-shung* up and running.'

He helped Lottie down from the truck. 'There's no rush,'

151

he said. 'First we make camp. Then we see what's what.'

'We know what's what.'

Blazer shook his head. 'Not yet. Daniel Boone here's been waiting for hours for us to show up. Now we've got to wait for his mates. They'll give us the latest picture.'

'Have they seen it?' asked Patrick.

'As good as. Loads of droppings.'

'Is that all?'

Blazer sighed gently. 'Haven't I made myself clear? You can't have too much panda shit. It's the best news there is. If he's in the neighbourhood that's what he's doing. In one end and out the other. Thirty dumps an hour they reckon. Highly insanitary, of course, but don't knock it. Just count your blessings and follow the yellow brick road.'

The soldiers made a fire and dug a latrine pit. Smoke rose in a steep blue column and, like smoke returning, men with dogs filtered through the surrounding trees. They made no sound until they entered the clearing, when the dogs – suddenly off duty – raced up to inspect the newcomers. In rapid succession they peed on the wheels of the truck and barked at whatever moved. Patrick felt a wet muzzle on the back of his hand and made encouraging noises. There were nine dogs, large and small. He recognized no particular breed, but mostly they were terriers and lurchers. There was one hound, with ears like extended tear-drops and a nose already scraped raw.

'He's the one who finds the scent,' said Blazer. 'Trouble is, he stays with it till he bleeds.'

Lottie took photographs head-on and in profile. 'Does he have a name?'

Blazer spoke to the owner. 'He calls it Dog.'

'Is that all?'

'It's not a pet,' said Blazer. 'They don't think of animals as we do. Sometimes they eat them. When they've got nothing else. Except that this lot earn their keep. It's a hunting pack. They're worth looking after.'

'What do they hunt?' asked Patrick. 'Apart from pandas.'

'Rabbits mostly,' said Blazer. 'Whatever there is.' He fondled the hound's ears. Their tips were swollen from being trailed over rough ground and thorns were embedded

152

in the fur. He plucked them out, one by one. 'Silly old sod,' he said fondly.

The hunters gathered around the fire and rolled cigarettes. Blankets were shaken out and boots taken off. Tea was served with slices of fruit cake and more of the sausages in tomato sauce. Each man sat with his rifle stacked beside him, his dog at his feet. It was intensely formal, thought Patrick, like a picnic on manoeuvres. He wondered whether Lottie's pictures would convey the atmosphere; the repose, the strange juxtaposition of things rustic and things military. She was using a tripod again, he noticed, as though the components of the scene determined the style of the photograph. When she moved, she moved slowly, giving them time to see what she was doing, taking care not to startle, not to alarm. Even her smile was toned down; open but demure. No one turned away, no one mugged for the camera and his estimation of Lottie's performance rose yet again.

'Good girl, that,' said Jack Blazer. 'I was going to tell them what she was about, but there's no need.'

Mr Lee shook his head. 'Some of the men will wonder.'

'Not for long. She's part of the team. They can see that.'

'What about me?' asked Patrick.

'They know about you,' said Blazer. 'I had a word. They know you're a *bei-shung* expert from England. Someone they have to impress.' He rested an arm on Patrick's shoulder. 'Mind you, it cuts both ways. You'll have to do a bit of impressing too. You'll have to keep up and stay lively. They've found a trail and we'll be taking off in about twenty minutes. We won't be going very fast, but it's hard going. This'll be our base for tonight. We're about twenty-five miles from the village and we could be going that far the other way. From here on, we walk.'

'What if we see the panda?'

'That won't be for a while. They've done about five miles to get back here.' Blazer prised a thorn from the hound's nose and stroked its mottled head. 'What we do now is go back the way they came and follow the signs. If we see the old *bei-shung* we plug it with a dart and bring it back here to the truck. Then we radio for the chopper and drive to where it can pick us up.'

'Why not here?'

Blazer shook his head. 'Too many trees. Too close together. You need room for a decent lift-off. We don't want
any accidents.'

'Where's the chopper coming from?'

'There's an army base due west. Forty miles or so.' Blazer
pointed away from the sun. 'The chopper gets us back to the
village. Then the plane flies us home.'

Patrick tried to make sense of the schedule. 'It's compli-
cated.'

'No other way,' said Blazer. 'But keep your fingers crossed.
Just hope we catch up with chummy soon.'

'Why's that?'

'Think about it,' said Blazer. 'We're on foot. No transport.
When we catch it, we carry it.'

The hunters were already putting on their boots. One of
them stepped behind a bush with his back turned towards
Lottie and urinated loudly. It was like preparing for any
journey, thought Patrick. He could still hear his mother's
voice as they were about to leave on a drive to the sea.
'Have you *been*? We don't want to stop on the way.' For
several weeks after he and Cassandra had split up he had
been unable to pee in public. Visiting a urinal at the theatre
or after lunch was an embarrassment. He could not perform
until he was alone. There was nothing physiologically wrong
his doctor told him. 'It's all in the mind. It's what we call a
nervous bladder. Try not to think about it.' But, of course,
he did and even now he could not be sure that the flow would
be free and uninhibited. When he was successful – splashing
his fell boots with a sudden cascade – he felt reassured. The
day was still on course. He was leaving his hang-ups behind
him.

Half a mile on the bamboo began. He was aware, first of
all, of the noise that it made – a leathery creaking, like harness
being flexed – and then, of how densely it was planted. The
sound came from the stems rubbing together. They looked
like rubber tubing, he thought; segmented, the colour of
verdigris. Some were as high as a house. Others fanned
out into an undergrowth that linked one tree with another,
forming a mesh that appeared fragile but which snagged the
knees and ankles.

'Look for the trail,' said Blazer. 'That's where the droppings are.'

He pointed to a barely defined path, hidden by the leaves. On either side of it some of the smaller bamboo shoots had been ripped out. The chewed remains lay all around. The stems were gnawed and, just as Blazer had promised, there were droppings; small mounds like garden compost in which the gristle of fibre retained its shape.

Somewhere ahead the dogs gave tongue. 'It doesn't mean much,' said Blazer. 'They sound like that whatever it is. It's never about nothing, but there's no guaranteeing it's the right article.'

One of the hunters called back to him and he grinned. 'It was only a squirrel. Miles to go for the old *bei-shung*.'

They each carried a water bottle and a small pack. Inside it there were matches, salt tablets, a poncho, a pair of dry socks, a tin of sausages and a packet of barley sugar. Patrick wondered whether it was too early to break open the rations. His watch claimed that it was nine o'clock, but it seemed that more than two hours had passed since they set out. He was not exactly hungry, but he felt the need for something to chew. Seeley would call it a displacement activity.

He was a clever bloke, thought Patrick, but he had never seen *bei-shung* droppings in the wild.

He was breathing heavily and sweat ran into his eyes. He was not wearing his glasses. Although he carried a spare pair he was afraid of breaking them and at times like this, with branches whisking across his face already greasy with perspiration, he saw the world as a green blur. It was no great disadvantage. Close up he could see perfectly well and if there was anything further away which seemed interesting he relied on those with better vision to give him warning.

Cassandra had complained about it. 'It's just attention getting,' she said. 'It's a way to make people like you.'

'How's that?'

'You put yourself in their debt. You ask a favour which it costs nothing to perform.'

'And that makes them like me?'

'You allow them to feel superior. That's a bribe.'

'I never thought of it like that,' said Patrick.

'Think of it now.'

He did, for a count of five. 'You're talking balls,' he said.

But now he wondered. He had not actually appointed anyone to be his ears or his eyes, but there was a tacit understanding that, now and again, he needed help. He had never regarded it as a tactic on his part, but he was clearly following a behaviour pattern to which others responded. He shook his head and beads of sweat flew away brilliantly into the boskage.

Since the start of the bamboo they had marched in single file. The hunters led the way, followed by Jack Blazer, the army vet and two of the soldiers. A third soldier carried Lottie's tripod and camera box, the white metal plastered with hotel labels. Lottie walked ten to fifteen yards ahead of Patrick and behind him came Mr Lee. For the past thirty minutes he had been limping badly.

Out of the corner of his eye Patrick saw him sink beneath a canopy of bamboo and, retracing his steps, found him braced against a bamboo stem tugging off one of his fell boots. He stooped over him. 'What's wrong?'

Mr Lee pointed to his right foot. 'Very painful.'

'Can't you walk?'

'Not at present.'

Patrick waved his arms and shouted and the column came to a halt. Jack Blazer joined them. 'First casualty,' he said and squatted on his heels. He peeled the sock off Mr Lee's right foot and felt the ankle. 'Is this where it hurts?'

'Hurts all over.'

'Bit swollen,' said Blazer, his fingers denting the puffy flesh. 'Had someone like you in my old mob. Got himself a season ticket with the MO. First one foot, then the other. Finished the war wearing plimsolls. They gave him a chitty: excused boots. That's what you need, my old son.'

'You told me to wear fell boots,' said Mr Lee. 'Best for the job, you said.' An ant crawled across his forehead but he did not brush it off.

'You didn't tell me about your feet,' said Blazer. 'Something seriously wrong there.'

'Nothing wrong with my feet.'

'Course there bloody well is. No one else is complaining.'

He pointed to Patrick and to Lottie. 'Is there anything wrong with your boots?' They shook their heads. 'Course not,' said Blazer. 'What we have here is a basic design fault, peculiar to all translators and minders.' He leaned forward confidentially. 'Weak ankles. That's what's wrong. What we need is a spot of support.' He opened his small pack and took out an elastic bandage. 'There's enough here for both scotches.'

'Scotches?' said Mr Lee.

Blazer ripped off the cellophane and measured the bandage. 'Tell him, somebody.' No one offered an explanation and he sighed his disapproval. 'Scotch eggs. Legs,' he said. 'Don't you know your own language?' He removed Mr Lee's other boot and sock and bandaged both ankles. While he worked he whistled through his teeth. 'Right,' he said. 'Up you get. Give us a few turns.'

Mr Lee stepped gingerly down the track. He balanced on one foot, then the other. 'Much better,' he said. 'Thank you.'

If pressed he could probably have applied the first aid himself, thought Patrick. So why had he summoned Jack Blazer? 'Where did you learn that?' he asked him.

'Here and there,' said Blazer. 'Made it up mostly. You can't do much harm with a bandage.'

'I suppose not.'

'Good for the morale to put things right without hanging about.'

Patrick watched Mr Lee lace up his fell boots and hook them over the bandages. He chattered to the soldier who carried Lottie's tripod and sucked on a square of barley sugar. 'He looks happy enough now,' he said.

'Course he's happy,' said Blazer. 'Why shouldn't he be? Out in the fresh air. No one to put the frighteners on him and more grub than he's had in years. It's the simple life. That's what does it. You should bear it in mind.'

They marched for another hour and the droppings multiplied. It was as though the panda was eating and defecating against time, with a penalty to pay if it fell behind schedule. 'Poor thing,' said Lottie. 'It's so humiliating. It just can't stop.'

'Lucky for us,' said Patrick. 'At least we know where it's going.'

The bamboo thinned, the track broadened and they walked side by side. 'Did you sleep all right?' he asked.

'Fine. How about you?'

He made a circle with his thumb and index finger. 'Terrific. No dreams.'

'D'you dream a lot?'

'Quite a bit.'

'Bad dreams?'

'Not nice.'

'You should write them down,' she said. 'Then burn the paper. That's how to get rid of dreams. You can see them go up in smoke.'

'Not mine,' said Patrick. 'They're about real people. It's like the song says. Always something there to remind me.' He hummed a few bars but she shook her head.

'I don't know that one.'

Too young, he thought. 'Dionne Warwick sang it,' he said. 'In my youth.'

They paused to draw breath and distantly they heard running water. The bamboo was still patchy and there were other trees, some of them tall and bushy, which marked the spine of the ridge they were climbing. 'Is it your wife you dream about?' asked Lottie.

'Mostly.'

'It was the first time I met her, down at Beechers. She's very striking.'

He nodded. 'You made an impression too. When you came out of my room. She told the Admiral about it.'

'She did what!'

'She told him what she'd seen and he warned me off.'

'What did he say?'

'It doesn't matter,' said Patrick. 'He just made it very plain that I should keep my distance. What we have is a professional relationship. Full stop. He's very protective.'

'He's bloody interfering,' she said. 'I can look after myself. And your wife can mind her own business.'

'Ex-wife,' said Patrick. 'I take no responsibility for Cassandra.'

'Bloody nerve,' said Lottie. 'Was she like this when you were married to her?'

'Not exactly. There were variations. She believes she was born to command.'

'She should mind her own business.'

'Everything is her business. Read her column. She likes to meddle. She likes to give advice. She's a Compassionate Woman. She's worse than AIDS.'

'I never said that,' said Lottie.

'I did,' said Patrick.

Her breathlessness was catching. He felt the familiar ball of helium in his chest and a corresponding rise in temperature. Anger, he thought, was supposed to make you light-headed. But his entire body seemed to lose weight as his irritation grew. Talking about Cassandra always had the same effect. It was like embarking on a binge, knowing in advance that another drink, another burst of recrimination would loosen the brakes and that he would say the unsayable, feel what he no longer wished to admit. He no longer loved her. He would swear to that. But to admit remembering her, even at this distance, was a risk. The Worst Fuck was still with him. The exorcism was not complete.

'Are you all right?' she asked.

'Certainly I'm all right.'

'It's me that should be upset.'

'I know.' He nodded violently. 'I shouldn't have told you. It doesn't matter what people say.'

'Of course it matters. It means they're trying to make decisions for me. I'm not having that.'

Patrick saw legions of do-gooders wilt under her fury. He made soothing noises. 'It's me they're getting at.'

'They're getting at both of us.'

'We'll tell them to piss off.'

'You'll tell the Admiral?'

'In a manner of speaking.'

She tugged off her cap and her hair fell to her shoulders. 'Let me know when you do,' she said. 'I want to be there.'

'And you can talk to Cassandra. I'd like to see that.'

They walked on in silence. The track turned suddenly to the right, and as they emerged from the thin clumps of bamboo they saw the hunters and the soldiers gathered around a tree that stood on the brow of the hill. They were like witnesses at a crucifixion. Everyone was looking skywards and, following their gaze, Patrick saw Jack Blazer wedged in a fork of the tree, scanning the landscape ahead through a pair of field-glasses.

'Glad you could join us,' he said.

'What's happening?'

'Something in view. Could be a false alarm but it's worth a look.'

He helped Patrick up and handed him the glasses. 'Straight ahead,' he said. 'Past the bamboo. Over the broken ground. Half a mile or so. Look for the bushy-topped tree. Follow the trunk and bear right.' He waited while Patrick followed his directions. 'What can you see?'

'Nothing.'

'Try a different focus.'

He did as he was told. The lines of the foliage sharpened and he saw a bird perched on a broken branch. Magpie, he told himself, the species that Mr Lee can identify. He saw patches of sunlight, pools of shade and, in a litter of leaves half-way up the trunk, a clump of white fur, as though a party-goer had flung a coat there and abandoned it.

'Well,' said Blazer. 'What d'you think?'

'I don't know.'

'Do you know what I think?'

'Tell me.'

'I think we might have struck lucky,' said Jack Blazer. 'I think we could be looking at the old *bei-shung*.'

twelve

'It's all systems go on the panda front,' said Dominic Downey. We'll be syndicating your series in *The Arbiter*. Then there'll be the official presentation. Education packs and posters. Competitions. Trips down Memory Lane with all the old zoo buffs. And Cassandra's TV stuff to keep it on the boil.'

'You didn't tell me about that,' said Patrick.

'I'm sure I mentioned it.'

'Not a word.'

'*Mea culpa*,' said Downey. 'Not that it really matters. I'm telling you now. We have plenty of time to lay down the track.'

Downey's use of metaphor deserved study, thought Patrick. Most often he employed it to distance himself from the action, as though jargon itself could create a barrier from behind which he could watch others tote that barge and lift that bale. 'Laying down the track' was fairly straightforward. What the phrase evoked was a series of drawings, executed in bold perspective, in which railway lines emanating from the four points of the compass converged on a single destination. It was like a cartoon strip in which the happy ending was announced before details of the plot had been worked out.

'Tell me again,' he said.

'It's the same as it's always been,' said Downey. 'Same

title, same format. *Open Heart*. People with problems and Cassandra solving them. Seven p.m. Tuesdays and Thursdays. What else is there to know?'

'How does the panda come into it?'

Downey sighed. 'Use your imagination. Pandas are love objects. Pandas have problems with their mates. Do we have the same sexual hang-ups? Get the right panel and you're up and running.'

'I can imagine.' At least he understood why his memory was a blank. It was possible, he supposed, that over the past few weeks someone may have let slip that Cassandra's programme was finally to achieve lift-off. But he had developed an early warning system which rendered him deaf whenever the topic was announced. It was Cassandra's bid to be Big, the giant step which had plucked her from the ruin of their marriage and it was something which he preferred not to know about. Now his ignorance had been breached and a little knowledge had become a worrisome thing. It was better to face up to what was happening.

'When does all this start?'

'We've made a couple of pilots. The first transmission's next week.'

'But what about the panda? I don't even know when I'm going. Nothing's been fixed.'

'Yes it has. That's next week too.' Downey shuffled through his papers. 'You're off on Friday. I was going to tell you. It'll be via Moscow, so you need a visa. Better get on to it right away.'

They were sitting in Downey's office at Beechers. It was a tall and airy room, with a three-piece suite furnished in Liberty fabric and a view of the rose garden. It was everyone's image of an English country house, thought Patrick, but it had been the setting for some of the worst moments in his life. This was where he had been made to feel incompetent, outmoded and insignificant. It was where decisions had been sprung on him without warning, where he had been humiliated without reason and where, on several occasions, he had contemplated murder. He wondered if Downey knew how comprehensively he was loathed. It was the only common ground on which warring factions on the *Arbiter* staff would be willing to stand.

162

Not that it worried Downey. His insensitivity was his strength. He could always be relied on to say the wrong thing at the right time, to omit the piece of information which would make a job easy or difficult, to ignore the statistic which any other planner would have known to be vital.

The chances were that he had known for weeks that Cassandra would be plugging the panda on TV. He must also have known the date of Patrick's departure and that a visa from Moscow was necessary. But by delaying his announcement he had turned it into an emergency. It was a technique which made people run rather than walk. It was a sight which he knew the Admiral enjoyed.

'Cassandra's earning her keep,' said Patrick.

'She always has done,' said Downey.

'A bit more than usual.'

'Not at all.' He looked up at the ceiling as if a text had been projected there. 'From each according to his means. To each according to his needs. Isn't that how it goes?'

'What's that got to do with it?'

'It's how we operate. You, me, Cassandra. It's what we're all about.'

It was just possible, thought Patrick, that the room was bugged and that somewhere, fairly close at hand, the Admiral was eavesdropping on the conversation. It was one way of determining loyalty, of deciding who was for promotion and who was for the chop. Another explanation was that Cassandra was being encouraged to stretch her wings. The higher she flew, the more use she would be to the organization. Between them, the panda and Amos would put her squarely in the public eye. There was a marked imbalance between needs and means, but it looked as though Cassandra would get what she wanted. Bigness was about to descend.

'When do I start filing copy?' he asked.

'When everything's in the bag. We don't know how long it'll take.'

'What about Cassandra?'

'Don't worry about that. It's our show.'

'I hadn't realized.'

Downey rolled his eyes. 'You don't pay attention. We're increasing our investments all the time.'

'I suppose we are.' He was struck by a sudden possibility. 'Do we own *The Fogey?*'

Downey smiled and he knew the answer. Everything was for sale, but the buyers were becoming fewer and fewer. Power was still distributed among the very rich, but every day the club grew more exclusive. It was like an Oxo cube whose essence would, in time, flavour the world.

He had been invited to lunch, or, rather, ordered to attend what he imagined would be an Admiral's briefing. Orders would be given, final touches applied. He would be expected to take notes. If he was very lucky he might also be given a mite more background information. He did not yet know details of the newsprint deal, or how positive the signals were that the Admiral would figure in the Honours List. He did not expect to be given precise facts, but he had learned to look for signs and portents. If he read them incorrectly it meant that he would be left with a false rumour to circulate. Not that it mattered. Tomorrow or the next day it would be overtaken by a story which was even further from the truth.

For an hour he discussed details of the trip with Downey. 'You've told no one where you're going, have you?' he enquired.

Patrick chose to forget his conversations with Seeley and Benn. 'No one.'

'I hope not. We don't want anyone to run a spoiler.'

'Why should they do that?'

'Malice,' said Downey. 'They don't like us coming first.'

It was not the customary complaint about *The Arbiter*, but the point was not worth debating. A succession of clocks struck noon. They were all over the house, a reminder, said the Admiral, that time cost money.

'Lunch in half an hour,' said Downey. 'Why don't you get a breath of air.'

No alternative, such as a drink was offered. 'I thought I might read the papers,' said Patrick.

'Lady Larkin will be looking for you.'

'What's she doing here?'

'The same as you. Lunching. Just walk her round the garden. Tell her the bar opens in twenty minutes.'

Lady Larkin was sitting on an oak settle, her hands

folded on the knob of her cane. She smiled as Patrick approached her. 'Loyal Mr Lamb.'

'My pleasure,' he said.

'Gallant too.' She gripped his arm and hauled herself upright. 'When is that wretched Downey opening the bar?'

'He said in twenty minutes.'

She sniffed loudly. 'Once around the roses then. Better get on with it.'

There was no one else in the garden. Once down the short flight of steps they were out of the wind and the scent of the flowers enclosed them. Butterflies basked on the sun dial and bees grumbled in the shrubbery. 'I had roses in Africa,' said Lady Larkin. 'But not like this. They were gone in a flash. Too much sun. Nothing lasted.'

'What part of Africa?'

'Rhodesia,' she said and put a finger to her lips. 'Mustn't call it that any more. Not since they put old Smithy on the shelf. It's Zimbabwe now.' She exaggerated the middle vowel. 'That's where we all met. Long, long ago.'

The bar was not yet open but Lady Larkin had already been at the gin. 'You mean you and the Admiral?'

'And Nora. And my husband. Sir Charles that was. Quite jolly for the end of empire. Lots of dancing on the Titanic.' She tightened her grip on his arm as she performed a half pirouette. Her skirt swirled. She leaned back and, mingled with the gin, he could smell perfume. 'Nobody dances now,' she said. 'Do you?'

'When I'm asked.'

Lady Larkin squeezed his arm. 'Now I remember. Good for you. It's a social accomplishment. Very useful.' She walked a little way in silence. 'We all have our uses. In Africa we were useful. Putting people in touch. Much appreciated.'

Patrick nodded encouragement. It must have been a dance of another kind he thought. Up and down the garden path. In and out the sanctions. 'I'm sure it was,' he said.

'And still is,' said Lady Larkin. She pointed the way with her cane and, obediently, he steered her towards the house. 'People like to be appreciated. They can turn quite ugly if they feel they've been overlooked.'

'I can see that.'

'Did you ask anyone about that boxing match?'

'Not yet.'

The sun beat down and a thousand roses breathed out their perfume. 'I think you should,' said Lady Larkin.

Downey had not warned him that Cassandra would be with them for lunch, but it was just conceivable that he had not known. On the other hand it was more likely that he had decided to spring a small surprise, no less irritating because it could have been predicted. It was his own fault, Patrick decided, for not asking if she was going to be there. He still had to learn how to think ahead.

'I've just been hearing about your programme,' he said.

She rolled her eyes and fluttered the fingers of one hand. 'Terrifying.'

'You don't mean that,' said Patrick. 'You're not in the least afraid.' Her dress was the giveaway. During their marriage he had learned to read her mood not by what she said, but by what she wore. Black meant resolve; blue meant affection; sludge green – a colour she chose only on her worst days – meant a nagging uncertainty. Today she wore a tunic of cherry red, with golden buttons and matching ear studs. Cassandra, he judged, was feeling confident; perhaps over-confident. There were times when she went over the top, talking intemperately, laughing wildly as though she had drunk too much champagne. It was not like a whisky drunk. There was no slurring or slowing down, but an effervescence which made her sound quite hysterical. She laughed a lot, with corresponding body language, her head thrown back, her belly heaving. It was behaviour which Patrick interpreted privately as being one of the chaps. He could not bear to watch it. Embarrassment made him sweat.

'You don't understand fear,' said Cassandra. 'It can be used creatively.'

'How's that.'

'It tunes you up. Gives you an edge.'

'I suppose it does.'

'Fear of failing,' she said. 'Anyone creative suffers that. But I have help.' She turned towards the Admiral, her wan

166

smile flowering into a full beam. 'I have a wonderful crew. A wonderful director. Wonderful support from everyone.'

The Admiral raised his glass. 'No more than you deserve.'

Patrick swallowed hard. 'About the panda . . .'

'Great for the programme.' The voltage had changed. Her smile was no longer melting but clipped out of foil. It signalled a change of character. Sitting opposite him now was Career Woman; sassy, stylish, indomitable. It was like meeting an old acquaintance and he remembered how he had introduced her to the role model. They had been in bed, grazing on each other's flesh while a late night movie played on TV, when he realized that Cassandra had switched her attention from his penis – still standing hopefully erect – to the actress occupying the screen. She was tailored and rakish, wearing an absurd hat and a pin-striped costume, giving as good as she got to a room full of hard-nosed reporters.

'Who's that?' she asked.

He squinted over the tumbled bedclothes. 'Rosalind Russell.'

'And the film?'

'*His Girl Friday.*'

'I'd like to be like that,' she said.

It was love at first sight, or rather an admiration so intense that Cassandra was quite shameless about copying her. But Cassandra's swagger came second-hand. She did not go into her act intuitively. There was always a moment's pause, a split second deliberation which no one else seemed to detect.

He wished that he could be less aware of the process. But love did not make him blind, only more perceptive and, for a while, more forgiving. How else could he have endured the performance which became Cassandra's stock-in-trade? Occasionally he played a cassette of the film. Fifty years old, it was still terrific. The black and white print framed the actors like aspic, preserving their attack, their youth, the jauntiness that shaped their style. That was what Cassandra had envied; the assurance which gave them heart and buoyancy. She had tried to make it her own. But while she could mimic, she could not create. There was something forced about her vivacity which made it dogged instead of inspired.

It was too late to tell her now, he thought; better to concentrate on more pressing problems. 'The panda won't be in the studio,' he said.

'Why not?'

'There'll be quarantine for a start. And it's not a pet. People could be hurt.'

'Not by a panda . . .'

He fought the temptation to slap her wrist. 'They bite people,' he said. 'There was a keeper who had his arm chewed. And they have long claws. Think of them as bears. You can't play with them.'

'I could.'

'The zoo wouldn't let you,' he said patiently. 'I wouldn't let you. I know it would make good telly. But you can forget about it.'

'I've seen people with pandas.'

'Once upon a time. Before they knew better. Or when the panda was very small.'

'How big is ours?'

'We don't know. We haven't got it yet.' He appealed to Dominic Downey. 'Just explain to her what the situation is.'

It was all for the Admiral's benefit, he thought, and he kicked himself for rising to the occasion. Yet again in the continuing saga of Cassandra becoming Big he had been given a part (a small one), with lines (largely feed) which allowed her to star as the feisty female challenging a dull, male-dominated world. He felt desperately bored. The scene was played out. Someone should say 'Cut'.

'Cut,' he said.

'What do you mean?'

'Come off it,' said Patrick. 'You've got the programme. We'll get the panda. We'll work something out.' He saw Harry Miller hovering at his elbow with a bottle of wine. 'Don't go away,' he said. 'I'll have some of that.'

He was behaving recklessly, but a brush with Cassandra invariably had that effect. It was a dangerous tonic, like taking small doses of arsenic. While the toxin raced through his bloodstream he did not consider the consequences. He saw the Admiral reach for Cassandra's hand and enclose it

168

in his old, red paw. He smiled and she smiled. 'He's right for once,' said the Admiral. 'We'll work something out.'

After lunch the discussion took two hours. At the end of it the panda had been pencilled in to several future editions of Open Heart. Patrick had agreed to write not only his series of articles for *The Arbiter* (with only a minute share of syndication), but also a panda book, the script for a panda comic strip and a speech for the Admiral to deliver when the panda was handed over to the zoo. 'Put in a few panda jokes,' he told Patrick. 'I'd like it to be a festive occasion.'

'I don't know any panda jokes.'

'Make them up.'

It was not why he had become a journalist, he thought.

If, several years back, he had been granted a glimpse into a future where the Admiral ruled he would have chosen otherwise. Now there were fewer options. Fortune had always favoured the shit. But to take advantage of the fact, one had to have not only the knowledge but the proper disposition.

He excused himself from the meeting, which seemed good for another hour, and found a lavatory. The claret had left his brain for his bladder and he sensed the beginnings of a hangover. He pressed his forehead against the tiled wall and unzipped his fly.

'Excuse me,' said Harry Miller. He was standing behind the door which Patrick had pushed open and now emerged, clutching a dustpan and brush. 'Mr Downey says there was mud on the floor.'

'I saw the newsreel the other night,' said Patrick. 'Great fight. You were doing pretty well to start with.'

Miller sniffed loudly. 'I don't watch it any more.'

'Why not?'

'I know how it ends, don't I.'

'Lady Larkin thought there was something funny about the knock-out. Not the actual punch. The one before.'

'It's a long time ago,' said Miller.

'But you must remember . . .'

Miller shrugged. 'I had a lot of fights.'

His face could have been carved in stone, but something

seemed to shift behind his eyes like a match flaring in a darkened room. Memory had been set in train and it was having a bumpy ride. Patrick shook loose the last few drops and hoisted his zip. Lady Larkin was on to something, he thought. The fight with the Admiral had been lost and won fifty years ago, but one thing was certain. Harry Miller was still unhappy about the old one-two.

Cassandra begged a lift when it was time to leave for London. 'But you hate my driving,' he said.

'I did once. I don't mind it now.'

'You always said I was absent-minded.'

'Not absent-minded. Inattentive. You never notice what's in front of you. Or behind you. You simply don't see it.'

He recalled his last journey with Amos when the complaints had been much the same. 'You've been comparing notes. Passengers Anonymous. You could form a club.'

'I just want you to take care,' said Cassandra.

She was a bad passenger, just as he was an indifferent driver. Her special tactic – devised, he thought, to exasperate him – was to clutch the rim of her seat whenever he braked or accelerated, so that his competence was always under review. Her criticism was mute but implacable.

Lady Larkin waved goodbye from the front steps and he waved back. 'What a sweet old thing,' said Cassandra, getting it wrong yet again.

Lady Larkin, thought Patrick, was an old mercenary and while he both liked and admired her, he had never discerned an ounce of sweetness in her nature. He settled behind the wheel and tried to ignore the gust of perfume which Cassandra was spraying on to the base of her throat. It was one of her musky numbers and it reminded him of other anointings.

She showed him the bottle. 'They've asked me to try it out. 'D'you like it?'

He sniffed cautiously. 'Nice enough.'

'They want me to endorse it.'

'What are they paying?'

'Lots.'

It was the prime perk of becoming Big, he thought. There was no point in feeling resentful. 'What does the Admiral have to say about it?' he asked.

'Not much. He has product approval. The image has to be right. But he thinks the exposure's useful.'

She applied more perfume and he held his breath. 'What do they call it?'

'Dominate,' said Cassandra.

Patrick leafed through an imaginary thesaurus. 'Tyrannize,' he suggested. 'Subjugate. Enslave. Oppress.'

'Don't be ridiculous.'

'Or you could keep it simple. You could call it Boss.'

She stared through the windscreen without replying and he supposed that she had gone into a sulk. He was wrong. 'I like that,' she said. 'I'll pass it on.'

She was still in character, he decided, but Career Woman had been modified into Cynical But Loving Old Chum. The part was not taxing, but there were several nuances she had still to perfect. The weariness needed to be a touch more worldly. The fondness had to be underlined. This was someone, said the subtext, with whom he had shared a life, including a bed and although all passion was spent they were still joined by a rueful affection. Nostalgia hung in the air, competing with the spray from the aerosol, and he wound down the car window to let it out.

She sighed loudly and patted his knee. 'I wish we were better friends.'

'Why's that?'

'I need someone to talk to. Someone who knows me really well.'

He grunted as he changed gear. It was better to say nothing until he knew precisely where the conversation was leading.

'I've always cared for you,' she said. 'I still do.'

'It was you that walked out. I never wanted you to go.'

'I never wanted to go. You made me.'

It was as though she was playing with possibilities, trying them out for size before they were finally discarded. And he was joining in, returning the service with a promptness that made him seem eager, even optimistic. But it was a game he could not win. There was no chance of another chance.

'Mind you,' said Cassandra, 'it was the right decision.'

'What was?'

'To go. It was all over. We were heading in opposite directions.'

He nodded without speaking, thankful that he had said no more.

'I blame myself,' she said. 'You needed help and I didn't give it. I've learned so much since then.' She drew herself up like a singer who had reached the chorus of her song after a series of preliminary trills.

'Such as?'

'Patience. Humility. That's what Amos says.'

'He said you were misunderstood.'

'He's a wonderful man.'

'A bit long in the tooth perhaps.'

'Age doesn't matter.'

'Probably not.' He recalled the midnight noises he had heard emanating from Amos's flat.

'I see him as an example,' said Cassandra. 'He gives people hope. He gives them something to look forward to.'

Suddenly everything was made plain. Amos and the Admiral were roughly the same age. When Cassandra spoke of hope being offered she had only one recipient in mind. The Admiral had bought *The Fogey* not as an investment, but an act of faith. He was seeing off *anno domini* and Amos was his champion. When he posed as a Senior Centrefold he was reminding the Admiral he could do likewise. When he was seen as Cassandra's consort he was acting as the Admiral's stand-in. Fantasies were being played out here but, so far, they were all in the mind. It would be interesting to see what Cassandra would do if they took a more practical turn.

'How long do you give it?' he asked.

'Give what?'

'You and Amos. True love.'

'Don't be absurd,' she said. But there was no sting in her reproach. It was possible, he supposed, that she had not yet taken in how she was being put to work. Cassandra was not slow; quite the contrary. Her problem lay in being in too much of a hurry to see what was going on. She had no patience. What she would have preferred, if it could have been arranged, was learning by implant.

'Don't get too involved,' he said.

She stared at him as he swung the car through flounces of razor wire and parked it in the shadow of Falkland House. 'I think you're jealous.'

'Not this time.'

'I hope you mean that.'

He held up his right hand, palm extended. 'So help me,' he said.

'Is there anything wrong?' he asked Judith Wales.

'Why should there be?'

'Your message. Something about mutual concern.'

'You and me,' she said. 'That's what I meant. Isn't that worth thinking about?'

'Of course it is.' He tried not to sound too relieved. 'And that's all you meant.'

'I wanted you to return my call.'

'I've been busy. I've only just got in.'

There had been two more messages awaiting him when he spoke to the switchboard. By this time, he thought, curiosity would be running wild.

'I want to see you,' said Judith Wales.

'That would be nice. But I don't know when.'

'Tonight.'

'That's a bit tricky. I don't know when I'll be through at the office.'

'I'm not going anywhere.'

'I'd better ring you,' he said. 'I may have something to do.'

'Don't you know? Are you waiting to see what else turns up?'

She sounded drunk, thought Patrick. It would explain her apparent desire to have him report for duty. 'I'm not waiting for anything,' he said. 'I have to see a friend.'

'Aren't I a friend?'

'Of course you are. But this is different. It's professional. I have to explain something to him.'

He heard himself gabbling and, much too late, remembered

the listeners on the line. 'I'll call you,' he said. 'I promise.' He broke the connection and left the phone off the hook. It was a habit which enraged the switchboard, but it could not be helped. He felt persecuted and apprehensive. Judith Wales had all the makings of a nutter. He would have to proceed with care. For the first time he thought of his coming trip with relief.

When he had first considered shopping for women his imagination had rarely taken him beyond a first encounter. But now, he realized, he had been dangerously short-sighted. What he had hoped to do was restore the confidence that had been laid waste by the Worst Fuck. But exorcism was not instant. Spells and nostrums took time to work. Egos took even longer to mend.

He remembered his mother planting him back on his pony's saddle when he had taken a fall. He had not been given time to think before he was off on another round of jumps. But the principle of recovery was different here. He was not taking a jolly canter round a summer meadow. Relationships were being forged; claims being made.

He telephoned Felix Benn and arranged to meet him for a drink. While the number rang his mind wandered and, for several blissful seconds, he was back in the saddle with his mother urging him to grip with his knees and keep his back straight. It had all been so simple then, but already he was learning lessons for life. The coming ride, he thought, was likely to be rough.

'So Cassandra's writing the piece on Amos,' he told Benn. 'Tomorrow most likely. There's nothing I could do about it. Sorry.'

'That's a nuisance,' said Benn.

They were sitting at the bar of the Wig and Pen. In its heyday club membership had been restricted to lawyers and journalists. But now, Patrick realized, as he rubbed shoulders with men wearing unstructured suits and girls drinking spritzers, publishing and PR had taken over. They were all too young, he decided. They did not know that Clapton was God and that there was no Bond but Connery. They belonged

174

not only to another generation but another race. It was a topic he might have aired in Lamb's Tales if the column had not been mothballed.

'She was down at the Admiral's,' he said. 'Planning the future.'

'Her future?'

'Everybody's future. Did you know the Admiral owns *The Fogey?*'

'I should have guessed.'

'And taking an interest.'

'A keen interest?'

'You could say that.'

'How ghastly.' It was always bad news when a proprietor performed the laying-on of hands. Benn's sympathy was an acknowledgement that he too was vulnerable.

'There seems to be something going on between Amos and Cassandra,' said Patrick. 'It's perked the Admiral up no end. Almost as though he was taking monkey glands.'

'I hope not.'

'You know what I mean. He's over-stimulated.'

They drank, as if by drinking they could wash away the image of an energized Admiral. It was the moment, thought Patrick, to plant Lady Larkin's item of gossip. 'Did you ever see the Admiral in action?' he asked. 'The big fight at the Albert Hall. He's got it on film. We had it again the other night.'

'You mean the newsreel.'

Patrick nodded. 'The old one-two. The man he was fighting works for him now. Harry Miller. Not best pleased. He still doesn't like the verdict.'

'Nobody likes to lose,' said Benn.

'Especially on a foul.'

'Is that what he says?'

'What he feels. He has a job to consider.'

'Is he approachable?'

'Hard to say,' said Patrick. 'He's pretty pissed off. You could sound him out. It might cost a bit.'

'It might be worth it,' said Benn.

He was sitting perfectly still, as though any sudden movement would topple the house of cards he was building in his head. Patrick watched it rise, jack on queen on king. Most newspaper exposés were jerry-built, but they were not required to last. They were tacked together from truth and innuendo, lawyer-proof for as long as they were needed. This was not a story that was going to run and run, but it had possibilities. It combined famous names and dirty tricks. At present it lacked sex, but Benn could probably make good the deficiency.

'Who says Miller's pissed off,' he asked Patrick.

'I've talked to him. So has Lady Larkin.'

'Lady Larkin?'

Patrick explained. 'She put me on to it in the first place.'

'Why would she do that?'

'She's pissed off too. I think the Admiral's cutting down on her perks. She wants to remind him of old times.'

'Old times,' said Benn reflectively. 'I think we might be on to something here.' He signalled to the barman and indicated their empty glasses. 'Same again?'

'The same,' said Patrick. He felt a glow not so much of satisfaction, but of justice done. Nothing that Benn wrote could possibly harm the Admiral. But that was not the object of the exercise.

In the first place he had passed on the tip to replace the story about Senior Centrefolds which Cassandra was now going to break. Secondly, he was acting on behalf of Lady Larkin who had somehow been done down by the Admiral (he was short on specifics here, but trusted his instinct). Thirdly, he was following the old columnist's custom of making creative mischief. Lastly – and transcending every other consideration – he was curious to see what would happen when Harry Miller spoke his mind. The question of loyalty did not arise. The Admiral paid his wages, but he would always be the enemy.

He wondered briefly whether the unstructured suits had such a figure to execrate. It was not likely. The media had always bred the best villains. It was a tradition which no one had yet explored, but it required ambitions and appetites on a scale which no other business could provide.

'Much obliged,' said Benn as he drained his glass.

'My pleasure,' said Patrick, doing likewise.

They walked to their respective cars and drove off in opposite directions. Benn, he supposed, was going home. He, on the other hand, was paying his respects to Judith Wales. As he turned the corner a small, shiny object rolled beneath his feet. When he picked it up he saw it was the flask of scent which Cassandra had been using earlier. He sniffed its fragrance and remembered the name. Dominate. Judith Wales would appreciate that.

thirteen

The dogs showed them the way, streaking through stands of wet bamboo, leaping streams and plunging into beds of parched, yellow grass that closed over their heads, rippling as if someone was tugging a drawstring at the roots. All the while they gave tongue, singly and together, baying with an abandon that was mad and exhilarating.

Patrick struggled to keep up. His thighs turned to wood; his glasses fogged. His breath became solid, like a wedge of compressed oatmeal which he laboured to push in and out of his lungs. It was painful to breathe, but if he stopped breathing he would die. It was absurd, he thought; no one should be faced with such a dilemma. Worse still, it was his own fault. He had allowed himself to slide into unfitness. Another drink here, another takeaway there. It all added up and on a mountainside in North Korea he was paying the price of self-indulgence.

The hunters were half a mile ahead. Behind them he saw Blazer and Lottie, her hair flogging her shoulders. Mr Lee, nursing his blistered foot, was further back still. Patrick staggered to a halt and watched the field pull away. He leaned against a tree and wiped his wet face. Soon he would jog on, but for one or two or even five minutes the chase could continue without him.

His mother had once taken him beagling and he remembered the smell of wet earth, the medley of sounds – most of them shrill – and the way his breath had smoked in the still autumn air. Everything was the same, except that they were not chasing a hare but a panda, and this time the pursuit had more serious implications. What impressed him was Blazer's enthusiasm. He peered into the distance and saw him just about to disappear over the next hill. From far away the hair that sprouted from his ears looked like some kind of harness. But he was riderless and unencumbered, as well as being twenty years his senior, the same gap that lay between Lottie and himself. Historians would have fun deciding if they accurately represented their different generations.

His breathing returned to normal. The wedge of oatmeal became liquid, then air. The autumn smells intensified. At the back of his throat he could taste leaf mould and fresh sap. He saw Blazer reappear over the hill and slump into Lottie's arms. The hunters began to troop back, their dogs trailing at their heels. He went to meet them and found himself rehearsing a limp which he decided to attribute to a slight sprain, nothing to warrant concern, but reason enough to have lagged behind. He decided against it. There was no need to lie. He had done his best and there was no loss of face.

Blazer was pimpled with sweat as if he had walked under the shower. 'There he was, gone,' he said.

'You're sure?'

'Pretty well. You saw the dogs. They don't get worked up like that over a rabbit.'

'Dogs can be pretty silly,' said Lottie.

Blazer shook his head. 'Not this time.' He looked at his watch. 'We've got about three hours of daylight left. There's no point in pushing on any further. What we'll do is establish a scout camp and be back in the morning. Nice and early.'

'How early?'

'Five-thirty. Six o'clock. We know the old *bei-shung*'s around here somewhere. He won't go far overnight. We'll meet him in the morning.'

'Not all of us,' said Lottie. She indicated Mr Lee who was hobbling towards them, his weight supported by a cut branch.

'Wonderful,' said Blazer. 'That's all we need. Why didn't you just stay put?' He helped Mr Lee to sit down and laid the branch at his feet. 'How are you feeling now?'

'Painful to walk. All right tomorrow.'

'No chance,' said Blazer. 'You can stay here with the lads. They'll find a bed for you.' He held up a hand when Mr Lee opened his mouth. 'Don't worry. We won't let on. We won't tell old Kim that you fell by the wayside.'

The dogs lay around them in a semi-circle. Their flanks were streaked with mud and they grinned with fatigue. Patrick scratched behind the ear of the hound he had noticed earlier. 'Do they get fed?'

'Course they get fed,' said Blazer. 'At the proper time. These are working dogs. They're not on a picnic.'

'I know that.'

'Nor are we.' He looked back at the hill he had just descended and the bamboo they had still to explore. 'They can pitch camp here,' he said. 'It's as good as anywhere. I'll just have a word.'

He walked to the fire where the hunters were brewing tea and they watched him issue instructions. There was no consultation, no argument. 'He's the man,' said Lottie.

'Very masterful.'

'Very necessary.'

'I suppose so.' He tried not to sound grudging, but his enthusiasm was muted. Nothing that Jack Blazer had said or done over the past twenty-four hours had been half-hearted. Quite the contrary. But he could not shake off the feeling that they were going through the motions. Somewhere in the background there was a master plan in which everything had its place. It was not rigid. There was some room for improvisation. But the end had been determined long ago. It was like being on an adventure holiday. Every hazard was anticipated, every risk allowed for.

They made their way back to the middle camp. The hunters watched them go and Mr Lee waved his stick. 'It's his shoes that did him in,' said Jack Blazer. 'All those years with his toes pinched up like sardines. It's not just the blister. It's the whole bag of bones.'

Ahead of them Lottie whacked aside the bamboo and he

stared at her buttocks as they rose and fell beneath the skin of her jump suit. 'Honest admiration,' he said. 'There's nothing wrong with that.' He shot a sideways glance at Patrick. 'You got plans there?'

'Certainly not.'

'That's all right. I just wondered.'

'We're colleagues. I'm responsible for her.'

'Are you really?'

'Really,' he said, sounding as positive as he could.

'I thought she looked after herself. She's done all right so far.'

'She's very capable. A bit impulsive.'

'That's what I like,' said Blazer. He flicked beads of moisture from the hair that jutted from his nostrils. 'I love a nice arse,' he went on. 'But it's got to have some go.'

'What kind of go?'

'Knowing what it wants. Taking the lead.'

He should be back in Britain, thought Patrick. 'Women on top,' he said. 'That's what they call it now. The new orthodoxy. Politically correct.'

'Is it really?'

'Trust me,' said Patrick. 'I have experience.' He would have liked to have continued with the discussion but he felt himself seizing up. Not only were his thighs stiff, but when he climbed over a fallen log that spanned the track, his spine contracted as though giant fingers were nipping the gristle that linked the lower vertebrae. He found himself walking awkwardly to avoid putting pressure on where it hurt.

Blazer noticed. 'Have you put something out?'

'I don't know. Possibly.'

'D'you want to rest?'

He shook his head. 'Let's get back to camp. I don't want to slow you down.'

'Can't be helped. Is it the same as before?'

'Not as bad,' he said. 'It comes and goes.' He concentrated on Lottie's buttocks. They were a useful distraction, but he reminded himself never to mention the fact. Sexism, even when it was therapeutic, would not be approved of. Cassandra, he supposed, would make an exception when she was being one of the lads. But the circumstances would have to be extreme, the rewards outstanding. He tripped over a branch of bamboo and felt his spine ignite. It was not a major conflagration, more of a thunderflash, but the unexpectedness of it made him shout. Lottie swung round. 'What is it?'

'His back,' said Blazer. 'We've got another bleeding casualty?'

There were three more miles to go and they carried him for the last two. Patrick lay on a stretcher made of blankets torn and woven between small saplings and Lottie walked beside him, her fingers trailing against his cheek.

'I feel a fraud,' he said.

'You're not faking anything.'

'How do you know that? Suppose I just wanted a lift.'

'I think you should be in hospital.'

'I'm not going to hospital. If you mention it again I'll get up and walk.'

'No you won't,' said Lottie, and held his hand.

He stroked the tips of her fingers. 'You bite your nails.'

'I do not.'

'Why are they so short then?'

'It's best for work. There's nothing to snag. Nothing to get in the way.'

A late shaft of sunlight pierced the canopy overhead and he closed his eyes against the glare. He could be in a garden at home, he thought. In a hammock, perhaps, with a view of clouds cruising behind a pantiled roof, baked by August. They were conducting the right, inconsequential kind of conversation – the sort which usually concealed a crisis. 'I shall be all right,' he said. 'I promise. I simply have to take my time. Just for a while. I shall be okay tomorrow.'

'Does massage help?'

'Nothing better.'

'I'll give you one then,' said Lottie. 'One of my hidden talents.'

'Sundown in half an hour,' said Blazer. 'We'll just about beat the dark.' He tucked a loose strip of blanket into the cradle of the stretcher. 'Plenty to write about. Should make you a nice little story.'

'I could do without this bit.'

'I expect you could.' Blazer peered along the track and

shook his head. 'Silly buggers. They're taking a wrong turn. He shouted and waved his arms. 'To the left. Follow the river.' He was as lively as when they had first set out, thought Patrick. Perhaps the hair that sprouted from his head like aerials attracted energy, sucking it from clouds and storing it in his liver and lights. He trotted ahead, light on his feet, looking half his age.

As they emerged from the bamboo the track became familiar. Patrick recognized a rock face and a stand of trees that he had noticed on the way out. It was suddenly less of a jungle. There were signs of management. When they paused on the brow of a hill he saw smoke rising from the far end of the valley.

'Middle camp,' said Blazer. 'Nice and steady now. Let's keep the patient in one piece.'

Patrick held on to the sides of the stretcher as they descended the slope. The light was draining away as if a hole had been punched in the sky. Bars of black cloud locked into place and above them stars glinted. He looked for familiar constellations, but recognized none. It was plain, though, why Blazer had chosen the site as the helicopter pad. There was a bald patch of ground surrounded by trees. As far as he could tell it was level and clear of boulders. From above it looked like a tonsure on an otherwise unbroken thatch of green. There was no indication that it was man-made, but to find such a spot so conveniently placed seemed too good to be true. Blazer knew the terrain. It was doubtless one of the reasons that he was leading the expedition. Everything made sense. But once again there was that creepy feeling of symmetry, of a scenario whose ongoing plot absorbed whatever the day threw up. Something was going on. He felt it in his bones like rheumatism waking to damp.

For the second night he was sharing a tent with Blazer. The soldiers who had been carrying the stretcher tipped him gently on to his bed. He stretched himself, limb by limb and inch by inch. Everything seemed to work, but he no longer trusted his own body. It was always letting him down and, although he was not to blame for its unreliability, word got around. He could not be depended on. He was the weak link in the chain; willing but not always able.

A fire burned brightly outside the tent. Beyond it he saw sleeping bags and a field kitchen. There was the whiff of something savoury and beneath it the smell of coffee. 'Fancy a cup?' asked Blazer. His head, appearing round the tent flap, cast spiky shadows on the roof.

'Love one,' said Patrick.

'How's the back?'

'All right now. At least, I think it is.'

'Dodgy things, discs.'

'Wearing out,' said Patrick. 'That's what they tell me. I don't think they have a clue.'

Blazer nodded emphatically. 'Bleeding doctors.'

'It comes and goes,' said Patrick. 'They don't know what they're looking for.'

He had lost count how many times he had held the same conversation. It was the dialogue of the helpless: resentful, resigned, with its own rhythms, its own idiom. He slid his feet on to the ground, but Blazer waved him back. 'You stay where you are. I'll get the coffee.'

Sparks danced above the fire. It was a still night and the logs burned evenly. One of the soldiers was singing, wordlessly but with great feeling. Patrick hoped that it was a love song, but decided not to ask. It could easily be a hymn to the Great Leader and he would rather not know. He was dozing when Blazer returned. 'It's pain that does it,' he said. 'There's nothing more tiring. If it starts playing up again I'll stay here. You can go on without me.'

'You have to be there,' said Blazer. 'You're supposed to be writing about it.'

'So I am.'

'We'll get you where you need to be then.' He nodded his bald, horned head. 'One way or another.'

On the face of it, thought Patrick, he was being done a favour. But Blazer's brusqueness suggested otherwise. It was a command performance. He was expected to be present and correct.

Tins clashed in the field kitchen and the savoury smell grew stronger. Patrick's mouth watered. 'What are we eating?'

Blazer sniffed long and judiciously. 'Hare, I think. D'you fancy that?'

'Wonderful.'

'After nursie's rounds.' He stepped back as Lottie pushed her way into the tent, a bowl of steaming water clasped to her breast, a toilet bag slung over her shoulder. 'Treat him gently,' he said. 'Leave no fingerprints.'

She steered him outside and knotted the tent flap. A sudden breeze rippled the roof and the flame of the lamp jumped in its glass chimney. Lottie tugged her sweater over her head and rolled up her shirt sleeves. The hair on her arms was like fine gold fur and, momentarily, Patrick thought of Miss Flynn, as dark as Lottie was fair. This was going to be different. He was not going to disgrace himself.

'Let's have your top off,' said Lottie and helped him undress. His head butted into her stomach as she peeled off his vest and he could smell soap and toilet water; not demure, but domestic. She had showered before coming, he thought and – without warning – came an image of water gilding flesh. It was disturbing but, as the picture sharpened, the censor in his head went to work. Vital parts were obscured. There were no full frontals. It was like turning the pages of an old naturist magazine, subscribed to and preserved by his father. *Health and Efficiency*, 1947. Desire was muzzled by nostalgia.

'Lie on your front,' said Lottie. 'We'll loosen you up with some hot towels.' They were already soaking in the bowl and as she wrung them out the steam clambered to the ridge pole where it hung in a small cloud.

Patrick felt his spine expand and relax. 'That's good.'

'Has no one ever done it before?'

'Not like this. My osteopath uses a heat lamp.'

'This is better,' said Lottie. 'Sexier.'

She crouched on the bed, his head nudging her knees, and dribbled oil down his back. She could have been basting a steak, he thought, but the oil smelled of geranium, so pungently that he could see the leaf crushed between his fingers. In the garden at home there had been tubs of geraniums whose proper name, his mother insisted, was pelargonium. At the end of October, before the first frosts, his job had been to bring them into the conservatory. They had flowered throughout the winter, braver than berries, vivid against the snow that covered grass and gravel. It was one of the memories that it was safe to invoke; prepubescent, pre-*Arbiter*, pre-Cassandra. He turned his head and squinted over Lottie's kneecap. 'Third and fourth vertebrae. That's where it hurts.'

She leaned over him as though she was scrubbing a floor and her thumbs eased his backbone apart.

'Does that hurt?'

'Only when you stop.'

Her breasts brushed the back of his neck as her hands made a wider sweep. 'You can lose weight doing this,' she said.

'You don't need to.'

'What about tomorrow? D'you think you'll be fit enough to come?'

'Blazer thinks so. He's practically threatened to carry me if I can't walk.'

Lottie sat back on her heels and he shivered in the sudden cold. 'Don't do anything silly.'

'I won't.' He looked up from between her thighs. 'What if someone sent a snap of this little scene to the Admiral.'

'Deny everything.'

'I wouldn't want to,' he said. 'I'd tell them how good it was.'

She wiped away the oil and dusted him with talc. 'On a scale of one to ten. How good?'

It was the same question that Judith Wales had asked and he gave the same answer. 'Wonderful,' he told her. 'Ten out of ten.'

They ate the hare from mess tins, sitting on logs arranged in a semi-circle around the fire. It was entirely appropriate, but at the same time, thought Patrick, it was not truly rural. He was reminded of a picnic area off some Home Counties motorway, fully furnished with rustic benches and tables, where wardens picked up the litter and, discreetly situated behind the boskage, there was a flush toilet. The lavatory here was a slit trench and there was no warden to police the site, but he could not shake off the impression that they were using a module which had been tried and tested elsewhere. A fool could put it together. It was not meant to deceive but ingratiate.

Blazer turned his watch face to the fire. 'Time to call old Kim,' he said. 'I won't tell him about your back. No need to complicate things.'

'Just as you like.' Patrick sucked the meat from a shoulder blade. His back felt remade. If necessary, he could walk miles. 'It's down to Dr Moffat,' he said. 'The lady with the healing hands.'

Blazer stepped out of the firelight and walked briskly to the truck. In silhouette they saw him put on headphones and throw switches. The cab door was closed and they were too far away to hear what was being said, but there was a good deal of head nodding, as if what he had to report was good news, positive thinking.

'He said he wouldn't mention Mr Lee going lame,' said Patrick. 'No black mark for anyone.'

'I should hope not.' Lottie swigged from her mug of coffee and watched the fire consume itself. There were no flames now. The embers throbbed red and black and as they fell apart they chimed like bells made out of carbon.

'Are you engaged or anything?' asked Patrick. 'I mean, do you have any attachments.'

'Not that you'd notice.'

'You don't mind my asking?'

'I don't mind.'

'I was just wondering if you wanted to get in touch with anyone. I suppose we could get a message passed on.'

'I live by myself,' said Lottie. 'I have a Mum and a Dad and they've stopped worrying about me. Does that cover the ground?'

'Completely.'

Rain was falling when they struck camp the next day. The sky was streaked with red and the wind blew fitfully from the north. 'We'll most likely get snow within the hour,' said Blazer. His face was purple with cold and his ear and nose whiskers stood on end.

They were all wearing bright yellow PVC jackets and trousers over their jump suits. Without them, said Blazer, they would be drenched through in an instant. The bamboo shed water the moment it was touched. There was water in the air and water underfoot. The crisp autumn weather of the previous afternoon had been washed away. The tops of the trees were swaddled in mist. Visibility was down to two or three hundred yards.

'Lax weather,' said Lottie.

'What's that?'

'Lacrosse,' she said. 'That's what we played at our school. Always on days like this. Very character forming. Cold and rain make English roses bloom. That's what they used to tell us.' She tucked her camera beneath the PVC. 'I hope to God it clears up a bit. It's like shooting through soup.'

'Blazer says we'll have snow.'

'Naturally,' said Lottie. 'It's sod's law.' She wiped her face and gave him a hard look. 'You're sure you'll be okay.'

'I feel fine,' said Patrick. And it was true. Despite the rain and the cold that numbed his ears, his spirits were high. He was doing what was expected of him and he would not have to make excuses. The yellow jackets started to move and he followed in their wake. One of the cooks waved goodbye. He was still standing with his hand upraised when they reached the first stand of bamboo. Patrick looked back at the camp with its neat line of tents and its twist of woodsmoke and he felt a fleeting pride of place. It was not like home, but it was somewhere to come back to.

The rain fell for an hour. The PVC kept him dry, but sweat formed a damp patch in the small of his back. He flapped his arms to activate the ventilation holes, but there was no rush of air. He was zipped into plastic like a boil-in-the-bag casserole. Small puffs of steam escaped from the neck of his jacket.

Blazer waited for him to catch up. 'How are we doing?' he enquired.

'No problems.'

'That's the spirit. An hour or so before we reach the others. Then we'll have a brew-up.' He accepted a square of barley-sugar and sucked it noisily. 'Have you copped the birds?'

'Which birds? Where?'

'Where d'you think?' Blazer gestured skywards. 'Buzzards, or something. We get them up here. Sailing about on thermals. The rain buggers it up for them. They get waterlogged. There's a couple cruising round the edge of the woods. Nothing to worry about. Just part of the local colour.'

'I'll keep an eye open.'

'I thought you'd want to know,' said Blazer. 'For the articles.'

'Very thoughtful,' said Patrick. He wondered if Mr Kim had expanded his briefing the previous night. It had been a long conversation during which his task may have been defined yet again. There was going to be no idling on the job. Jack Blazer was there to show him the sights.

Something stirred in the mist overhead, as though it was being churned with a paddle, and he saw a large bird disappear into the gloom. There were no distinguishing marks. It seemed to be all-over brown and remarkably clumsy. It was flying blind, he thought. Visibility was now close to nil. Minutes later he saw it again, perched on the top branch of a tree. It was the most miserable looking bird he had ever seen. Its wings were sodden. Its beak curved abruptly down as though it was about to deliver a verdict on the state of the world which allowed no grounds for hope. And, steadily and mechanically, its head jerked backwards and forwards as it tried to pull its immediate surrounding into focus.

'Mockpie,' said Mr Lee when he told him about it later.

'Not magpie. Buzzard.'

'Don't know about buzzard.'

Patrick flapped his arms up and down. 'Eats interpreters.'

Mr Lee laughed uneasily as though he still found the natural world a dangerous place. He looked seriously rumpled as though he had been stuffed into his sleeping bag and shaken like a packet of crisps. He was alone in the camp, except for a dog with a lame foot. It followed him as he came to meet them, limping down the narrow track, pausing occasionally to wave his stick as if warning the mist to stay back.

'Minding the shop, are we?' said Jack Blazer.

'Shop?'

Blazer sighed. 'Looking after things. How long have they been gone?'

'One hour. Hour and a half.'

'Did they find signs?' He pointed to the ground. 'Tracks? Panda shit?'

'Some shit.'

'That's all right then. We know where we're going.' Blazer slapped his arms across his chest and breathed deeply. 'We're going to be lucky today. I can feel it in my water. All we need is this mist to clear. Then we can get going.' He took a plastic wallet from his pocket and parted the velcro fastener. Six cartridge-sized phials lay snugly side by side. 'One of these should do the trick,' he said. He raised an imaginary rifle to his shoulder and squeezed the trigger.

'Does it work fast?' asked Patrick.

'Faster than Ovaltine.' He closed the wallet and put it away. 'Five seconds and you've got a dozy panda. Then you top it up if need be.'

'You know about the dosage?'

'Near enough,' said Blazer. 'You can't be exact.'

'But don't you measure it against the body weight? How can you know that in advance?'

Blazer waved him down as though he was directing traffic. 'It's thereabouts. Give or take a few pounds. It doesn't do any damage. It's only a tranquillizer.'

'I hate tranquillizers,' said Lottie. She breathed on the camera lens and polished it with a tissue. 'They turn people into zombies, build up in the system. Very nasty.'

'We don't have that problem,' said Blazer. 'We're talking about minimum dosage. We're not creating a habit.'

The mist lifted as they drank their tea. Patrick saw one buzzard, then another, circle the camp. There was a light wind, but the birds flew as though they were labouring to stay aloft. If the rain held off they could most likely drip dry within an hour or two. But the sky was the colour of slate. There was more rain to come. Fat, solitary drops shattered on his PVC and Patrick pulled the drawstring of his hood tighter. Beneath it he felt blinkered, but it was better than getting wet.

He drained his mug (army issue, he noticed, made in Taiwan), and as he set it down one of the hunters ran from the trees. He was close to collapse. Mud streaked his legs and thighs. There was a grey skid mark across his face, blurring

190

the features as though he had wiped them while they were still setting. His knees buckled and Mr Lee hobbled forward to catch him as he fell. He held the hunter beneath his arms and lowered him to the ground where he sat panting, his eyes closed.

Blazer waved everyone back. 'Let the dog see the rabbit. Give him a chance. Let him catch his breath.'

Patrick joined the small crowd and strained to hear what was being said. Everyone spoke at once, but two syllables made themselves clear. He caught Blazer's eye. 'Is he telling us what I think he's telling us?'

Blazer nodded vigorously. His hair stood on end and he bared his teeth in an enormous smile. 'Too bloody true,' he said. 'About three miles from here. They've cornered the old *bei-shung*.'

The hunters had laid a trap and baited it with boiled mutton. In a tiny pitfall they had hidden a wire noose attached to a bent sapling. The pitfall was just big enough for an animal's foot. Beneath a scattering of leaves it was invisible. The panda had stepped into the noose. The restraining peg had jerked free, the noose had pulled tight and now, somewhere in the bamboo, the panda lay captive.

The hunters sat on their haunches and rolled cigarettes. Their dogs whined incessantly. One of them inched forward and its owner cuffed it on the nose. 'What we do now,' said Blazer, 'is put the beast to sleep.' He unslung his rifle and fitted the dart. 'You'd better keep to one side,' he told Lottie. 'We have to pull back the bamboo so I can get a clear shot. I think it'll stay put, but you never know.'

He nodded to the hunters who began to peel away the branches, one at a time. The sapling, stretched taut, was like an arrow pointing to where the panda was hidden. The dog that had broken ranks threw back its head and howled. 'Keep that bloody thing quiet,' said Blazer. 'Let's have some hush.'

His voice was pitched low, as if he was soothing a fretful child or repeating an incantation. He was willing the beast to be there, thought Patrick. He was casting a spell to make sure that the hunters had been successful. Killing the cockerel had not been the villagers' idea. Blazer had planned it, staged it, paid for it. Whatever else he believed in, he believed in magic. He was not only a survivor, he was a sorcerer.

'You're in the way,' said Lottie, and Patrick stepped back. He heard the camera mutter. A branch, released too abruptly, flung water in his face. It had all worked out, he thought. He was bearing witness to something remarkable. It had nothing to do with the Admiral, or Dominic Downey, or Mr Kim. They had been instrumental in his coming to this place. But they had no part in the moment that was fast approaching.

The last branch was stripped away. He saw the tip of the sapling, the copper wire and, at the other end of it, a morose, medium-sized animal like a bear, with a furry, white face and eye-patches like black goggles. It did not move. It made no sound, but stared at them with button eyes.

Jack Blazer put the rifle to his shoulder. 'Sweet dreams,' he said and squeezed the trigger.

fourteen

Surrounded by the litter of his packing, Patrick wondered yet again whether to take the paper underpants with him to North Korea. He had bought the packet ten, or even fifteen years ago, in which time he had used only one pair. The idea was to wear them once, then throw them away. But while he warmed to the notions of hygiene and saving space, he had never trusted them completely. They did not inspire confidence. Paper was made to tear. It was not comfortable in the crotch and, although he could not be sure of this, he suspected that he rustled when he walked. They were the product of another age, a get-up-and-go decade in which travel was fun and disposability a plus. He thought differently now.

He put them to one side and pored instead over a pile of boxer shorts. No travel writer enthusing over the journey to come ever mentioned this part of the process. Patrick's passport was crammed with visas. He had been on the move for more years than he cared to count. But for most of that time he had managed to delegate his packing to someone else. His mother actively enjoyed it, tucking lavender sachets between his shirts, secreting goodnight chocolates in his pyjama pockets and Cassandra had accepted it, not so much as a duty, but as a project in which she was bound to excel.

He would be seeing her in a few hours' time. As Downey

had warned him, the TV version of Open Heart was being launched that evening and the Admiral was giving a party. It was going to be a major thrash. The hotel was booked, the guests invited. The champagne was on ice and the ballroom was now ringed with television screens. The programme had been pre-recorded and at ten p.m. it would be shown to a captive audience. Not once, but several times. Some people were bound to arrive late, but they would not be allowed to escape.

'I can't come,' he told Downey. 'I've got an early morning flight. I need my sleep.'

'Be there,' said Downey.

There was no argument; no excuse would be accepted as valid. Patrick slid his dinner jacket from its plastic shroud, remembering as he did so the soup stain on the lapel. He had intended taking it to be cleaned, but he had forgotten. Perhaps cold water would do the job, or one of those patent stain removers which comprehensively anticipated every calamity known to man. The range was daunting from blood to body fluids which he shrank from enumerating. He would have to be careful not to add to the damage. The suit was going with him to Pyongyang. Downey had warned him that he would be attending a lot of dinners.

He had decided to take Judith Wales to the party. His ticket was for two guests and although it was never actually stated, there was an *Arbiter* tradition that members of staff and their accompaniment were there to provide a claque to meet the Admiral's demands. They were expected to applaud on cue, beat on the tables and create the flattering hubbub that passed for approval. Patrick had always mocked the custom, but never actually challenged it. Judith Wales, he thought, would fall into line. However she behaved in private, she was not a dissenter. She would also prove to Cassandra that he could still find female company.

He sat with his back to the wall and counted out shirts and socks. He was joining an expedition, he reminded himself. Equipment would be provided and even in North Korea there would be a laundry service. There was a knock on the door and when he answered it, Amos Bennet was standing outside.

194

'Not disturbing you am I?'

'Just packing a bag,' said Patrick.

Amos dipped his shaggy head. 'So you are. Off on your travels. Looking forward to it?'

'Not a lot.'

'Could be fascinating. See what you mean, though. Tricky, dealing with foreigners. Mind you, John Chinaman's pretty straightforward.'

'I'm going to North Korea.'

'Much the same thing.'

'I don't think so.'

'Both lots are Commies aren't they?'

'I expect they are.'

'Orientals?'

'That's right.'

'There you are then. Same colour. Same ideology. Feet under the same table.' He nodded to himself. 'Play it by ear.'

Patrick looked for his bottle of whisky. 'Have a drink.' It was not a question. Amos always had a drink, just as he invariably pronounced opinions and offered advice that was either irrelevant or positively dangerous. He was xenophobic, politically ignorant and unshakeable in his convictions. What was scary was that he was so often proved right.

'I just wanted a word,' he said. 'Before you took off. About Cassandra.'

Patrick poured the whiskies without spilling a drop. He congratulated himself. 'Yes?'

'I told you I should be seeing more of her.'

'You did indeed.'

'Well, I have.' Amos went at his drink as though he had earned it.

He was embarrassed, thought Patrick, but strangely defiant. 'Congratulations,' he said.

'And I shall be seeing her more often. On a permanent basis. It's not official. Not yet. But I thought I'd give you early warning.'

He held out his glass and Patrick refilled it. There was no sense in being stingy. Something important was happening and he was not sure how to react. It seemed that he was about to be let off the hook, or rather pushed off it. But he could not decide whether he felt hurt or grateful. His own business with Cassandra was not over yet. He had not been given his emotional discharge.

He wondered whether he should warn Amos what he was in for. If he had been paying attention over the past few months, during which Patrick had endlessly dissected his marriage, he should already know what to expect. But, clearly, he saw Cassandra in a different light. In his eyes she was not the ball-breaker who had featured in Patrick's bleak saga, but someone kinder, wiser, less demanding. She was not vain, or over-ambitious or egotistical. Her name was Compassion and she was giving him something that he needed – a new self-image, which was reassuring, if it had not been ludicrous. The Senior Centrefold had found his mate and it was to be a marriage made in heaven.

'Will someone be making an announcement?' Patrick enquired.

'I don't know about that.'

'Why not?'

'We haven't discussed it.'

Which meant, thought Patrick, that Cassandra was holding it in reserve to drop like cutlery or a small bomb whenever she judged the time was right. He tried to guess when that would be; most likely when interest in the programme was flagging or about to transfer to some other topic. Cassandra hated that, and a short, sharp burst of wedding bells would bring the attention back to where it belonged.

He did not offer Amos another drink, which, in other circumstances, he probably would have done. Quite urgently, he wanted to be alone with his thoughts and his packing.

Amos saw the paper underpants and gave one of his most contemptuous laughs. 'You're not still wearing those.'

Patrick preserved his smile. 'Not at present.'

They're all right for eunuchs,' said Amos. 'But they don't give you the support. I mean they don't actually contain the goods.'

'Is that a problem?'

Amos nodded emphatically. 'You need to look after your tackle. It's the only set you'll ever have. I've looked after mine. I've never had any complaints. Good as new. Even better.'

'Because of the exercise, you mean?'

'Precisely.' He paused to scratch himself. 'Have we had this conversation before?'

Frequently, thought Patrick. 'Once or twice,' he said. His irritation had subsided. There was no point in being cross with Amos. Coals of fire were about to fall on his head. Until they did, he needed his vanity to keep him warm.

Judith Wales wanted to take her cats to the party. 'We have matching collars,' she said, and showed him thin leather bands blazing with *diamanté*.

She strapped hers round her neck. 'D'you like it?'

'I'm not sure.'

The white flesh puffed up around the strap and he ran his finger over the clasp. 'Isn't it too tight?'

'It's meant to be tight.'

'Can you swallow?'

She drank from her glass of wine. 'Easily.'

'Very striking,' he said. 'But no cats.'

'They're perfectly well behaved.'

'For some of the time.'

'Oh, that . . .' She licked her lips quickly as if trying to catch some elusive flavour. 'They were just joining in. They like company.'

'They stay here,' said Patrick.

It occurred to him that he knew very little about Judith Wales, although they had exchanged the usual biographical sketches. Neither was comprehensive. His own version of the Lamb lifeline, while in no way immodest, made him sound wittier, more confident than he actually was. Everyone, he thought, was allowed a certain licence. But instead of making use of it, the Screamer (over her shoulder he saw the photograph on the wall) preferred discretion. She had a professional life, she had told him as much. But how it was lived, who her friends were, what made her laugh remained a mystery. In fact, it was not as important as that. What she had not told him she regarded as irrelevant. It had nothing to do with what they did together. He knew more about the weight of her breasts, the taste of her sweat than he did about her every day concerns.

'Are you married,' he asked her.

'Not now.'

'But you have been?'

'For a time.'

'What happened?'

'What do you think happened? We split.'

'Were you divorced?'

She weighed a hairbrush in her hand, then put it down. 'Yes, we were. Not that it matters. I didn't want to be married.'

'That's it?'

'I didn't like it,' she said. 'It wasn't his fault. He was all right. He took the pictures.' She indicated the framed photographs of staged violence, the screaming women, their mouths like holes torn in fabric. 'He does catalogues now. Mail order stuff. More restful.'

'I'd have thought you were well matched.'

She arched an eyebrow at her own reflection. 'Would you really?'

'You must have had something in common.'

'I was useful to him. He was useful to me. We ran out of steam.'

'That sounds sad.'

'Not very.' She fingered the *diamanté* collar. 'Shall I wear this?'

'It's beautiful.'

'And a bit kinky.' She sleeked back the hair over her ears. 'There's nothing wrong with people making use of each other. But it doesn't have to last. There's no law which says it does. Sometimes you need a change. That's when you advertise.' She grinned at him in the glass. 'Was it such a let-down?'

'Absolutely not.'

'Will you do it again?'

'I shouldn't think so.'

'I will.'

Her tone was cordial, but the message was clear. It was time for a change. All his worries had been unfounded. Judith

Wales was moving on and someone else would suffer the ordeal by cat.

They were among the first guests to arrive at the party. The Admiral and Cassandra were greeting VIPs, but *Arbiter* staff were diverted long before they reached the receiving line. The invitation cards were colour coded. A gold card meant celebrity status. Black on white relegated you to the herd. He did not feel deprived. A handshake from the Admiral was not likely to make his day and, even from a distance, he could see that Cassandra had reached that pitch of excitement in which needles could have been driven through her cheeks without her feeling pain. Amos stood guard behind her. He seemed uncertain what he was doing there. He was not one of the official party, but his place in the line-up suggested that he was being considered for a part. When the plot unscrambled his role would emerge.

Judith Wales pointed across the lobby. 'Who's that man?'

Patrick peered through flurries of hugs, collisions of kisses. 'His name's Downey.'

'Not when I knew him it wasn't.'

'When was that?'

'A year ago. Maybe two.'

'What was he called then?'

She shook her head. 'Can't remember. Not Smith. Not Jones. But something like that. Something plain.'

'How did you meet him?'

'He placed an ad,' she said. 'Just like you. Stressed Executive seeks light relief. Not word for word. But close.'

'What was he like?'

'Excited.' She licked away a crumb of lipstick. 'Be fair. You wouldn't want me to talk about you. Who is he anyway?'

Patrick told her. 'He's a total shit,' he concluded.

'Is he indeed?' She watched Downey shake hands and direct the celebrity traffic. 'You still have something in common.'

'What's that?'

'Me.'

'It's not the same,' he said. But, of course, it was and what made it worse was that Judith Wales found the fact amusing. She grinned widely and shifted her collar so that the stones flashed. She was a woman without illusions. Knowledge was power and the coincidence that she and partners past and present met on the same tumbled bed was not shocking but comic.

She put her hand on his arm. 'I think you should introduce me.'

'Later.'

'Does he have a wife?'

'Does it matter?'

'I don't want to embarrass him.'

'Very thoughtful.' He shook his head. 'No wife.'

The room, though, was full of wives, which meant that the guest list had been screened more rigorously than usual. There would be news coverage as well as publicity shots so that it was important that you were seen with the right partner. ATI – Downey's shorthand for Attention to Image – was in operation and meeting Judith Wales was bound to give him a bad moment. It was a treat which lay in store and Patrick looked forward to it like Christmas.

The bar of the ballroom was crowded. Waiters were serving drinks which had already been mixed – suspiciously pale whiskies, over-fizzy gin and tonics – and he guessed that dilution had been the order of the day. He saw Lady Larkin sip from her glass, then screw up her face in disgust.

'Is there something wrong?'

'Taste it.' She waved imperiously at a waiter and as she did so several strands fell from the cape which hung from her bony shoulders. It was made from feathers no longer serviceable as plumage and when she moved, shedding wing tips and down in equal quantities, there was no mistaking that she was in terminal moult.

'A real drink,' she told the waiter when he appeared. 'Gin, ice and no mixers. Do I make myself plain?' Her voice, which Patrick had never considered musical, was several notches above the norm and would certainly give Downey cause for concern as the party progressed. Most likely, it was how she had talked to her servants in Zimbabwe. The tone was what he thought of as 'damn your eyes' and, democratically or not, Lady Larkin used it for every-one.

She yanked on Patrick's sleeve and obediently he bent his head. 'I'm with you,' she hissed and gestured towards the table plan. 'You're taking care of me. As usual.'

'That's fine.' He estimated the amount of gin in her glass and tried to work out how many more she could sink before dinner. Lady Larkin had enlivened many a dull function, but he hoped he would not have to carry her. She was a little old lady but she was heavier than she looked.

Felix Benn waved to him from the doorway and Patrick beckoned him over. Several other hacks were present, so were members of rival managements. This meant that the Admiral intended it to be an ecumenical evening. The fact that they were invited signalled that – at least while bread was being broken – they were not in competition. Every paper had its agony aunt. They were all in the same business and all that the TV launch of Open Heart signified was that someone had dipped his toe into the pond before the others. Patrick let his mind roam while he reviewed the possibilities. Some of them were immediate. He rested his hand on Lady Larkin's drinking arm. 'May I introduce you to Felix Benn,' he said.

For a moment he felt detached from the event, not with any sense of moral superiority but as though he had been gripped by two giant fingers and held above the room, boiling now with guests, while strategies were devised, games played. Going away always had the same effect. He was distanced before the journey had actually begun. He was not relevant to whatever was going to happen. Judith Wales would either place advertisements or reply to them. Felix Benn would pump Lady Larkin for her views on the Admiral's boxing skills. Harry Miller would be approached. Pens would be filled with poison and, in another part of the forest, Cassandra would be giving advice while Amos romped into his dotage. Patrick registered a slight curiosity about how things would work out, but it was largely mechanical. He was perfectly happy to hear the news at long range.

'I've been told so much about you,' he heard Felix Benn

saying. 'It's such a pity that you've not written your memoirs. You must have so many wonderful stories.'

And Lady Larkin was smiling, twirling her glass, losing feathers, warming to the rays of a sun which she thought had set long ago. At least, thought Patrick, he had made an old lady very happy. The underlying motives hardly mattered. Lady Larkin would have a great time telling all.

Judith Wales watched her raptly. 'She must be very old,' she whispered.

'Older than God.' He tried to recall an incident which would illustrate how much history she had witnessed. Lady Larkin had danced with the man who danced with the girl who danced with the Prince of Wales. It was the Thirties model, not the present incumbent; it was when royalty really mattered. 'She was with the Admiral in Africa,' he said. 'She saw the whole thing fall apart.' He saw Judith Wales's eyes glaze over and knew that he had chosen badly. The Prince of Wales made the better story.

The reception line had broken up and the Admiral moved between the ranks of the faithful. Nora was on one side, Cassandra on the other and Downey and Amos brought up the rear. It was like a royal progress. Some women actually curtsied. When they drew level Patrick kissed Cassandra on her cheek. 'Good luck,' he said.

'Bless you,' she replied. She said it again when Benn shook her hand and yet again when she was introduced to Judith Wales. The needle was stuck, the tape was looping endlessly. Not that anyone would notice, thought Patrick. The whole evening consisted of people going through the motions. He could almost hear the noises inside Cassandra's head, a magnified chirruping like an anthem for grasshoppers. There were no words, no music, just the reverberation of applause which varied in speed but never in intensity. He stepped aside to let her pass and as their bodies touched he smelled her perfume. Her habits had not changed. He could see her scooping between her legs, the shine on her finger as she stroked it behind one ear, then the other, and he felt weak with longing, and with loss.

He swallowed hard and closed his eyes. When he opened them he was staring at Dominic Downey. It was a relief to

202

engage with the real enemy. 'Dominic,' he exclaimed in a voice which promised nothing but good, 'there's someone here who's longing to meet you. Again.'

Dinner was served before the programme was transmitted. The menu was Admiral-inspired, with Spotted Dick sharing the bill with wild strawberries. Lady Larkin had managed to corral her own bottle of gin. 'Would you care for a drop?' she asked Judith Wales.

'I don't think so. Not now.'

'The good thing about gin is that you can drink it at any time,' said Lady Larkin. 'Very useful too. You can sterilize things in it.' She raised her glass and toasted the table.

There were eight of them. Benn had come alone, but they had been joined by two couples from middle management. Both wives smoked incessantly while their husbands discussed rugby. They sat close together as though they expected to be mugged or accosted by beggars and whenever Lady Larkin spoke their faces stiffened either in shock or disbelief. The experience was something they would talk about for weeks to come. Their idea of someone going too far, Patrick supposed, was for the sales director to make his entrance wearing a pair of knickers on his head. But Lady Larkin generated a different kind of unease. She conformed to no rules but her own. She could not be lectured or reprimanded or shamed into submission. She was a loose cannon whose priming and fire power had been made unpredictable by age.

Patrick stooped obediently when she jerked her head in the direction of Judith Wales. 'What is she? Some kind of tart?'

'Certainly not?'

'That's what she looks like.'

'I think she looks very nice.' Elegant was what he meant. But her dress of dark green silk, with its bolero jacket and shoes with malachite heels had the appearance of a uniform. The collar, burning around her throat, invited speculation. Lady Larkin meant no offence, he decided. She was simply going on form. Over the years she had seen too much to let it go unremarked.

'It's not that I mind,' she whispered more loudly than

she imagined. 'There's always room for a good tart.' She abandoned Patrick for Felix Benn and patted his hand over the table top. 'Do you come across much sex in your work?'

'All the time.'

'Is it interesting?'

'It sells papers.'

'Would it sell my memoirs?'

'Very likely.'

'But I've never written a line.'

'Anyone can write,' said Benn. 'It's just a knack. What you need is someone to listen, so that you can determine your own voice. That's where you begin.'

'Would you listen?'

Benn cupped his free hand round the ear that was closest to her furrowed lips. 'Yours to command.'

It was as easy as that, thought Patrick. The chances were that Benn would wind up with a good deal more than the story he had set out to get. It was not a single anecdote that was on offer, but the bones of a book which any sympathetic ghost could knock into shape. Lady Larkin had stories to tell and scores to settle. Revenge was the essence of good autobiography. But why had he never seen the possibilities himself? He chewed his rubber chicken, a speciality he had thought reserved for literary lunches, and scanned his immediate future. Was there some opportunity that he was missing? The Admiral and Downey seemed to have covered most of the panda options, but the story had innumerable angles. Perhaps there was some unconsidered trifle still to be snapped up.

He would have to watch out for Downey. Confronting him with Judith Wales had been highly satisfactory. The chagrin and alarm which had rooted him to the spot for several seconds was a memory to treasure. So was his desperate attempt to remember the identity he had assumed during his Walesian interlude. It was like seeing Dr Jekyll trying to locate Mr Hyde while pinned down by Scotland Yard's finest. Unless he brought up the subject himself ('Man to man, Dominic, how did you feel when the cats landed on your back?') he knew that it would never be referred to. But he had committed a serious indiscretion. With the Admiral looking on, he had put Downey at risk and he would not be forgiven.

'When are we going to see the telly?' asked Lady Larkin. She swivelled in her chair, the gin in her glass lapping the rim.

'Very soon,' said Patrick.

'Is it going to be dreadful?'

'I hope not.'

'We think she's wonderful,' said the blonde middle management wife. 'We read everything she writes.'

'Absolutely everything,' said her friend. Her hair was the colour of boiled ham, pink with highlights of pale blue. It was an unfortunate colour scheme, thought Patrick. At first glance it looked like a dinner plate, ravaged by mould.

Lady Larkin studied her with interest, then shook her head in disbelief. 'But don't you find her frightfully bossy? Always laying down the law?'

The blonde lit another cigarette. 'Somebody has to. Tell them where to get off, I mean. She's on our side.'

'Strange,' said Lady Larkin. 'I've never felt that.'

'It's the generation gap,' said the wife with pink hair. 'That's what makes the difference. She's one of us really.'

Lady Larkin nodded sympathetically. 'Poor thing.'

The toastmaster tapped the microphone and the Admiral made his speech. It was the one about looking to the future and broadening horizons. Patrick had heard it several times before, but television gave it a new impetus. What was remarkable was the enthusiasm with which the Admiral plugged Cassandra. Someone had decided that she was star material (had they taken a readership poll? Patrick wondered) and as the superlatives gathered momentum he watched her face glow as if someone had lit a candle in the hollow of her throat. Amos nodded at each compliment, confirming the rightness of the opinion. Dominic Downey surveyed the room, scanning each table for signs of mutiny.

'And readers have taken her to their hearts,' said the Admiral. 'She makes them laugh. She makes them cry. She speaks to Everyman and Everywoman. She looks into their lives and understands what makes them tick.' He blew his nose gently as though unwilling to disturb the sentiment.

'From the very start we knew we had something special,' he went on. 'Something, someone to cherish. Readers told us that they loved her and we knew then that she would win an even bigger audience. We're still behind her. You can still find her in the pages of *The Arbiter*. But from tonight you'll also find her on your TV screen.' He raised her hand to his lips and kissed it. 'Our very own Cassandra,' he said. 'And, for the first time on TV, your Open Heart.'

The lights went down and Patrick experienced a curious sensation as though every drop of blood was draining from his body down to his feet. He felt faint and wondered irritably what people would think if he passed out. Would they say he was jealous and trying to grab attention as Cassandra's name suddenly convulsed a dozen large screens around the room? He dipped his table napkin in his water glass and patted his face.

'Feeling all right?' asked Lady Larkin.

'A bit dizzy.'

All around him the screens were filled with red, satin hearts which pulsated in time to a drum machine. They split open and Cassandra stepped out. There was a close-up of her sincere smile followed by the titles.

'Try some of this,' said Lady Larkin and passed him the gin.

Patrick drank deeply. It helped to blur the details of the programme that followed, but some items were unforgettable. Even as they came and went he knew that the residue would cling to the memory like grit. There was Cassandra Confidential in which she spelled out her manifesto ('tell all and help all'). There was Love Gone Wrong in which maudlin men and women wept over their broken romances. There was Erogenous Zone in which harridans in white coats discoursed on the G-Spot and how to remove hair from nipples. There was a five minute plug for the Senior Centrefold and sex in old age. And there was Speaking Frankly in which a panel comprising a doctor, a female novelist and a footballer were invited to solve problems posed by mini-soaps in which actors played out embarrassing situations. Should the wife's best friend reveal all about her faithless husband? Should a lover complain about her partner's bad breath? Should an orgasm ever be faked? Patrick found himself shrinking into his chair. It was inevitable that people would assume he had inspired some of these intimate moments. Cassandra was notorious for finding her copy close at hand.

He peered through his fingers and saw a couple on a bed. They were evidently making love. Or rather, the man appeared to be committing rape on a woman who was letting it happen. She did not fight or try to escape. There was a close-up of her face, set hard and streaked with tears. She bit her lip as her partner pitched himself forward and then collapsed. The camera pulled back to contemplate the tangled bodies and Patrick groaned softly to himself. It hardly mattered how the question which the tableau was meant to illustrate was framed. No one would be deceived. Not his friends or his enemies, not the guests at the party, or several million viewers he had yet to meet. What they had all witnessed was the Worst Fuck in the World and he was the man responsible.

On screen the panel condemned the rapist ('brute, beast, fascist') and Cassandra said her goodbyes. The credits rolled, and as the screens faded to black, a spotlight raked the room and came to rest where the microphones clustered and the bouquets were thickest. Cassandra's smile, Patrick observed, was piteous as though she was still in shock from the assault on which everyone had eavesdropped. It grew in confidence as the applause began, warming and widening until it looked almost too painful to sustain.

'Thank you,' she said. 'Thank you everybody. Thank you for being here.' Her voice broke and her eyes brimmed. Patrick put his hands together for a performance that was no less sincere for being endlessly rehearsed. He recalled the dummy runs, the speeches which he had helped to write and which Cassandra had rewritten so that she sounded artless and gauche, reliant on those wonderful people who had helped her to become Big.

She stretched out her hand and led Amos forward to stand beside her. 'I want to introduce the man in my life,' she said. 'You saw him in the programme. And here he is in the flesh. Amos Bennet. The man I'm going to marry.'

Lady Larkin craned forward for a closer look. 'Doesn't that man write books?'

'He did once,' said Felix Benn.

There was an orgy of hugging and hand-shaking. The programme was unmistakably a success. Bigness was in the air. If one breathed in the right direction, thought Patrick, it might be possible to inhale some of the magic ingredient. Amos looked baffled as though his part in the proceedings had been briefer than he had expected. The role had materialized, but no one had warned him that it was a walk-on.

Ten minutes later the ballroom was half empty. The middle management wives and their husbands had gone. Lady Larkin and Felix Benn gossiped over the last of the gin and Judith Wales sat staring at him across the table. 'Well,' said Patrick, 'that's that. I hope you weren't bored.'

'Not a bit.'

'People seemed to like the programme. D'you think it will take off?'

She nodded slowly and fingered her collar. 'That was you wasn't it.'

'I don't know what you mean.'

'The couple on the bed,' she said. 'I don't mean that was you doing it on screen. But that's what happened. That's why it all went wrong.'

'Something like that.'

'You didn't tell me.'

'You didn't ask,' he said. 'You weren't interested.'

'I am now.'

'Not very,' said Patrick. 'Only because you know how it worked out. How it's working out. There's still some way to go.'

He yawned suddenly, as if the sleep that lay ahead had grown tired of waiting. He thought of the early morning plane and counted the hours that lay between now and then. He would place an alarm call, but it was hardly necessary. As usual he would wake every hour, on the hour. The more he worried about it, the more wakeful he became. He yawned again and his jaw cracked at the hinges.

'I must go home,' said Judith Wales.

'I'll take you.'

She shook her head. 'There's no need. I know you've a plane to catch.'

'It's just a taxi ride. It's no trouble.' Even to his own ears he had rarely sounded less convincing.

Judith Wales kissed him on both cheeks. 'Personable forty-three,' she said. 'Fellow explorer.'

He realized that she was saying goodbye, and watched her walk briskly away across the ballroom. She did not look back and at the far door Dominic Downey took her arm.

fifteen

Four men carried the panda back to the tracker's camp. It lay curled like a piebald comma inside a rope hammock. Poles were slotted through the open weave and the edges bound together with baling wire. When it was hoisted on to the shoulders of the men who were carrying it, the panda opened one eye, then closed it again. It began to snore loudly.

'She's right out of it,' said Jack Blazer. 'You can take it easy. No hurry, no worry.' He blew on to the panda's muzzle but there was no response. Its mouth was open and its tongue spilled over its teeth. It was shocking pink, the colour of salami.

'Did you say "her"?' said Lottie.

'Just a figure of speech. Only another panda knows for sure.'

'How is it size-wise? I mean, is it about average?'

'Biggish,' said Blazer. He poked one finger between the ropes and scratched behind the panda's ear. 'What we have here is a very fine specimen. As requested.' He turned to Patrick. 'Your lot should be well pleased.'

'Bound to be.' It was quite an occasion, he thought. All the trackers were drinking beer which Blazer had produced from his backpack. Even Mr Lee held a can to his lips. There was an air of holiday. Someone was whistling. The

210

dogs danced around the panda. But Patrick felt curiously detached. The fact that one of the world's rarest animals lay parcelled at his feet did not excite him. What he felt was ashamed, or at least apologetic. An hour earlier the panda had been blundering about its own affairs, devouring bamboo and defecating wherever and whenever it liked. Now, through no fault of its own, it was part of a plot, doing its stuff for a ghastly regime and a tycoon greedy for preferment. He was not proud of his part in the proceedings.

'Don't look so bloody miserable,' said Blazer. 'We're on to the easy bit now.'

As he spoke, the rain – which had been holding off since they caught the panda – fell with renewed vigour. It was bitterly cold. Patrick's face felt as though it had been varnished in ice. When he breathed through his open mouth, his teeth ached.

Lottie tucked her cameras inside her jump suit. The yellow of the PVC jacket drained all colour from her cheeks and when she blew her nose, her fingers left white indentations, as though blood was reluctant to flow back into the coldest parts. She stamped her feet and swung her arms. 'What are we waiting for?' she asked no one in particular. 'Let's go.'

The track was glazed with mud and going downhill they skidded as if they were treading in grease. Jack Blazer took one of the panda poles and looked for Mr Lee. 'Tell them to take small steps. Watch how I go. Steady as you like.' He edged his way down the hillside, digging his heels into the slope, bracing himself to take the panda's weight.

Mr Lee was still hobbling. He leaned on his stick and stared into the rain that sluiced through the bamboo. 'I shall be glad to be home again,' he said.

Patrick nodded doubtfully. 'It rains there too.'

'Not like this.'

He was a city boy, thought Patrick. He had not learned how to enjoy the country. Not that there was much to enjoy today. The rain was turning to snow and as it blew against the hammock it formed a frail, white shell which fell apart and reformed every few minutes.

'She's worth a bit!' said Jack Blazer. 'Last time a panda

came on the open market it fetched half a million quid. Or thereabouts.'

'When was that?'

'Twenty, thirty years ago.' Some kraut had one on offer. It's different now. Pandas are what governments trade for favours. They help to make deals happen. They're the new currency.'

They marched on in silence. Patrick watched Lottie's yellow-clad back bob on ahead and tried to ignore the occasional twinge in his own. 'How long before we reach camp?' he asked.

'Tracker's camp, half an hour. Middle camp, late afternoon.'

'It's a long day.'

'A bloody sight longer if we don't move.' Blazer quickened his pace and the porters stumbled as they tried to keep up.

'You said there was no hurry.'

'That was then. We're going to get more snow.'

It was an accurate forecast. The sky was an inky black. Sometimes, abruptly, it would clear and through chasms of cloud the sun shone before being blotted out by brief but intense blizzards. Snow gathered on the leaves of the bamboo and slid off as they brushed past. They waded through drifts and tripped over fallen branches. The panda was invisible in its white cocoon.

At the tracker's camp they made tea and ate field rations. The sausages that Blazer said were American tasted of soy. Patrick gave his to one of the dogs which gulped it down, then sicked it up moments later. In another hemisphere, he thought, GIs were probably experiencing the same reaction. It was a shame they could not compare notes.

There was a strong wind blowing from the north which made hearing difficult. But, periodically, between gale force blasts which ballooned his jacket hood and scooped tea from inside his mug, he was aware of a distant roaring like a foghorn far out at sea, or a bull bellowing across miles of open country. He could not identify the sound or where it came from. It rose and grew faint. When the wind fell he grabbed Lottie's arm. 'Listen,' he said.

'To what?'

'That noise.'

'What sort of noise?'

'I don't know. Something calling.'

She cocked her head, turning one way and then another. 'I can't hear anything.'

'It's stopped,' said Patrick.

'It's just the wind.'

'No, it's not.' He pulled back his hood, but it was no use. 'There was something there,' he said. 'I wasn't imagining it.'

'Wind devils,' said Jack Blazer.

'What are they?'

'Christ knows. It's what the locals say when they hear things. Wind in the chimney. Wind in the tree-tops.' He pointed to the threshing branches. 'They say a ghost walks up there on burning feet. Look at him go. Anything's possible if you listen long enough.'

They buttoned up and marched on. 'How's the panda?' asked Patrick.

'Still out cold.'

'Is that normal?'

'What's normal? How many tranquillized pandas do you know?' Blazer shifted the pole to another notch in his shoulder. 'You ought to take a turn with this. If your back's not playing up, that is. Just so you can say that you've done it. For the articles, I mean.' He beckoned to Lottie. 'Come and take his picture. Journalist attempting honest day's work.' He halted the column and transferred the pole to Patrick's shoulder. 'There you are then,' he said. 'Sing out if it gets too much.'

It was like carrying a coffin, thought Patrick, as he took his first step. Not only was it heavy and uncomfortable, there was also the fear of dropping something precious. He could not decide whether to try and march in step with the others, or set a rhythm which they had to follow. He managed neither. After two hundred yards his right foot slid forward and his left foot slid back as he performed an inelegant splits. The panda thudded into the back of his neck and Blazer caught the pole as it impaled itself in the mud.

'Sorry,' said Patrick. 'It's like glass.'

Mr Lee helped him up. 'Glass which breaks?'

'Glass which is smooth.' It was a hell of a time, he thought, to be refining the interpreter's English.

'You okay?' asked Blazer. 'No damage done here.'

'That's good. I'm all right. Just clumsy.'

Blazer passed the pole to another porter and waved them on. 'I don't think it's for you,' he told Patrick. 'But you can say you had a go.'

It took them four hours to reach the middle camp. Snow gave way to rain and Patrick's face lost all feeling. When a thorn raked his cheek he did not know he was bleeding until Lottie dabbed the scratch with her handkerchief. The mud was worse than the cold. It was thick and viscous, the kind which made bad wars terrible. Years ago, farther back than he now believed possible, he had interviewed a veteran of the Kaiser's War. He was an old man who still had nightmares, not about bombs or howitzers, but about the mud which had filled the trenches and in which half his platoon had drowned. Did Blazer have the same dreams? He showed no sign of it. In fact, thought Patrick, the worse conditions grew, the more cheerful he became.

'Halt!' he shouted, and threw up his right hand, the index finger stabbing the chilly air.

Patrick stared at him groggily. 'What is it?'

'Take a good sniff?'

'At what?'

Blazer did not reply, but cast his head slowly from left to right like a bloodhound, snuffling loudly through his clogged nostrils.

Patrick imitated him, a trifle self-consciously. He smelled soil and sap and his own sweat, but nothing unusual.

'Try again,' Blazer urged him and, without warning, it was as though he had tuned in to the right wavelength. He could smell wood-smoke and something cooking; meat certainly, with garlic and herbs. His mouth flooded with saliva and he swallowed hard.

'Are we nearly there?'

'Just over the hill. If you can last that long,' Blazer grinned triumphantly. 'It's like my old mum used to say, keep on keeping on and you'll get there in the end.'

The wind shifted to the east and the sky lightened. Patrick took Lottie's hand and they ran down the hill together.

The panda came to as it was being shunted into its cage. Blazer had unthreaded the wire from the lips of the hammock and two of the soldiers were rolling it free when it came out with a rush.

'Stand back,' said Blazer and slammed the door shut.

The panda swiped at him with one paw, but missed by several inches. It was still unsteady on its feet and tripped over nothing as it shambled to the far corner, where it sat with its nose to the bars.

'The cage is too small,' said Patrick.

'It won't be for long. We'll have the chopper tomorrow.'

'It can hardly turn round.'

'It'll be all right. It's only for a few hours.'

It was true that the cage was designed for travelling, purposely small so that the animal was safely confined while it was in motion. But it looked like a place of punishment, a cell of little ease. It was quite possible, thought Patrick, that north of Pyongyang they were still a feature of prison design.

Lottie took her pictures and sighed. 'It's pathetic.'

'It's not for long,' Blazer said again.

'How do you think it's feeling?'

'Confused.'

'Terrified,' she said. 'That's how I'd feel.' She turned on her heel and walked away.

One of the soldiers brought bamboo, boiled mutton and a bowl of water, but the panda showed no interest. Patrick tried to visualize it in a paddock at London Zoo or Whipsnade, but the prospect brought no comfort. The truth was that it did not want to be there.

'Is there anything to drink?' he asked Blazer.

'Beer or something stronger?'

'Whisky would be nice.'

'Whisky you shall have.'

They had several large ones, squatting by the fire while the cook sang his way through preparing dinner. Blazer studied him through the bottom of his glass. 'It'll all be over soon,' he said.

'Then it starts again.'

'It usually does.' He topped up Patrick's glass. 'Is it as bad as all that?'

'Sometimes it is.'

'And sometimes it's not.' Blazer stroked the twin plumes that spiralled from his nostrils, grooming them as if they were the fronds of a moustache. 'You have to take the long view. Don't let the bastards grind you down.'

'It's a bit late for that.'

'It's never too late.' He raised his glass as Lottie came to join them. 'How can you say that when there are lovely things like this about?' He pressed her hand to his lips and kissed it soundly.

They ate from their mess-tins and, afterwards, the hunters sang for them. The first song went on for a long time. Mr Lee attempted to translate, but after two or three verses he dissolved into giggles.

'What's so funny?' asked Lottie.

'Rude,' said Mr Lee. 'Too rude to tell.'

'Give us a rough idea.'

'About a farmer who drinks too much. Mistakes his lady's bottom for the moon. Realizes his mistake when . . .' he hesitated.

'When she farts,' said Jack Blazer. 'Very rustic.'

The song came to an end and everyone applauded. Mr Lee tapped Lottie's knee. 'Your turn.'

'I don't know any songs.'

'Everybody knows one song.'

She scowled at the fire and scuffed her feet. 'There's one we did at school.'

'Let's be having it then,' said Blazer.

'It's not very proper.'

'Don't you worry about that. What's it called?'

'Abdullah Bul Bul Amir,' said Lottie and began to sing.

There was no time to wonder which version she knew. It was the full and filthy one, preferred by the army and members of rugby clubs. Patrick remembered it from his days in the cadet corps when it was sung by a platoon of horny adolescents. Now Lottie was singing it for England.

There were eight verses and she knew them all. The ballad of Abdullah and his rival, Count Ivan Skavinsky Skavar, was heard in respectful silence. Mr Lee made no pretence of trying to translate, but listened carefully and took notes. At the end of verse seven he looked hopefully at Patrick and showed him what he had written.

Patrick read the line aloud: *'He felt a big poke up his old artichoke.'* He handed the notebook back. 'What's the problem?'

'Artichoke is vegetable?'

'In a manner of speaking.'

'How does one feel poke?'

'With amazement.'

The fire died down and the hunters went to their beds. Across the compound Patrick had a clear view of the panda's cage. It shuffled one way and then the other, sandwiched between the wire and the plastic wall. The wind had dropped and it was a still night. The owl was hooting again and further away Patrick heard the sound that had perplexed him that morning.

'Can you hear it now?' he asked Lottie.

'I'm not sure.'

They listened together, but it was no clearer than before. The bellowing grew fainter, then stopped. 'Deer, perhaps,' said Patrick. 'Blazer said there were some about.'

'Or pigs. Do they have wild boar?'

'I expect so.' It was not the forest primeval, but something with tusks was a distinct possibility. He saw Blazer checking the door of the cage, shaking the lock, making sure the wire was fast. The chopper was due to leave in eight hours time and the panda would be on it. Mr Kim had ordered an early start and he did not expect to be let down.

He awoke to a grey world. The fog was dense and he could not see beyond the fire, sulking within a cradle of damp logs. 'Don't you worry,' said Jack Blazer. 'They'll get here all right. It's clear as a bell above this lot. It's just low cloud. Nothing to it.'

217

'Rather them than me,' said Patrick. He hated helicopters. He had been on a film location in Thailand when a Chinook crashed, killing twenty passengers. 'They said the gear box froze,' he told Blazer. 'Then the oil seals broke. It fell out of the sky.'

Blazer shook his head. 'Very dodgy, Chinooks.'

'What are we getting?'

'The safest thing there is. Everybody's workhorse. The Sea King. Carries troops, passengers, five thousand pounds of cargo, torpedoes, anti-ship missiles.'

'And pandas,' said Lottie.

They all stared at the cage. The panda ignored them, just as it had ignored the food, but it seemed alert, with bright eyes and a wet nose which swung from side to side, teasing scents out of the soggy air. 'What can she smell?' asked Lottie.

'Us,' said Blazer. 'Dogs. Whatever's going.' He cocked his head to one side. 'Is that the chopper?'

They listened with him. It was becoming a ritual, thought Patrick, but he could hear nothing except the steady drip of condensation sliding from leaf to leaf, until it reached the lowest level of bamboo from which it fell silently to earth. He glanced at his watch. It was only half past seven. 'Too early yet,' he said.

The buzzards were back, he noticed, circling the camp, then dissolving into the fog as if they were diving into a sauna. Blazer waved his arms and shouted: 'Get off you buggers.' At some time between going to bed and getting up that morning, he had polished his boots. The toe-caps twinkled as he marched up and down, bawling at the birds. Patrick studied his own footwear. Each boot had an outer casing of mud which had set like concrete. He was glad that he had no serious walking to do.

'Perhaps they'll turn back,' said Lottie.

'Not them,' said Blazer. 'They've got their orders. They can't be messing about. We've done the hard graft. All they have to do is pick up Lulu and fly her out.'

'Lulu?' said Patrick.

Blazer gestured towards the panda. 'Her. It's easy as pie. We load the cage into the chopper and they're away. We could light a few fires. That might help.'

He called out orders and the hunters piled stacks of dry wood around the landing patch. The wood was doused with cooking oil and Blazer made the rounds with a Zippo. Columns of red and black bloomed through the mist and the smoke made Patrick's eyes water.

High above and some way to the south he heard the thrashing of rotor blades. The chopper was right on time, but it was still invisible. The fog was silvery, almost synthetic-looking, as though dug into the hill-top there was a dry-ice machine which pumped the stuff out to order. The engines came closer and, mixed in with the roar, there were subsidiary sounds: the rasp of metal against metal, the hammering of loose parts, the percussion of blades beating air. Between the corridor of bonfires, descending like a lift, he saw a black oblong which grew metal sides and a tail on which something spun like an electric fan. It hovered rowdily above the landing patch and, as it hung there, he sensed something else approaching from where the fog was thickest. He shouted a warning, distantly aware that Blazer was doing the same. But as their voices piped uselessly below the clamour, the shape took on definition and the buzzard beat down with its sodden wings to drive itself, like meat through a mincer, into the rotor on the tail.

The helicopter veered to the left, skidding on its own turbulence. It strained upwards, then staggered as if it had been struck by an unseen hand. For a moment it paused before spinning, first to the right, then to the left, then in a tight circle that aimed it like a corkscrew at the roof of the radio truck.

Bits flew off and Patrick saw Jack Blazer reel backwards, blood streaming from his head. He ran on towards the helicopter. There was no fire yet and men in uniform began to jump out, seemingly unhurt. The pilot slid back his door and crawled over the sill. There were people screaming. He wondered why then realized that his own voice was adding to the din. A trickle of flame ran over the back of the helicopter. There was a small explosion, then another like the slamming of an enormous door which threw Patrick on to his back and scattered the landing patch with fireballs.

He lay there stunned and saw Lottie close to the blaze taking pictures. He crawled towards her, with some vague idea of ordering her to safety. Someone hauled him back and he saw that it was Mr Lee.

'Get Lottie,' he gasped.

'No need. Lottie's okay.'

'See to Jack Blazer.'

'Others first.' Mr Lee bent his head against the flames and edged towards the burning helicopter.

Patrick forced himself to his knees and peered about him. Most of the fog within a radius of a hundred yards had evaporated in the fire. Some of the bamboo was burning and there were large, smouldering holes in the roof of the nearest tent. The truck had been demolished and when he looked closer he saw hands and legs, all patched with blood, hanging from the back. Clouds of thick, black smoke billowed from the wrecked helicopter.

He remembered why it was there in the first place and swung round to see that the roof of the panda cage was alight. Gobs of melted plastic were rolling down the walls and the panda was burrowing desperately into the furthest corner. He heaved himself upright and looked for something to put the fire out. There was no water, nothing with which to muffle the flames. A padlock held the door fast and he could not prise it open. He tore at the wire with both hands and saw blood spurt from the tips of his fingers. One corner came free and he ripped it away as if he was tearing the cover from a book. The panda did not move.

'Go on,' said Patrick. 'Shift.'

The panda remained where it was, squinting into the smoke that filled the compound. 'For Christ's sake,' said Patrick, 'get a move on.'

He got behind the cage and tipped it forward. Pain blazed through his back but he ignored it and pushed again. The panda scrabbled with its claws to stay in place, but its feet had no purchase on the plastic. Like a large bale of wool, it tumbled to the ground. Cinders stuck to its fur and there was an acrid smell of burning that cut through the reek of oil. Patrick booted it gently in the ribs. 'Piss off,' he said.

The panda looked at him fearfully and he booted it harder. 'Go!' he shouted and ran at it with open arms, as if he was herding sheep.

The panda fled. It swung about face and shambled swiftly into the bamboo. Close to camp the growth was patchy and for half a mile he watched it tumbling uphill, following the track to disappear finally into a haze of green leaves and fog. And so, farewell, he thought. Goodbye to the Admiral and Regent's Park and TV fame and doing your bit for the Great Leader. It was goodbye, too, to pats on the back for a job well done and the return of Lamb's Tales and job security in lean times. He heaved a sigh. But mostly, he realized, it was from relief and not regret.

'Good for you,' said Lottie, close behind him, and when he turned round she kissed him on the lips.

They counted three men dead and four with injuries which Jack Blazer classified as minor. 'They can still stand up,' he said. 'They can walk out of here.'

Not that they would have to, thought Patrick. The truck had been destroyed. The helicopter was a charred shell. But someone at base would soon clue in to the radio silence and come looking for them. They would find a disconsolate crew. 'It was no one's fault,' he said. 'There are more helicopter crashes due to bird strike than anything else.'

'Who told you that?' asked Blazer.

'I read it somewhere.'

'Bloody birds,' said Blazer. A crust of dried blood masked his right cheek and forehead and fire had cropped the hair in his nostrils and ears.

'No beauty prize for you,' said Mr Lee.

'None wanted.'

The fog had thinned to the colour of watered-down milk and a faint breeze stirred it as though someone was breathing gently through the bamboo. The wire swayed on the side of the panda cage. 'I bet she's miles away by now,' said Patrick. 'Saved by the bell.'

'Good for her,' said Lottie.

Blazer scratched at the blood on his forehead and picked it from under his fingernails. 'How's that?'

'It was like kidnapping,' said Lottie. 'It didn't feel right.

Taking her from home. From where she lives. For all the wrong reasons.'

Blazer shook his head. 'Oh dear, oh dear,' he said. 'How can I start to explain?'

'Explain what?'

'We have to catch her again,' he said. 'Even if it takes years. She doesn't belong here. We brought her here in the first place.'

He was smiling a trifle hesitantly, as though apologizing for some small social gaffe – using the wrong cutlery, opening the wrong door. The enormity of what he was saying was slow to register. Patrick tried to put first things first. 'Where did she come from?'

'China. The zoo at Beijing let her go.'

'Why?'

'Favours,' said Blazer. 'You scratch my back. I scratch yours.'

'I mean why did you need her?'

'No pandas here,' said Blazer. 'Not for ages. Not as far as we know. And we needed one in a hurry. Special request. Part of the package.' He leaned forward to emphasize the point. 'It was your lot made such a fuss about it. All we wanted to do was sell newsprint. The panda was the special offer.'

'A sweetener.'

'Right you are,' said Blazer. 'We make the sale. Your boss gets his knighthood. Simple really.'

'I see.' His legs were wobbly. He could not be sure whether he felt angry or sick. 'But what about us? What about Lottie and me? What are we doing here.'

'Making it real,' said Blazer. 'Making it authentic.'

The quake in Patrick's legs became an all-over trembling. He was not feeling sick, he decided. Rage was shaking him like a dog with a bone. 'How many people were in on it?' he demanded. 'How about Kim?'

'He knew.'

'And in London?'

'Just the top brass.'

Which meant the Admiral and Dominic Downey; no one else needed to be let in on the act. 'How long ago was it planned?'

'Six months or so. We had to get the panda in place.'
He sighed softly. 'I'm surprised they didn't tell you.'

'Are you really!' Now the truth was out he was not in the least surprised that he had not been told. For a fraud to succeed someone was required to play the innocent. Or rather two someones; gullible suppliers of words and pictures which told lies like truth. He remembered how Blazer had played his part; how the itinerary had been orchestrated, how his appetite had been whetted and how he had suppressed his suspicions when the neatness of design had seemed overwhelming.

'There's no sense getting in a state about it,' said Blazer. 'It's not that important.'

'It is to me,' said Lottie.

Jack Blazer dug his fists into the pockets of his jump suit. 'Sorry, my love. But look at it this way. What if you'd never known? What difference would it make?'

'They'd have known,' said Patrick. 'Those bastards who set it up. And they'd have enjoyed it, knowing how smart they were and how bloody stupid we were. That's what matters. That's the difference.'

Blazer wagged a warning finger. 'If you're thinking of blowing the gaff on all this, I wouldn't bother.'

'What's to stop me?' He pointed to Lottie. 'What's to stop either of us?'

'Common sense,' said Blazer. 'Old Kim's not going to let you take any pictures home. Even if he did, what would they prove? And what can you write that doesn't make you look a complete berk? If I were you, my old son, I'd forget it. Put it down to experience.'

He turned on his heel and crossed the compound towards the truck. The bodies had not been moved. 'Is that what you'd tell them?' Patrick called after him.

Mr Kim flew in late that afternoon. He sat in the tent shared by Patrick and Jack Blazer and counted the canisters of film piled on the table. 'Is that all there is?'

'That's all,' said Lottie.

'You give me your word? Do we need to search your belongings?'

'You will anyway.'

Mr Kim lit another cigarette. 'All film that is exposed in this country has to be processed here. It is the law.'

'Do I get it back after that?'

'You may apply.'

'Is there any point?'

'Each case is judged on its merits.'

Mr Lee nodded as each sentence was pronounced. He was being done out of a job, thought Patrick. He hoped that someone would mention how brave he had been when the helicopter crashed. He had burned his hands pulling one man from the wreck. The blisters, when Lottie had bandaged them, had been inches across.

'I have spoken to London,' said Mr Kim. 'They want you to return immediately.'

'You told them what happened?'

He nodded. 'They were most unhappy.'

'Are they still buying the newsprint?'

'We are re-negotiating.'

The ash on his cigarette was still intact and Patrick felt an impulse to unsettle either it or him. 'A pity about the panda,' he said.

'I gather you think otherwise.'

'I'm glad I let it go.'

Mr Kim put out one cigarette and lit another. 'So am I. The panda is a threatened species. An accident would have been very sad. You did well.'

'London won't agree.'

'What does London know?'

The camp was returning to normal. The bodies had been flown out and the cook was preparing the evening meal. The owl was hooting again and beyond it, faintly and far away, Patrick heard the sound that had haunted him since the previous day. He put his head through the tent flap and listened more intently. Between the clatter of pans and the sporadic drumming of engines, something was calling urgently and often.

He went outside and Mr Kim joined him. They stood side by side in the gathering dark, the wind gusting from the north. That was where the mountains began and where the sound was coming from. It was wild country and unpopulated. So far they had only seen the foothills. Not even the hunters did much exploring there.

'I'm sorry it should end like this,' said Mr Kim.

'So am I.'

'The deception was necessary.'

'I don't agree.'

'Then we must agree to differ. We must not part on bad terms. I have grown fond of you. And Miss Lottie.'

'You stole her pictures.'

Mr Kim sighed gently. 'I have explained the situation.'

'Not good enough,' said Patrick. 'We're going back with nothing.' He pursued the thought. 'When do we leave?'

'Tomorrow,' said Mr Kim. 'If it can be arranged.'

'There's not much you can't arrange.'

Mr Kim shot his cuffs like a conjuror announcing his act. 'Tomorrow, then. Will you be happy to be home?'

'I suppose so.'

'You don't sound sure.'

'I have problems at home.'

'Every problem has its solution.'

It was not the moment for old Korean proverbs, thought Patrick, especially this one which fell even below Cassandra standards. 'You really believe that?'

'Of course.' Mr Kim faced him squarely and the fur on his hat bristled in the wind. 'All problems must be confronted and resolved. No one can afford loose ends.'

It was too snug, too smug to have been coined by anyone but the Great Leader. But the proposition was not open to debate. Something else had claimed Mr Kim's attention. He walked past the camp fire and up to the picket line. His head was cocked to one side and he seemed to be straining to hear whatever sounds were coming from the north.

Patrick listened too, but he could hear nothing. The roaring had stopped. There was the steady sussuration of the bamboo, like surf on dry land. But all around it lay square miles of utter quiet; no engines, no explosions, no traffic, no words. Especially no words: it was something to be thankful for. Patrick thought of the babel to come and stocked up on silence.

sixteen

'Words fail me,' said the Admiral. 'All I can say is that you've made a balls of it.'

'I did as I was asked,' said Patrick.

'You let the panda go.'

'Its cage was on fire.'

'That's beside the point. It was not yours to release.'

'I beg your pardon.'

'It was mine,' said the Admiral. 'It belonged to me.'

Patrick studied the cross, red face of his employer and wondered if he had ever tried to comprehend anything that was not concerned with his immediate profit and loss. An apology was too much to expect, but he had thought that there might have been some acknowledgement that he had done his duty by the paper and been let down in the process. 'It was an emergency,' he said. 'Setting it free saved its life.'

'Of course you'd say that.'

'It's the truth,' said Patrick. 'Speaking of which . . .'

He was not allowed to proceed. 'The truth,' said the Admiral, 'is that you panicked. As I understand it there were some nasty bangs and a lot of smoke. And you lost your head.'

'The three men were *killed*.'

The Admiral ignored the interruption. 'You released a

valuable animal. Priceless, in fact. You knew what it represented.'

The knighthood, thought Patrick. A slot on TV. The snapshot outside the Palace gates. 'No one warned me it had been planted,' he said.

'That's irrelevant.'

'You expected me to tell lies.'

'I expected you to behave like a diplomat. You were representing this organization as you'd represent your country. You had a brief to follow. You had tasks to carry out. You went on an expedition. You caught an animal. You were supposed to bring it home and report on what happened. No more.'

'Why didn't you tell us the panda came from Beijing?'

The Admiral's eyebrows rose to meet his hairline. His expression portrayed honest bewilderment; the bluff sea dog all at sea. 'What does it matter where it came from? A lot of people went to a great deal of trouble. And for what?' He shook his head dolefully and heaved a sigh.

It was one of his best-ever performances, thought Patrick, and it was being given for an audience of two. Dominic Downey stood behind and slightly to one side of the Admiral's chair. It was a position which accurately defined their relationship. He was out of the spotlight, but conveniently placed to act as chorus or prompt. He was there to pass the dagger and catch the bodies as they fell.

'You could have saved all this aggravation,' he said. 'All it needed was a bit more initiative.'

Patrick remembered the flames and the screaming. The temptation to land one killer punch on Downey's sleek jaw was almost irresistible. But he would probably botch it. He was still jet-lagged after the flight from Pyongyang.

They had driven to the airport through empty, early morning streets where sweepers were already at work, chipping ice from the pavements and chasing stray leaves. There was no other sign of life; no lorries or cars. The city seemed to have died in its sleep.

'I'm sorry about the pictures. There was nothing I could do,' he told Lottie, as their plane took off into the dark winter sky.

'I'm not blaming you,' she said. 'It just makes me feel sick.'

'Don't think about it.' He held her hand. 'Close your eyes.'

She slept through two dawns and one sunset as they flew west, rousing herself occasionally to drink apple juice so thick that it had to be sucked from the glass. As they flew over Lake Baikal he woke her up. 'That's where the freshwater seals live,' he told her.

'Can we see them from up here?'

'I shouldn't think so.'

She pulled down her sleeping mask. 'Goodnight.'

The sun was rising on the port side like a blood orange, but he did not contradict her. At Heathrow he had seen her into a taxi and waved goodbye. He had supposed that they would meet in the office after the panda inquest had been held. He did not know her home address or telephone number; it was not the sort of information which journalists circulated among themselves. Work was what they had in common, assuming that it would always be there to be done. Now it was a doubtful assumption. The interview with the Admiral was not going well. He was standing on Execution Dock and the trap door on which he stood trembled beneath his feet.

'What would you have done?' he enquired.

'Put the fire out,' said Downey promptly.

'With what?'

'Water. Sand.'

'You could have pissed on it,' said the Admiral, needlessly coarse.

'As it is,' said Downey, 'the whole transaction is in jeopardy.'

Patrick registered a small spurt of satisfaction. 'Oh dear.'

'Of course, we're thankful there were no more casualties,' said the Admiral. 'It could have been worse. But you come out of it badly.'

'Very badly,' said Downey. 'And there's not much to be saved.'

'Saved?' Patrick saw the wisp of an idea, lying like thread on the sleeve of Downey's disapproval. If he gave it a tug something more substantial might emerge. 'Do you have something in mind?'

'We were talking to Mr Kim,' said the Admiral. 'He tells me that business possibilities in his country have been gravely under-estimated.'

'They sell a lot of weapons.'

'I wasn't talking about weapons.'

'They've got the Bomb now. There should be a few customers for that.'

'They have other things to sell,' said Downey. 'They need encouragement.'

'What we want from you,' said the Admiral, 'is something positive. Something up-beat. Something that says there's a new market out there and we're the ones to crack it.'

Patrick remembered the drunken salesmen in the hotel bar. It was not their story, not their experience. They had no place in the Admiral's prospectus and no amount of cheer-leading on his part would persuade them otherwise. Something else was in the air, he thought. The panda, which seemed to have been dropped from the discussion, had been the bait to coax the Admiral into buying newsprint. Now that it was gone, the deal must have been restructured in a way which was making him a fortune. The puff which he was proposing was a *quid pro quo* which would probably run to two or three parts. But the Admiral did not believe in giving something for nothing. Patrick tried to do sums in his head and gave up when the millions ran off the page.

He was not new to advertising supplements, whether they were described as such or not. But this would entail lying on a scale which he found difficult to imagine. 'Do I mention the prison camps?' he enquired.

'What prison camps?'

'Where they put the dissidents.'

'Don't be absurd,' said Downey. 'People don't want to know about dissidents.'

'I suppose not,' said Patrick. 'What about the censorship?'

Downey clicked his tongue in a way that reminded him of Mr Kim. 'Nobody cares about censorship.'

'I care.'

Downey sniggered behind his hand. 'I haven't seen you on the barricades.'

'There haven't been any barricades.'

'Precisely.'

The telephone rang and Downey picked it up. A woman's voice sounded distantly, like a bee in a bottle. 'How dreadful,' said Downey. 'How absolutely appalling.' He gestured with his free hand and nodded vigorously as if the person on the line could read the signal. 'Right you are,' he said. 'I understand. I understand perfectly. I'm handing you over now.' He placed his hand over the mouthpiece and passed the phone to the Admiral. 'It's Cassandra,' he said. 'Amos Bennet's just dropped dead.'

Patrick drove with Downey to Cassandra's flat. 'She needs her friends about her now,' said the Admiral.

'I wouldn't say I was her friend.'

'What are you then?'

'Her ex-husband,' said Patrick. 'She left me.'

The Admiral rolled his eyes. 'Don't split hairs. You were close to her. She needs your support.'

It seemed in bad taste to object. Death imposed its own standards of behaviour. The bereaved and the nearest and dearest were indulged to a degree which said more about the indulgers than those who suffered the indulgence.

'I don't know what I can possibly do,' he told Downey.

'Weren't you writing his obit?'

Patrick had quite forgotten. It seemed a long time ago. 'Yes, I was. It's bang up to date, except for Cassandra. Did they actually get married?'

Downey shook his head. 'It was going to be next month. At the end of the TV series. Cassandra had it all planned. She said they were still road-testing.' He risked a quick sideways glance to see how Patrick reacted. 'She was writing about it in her column. Sex in middle age.'

'Old age,' said Patrick.

'A matter of interpretation. In any case, he knew what she was doing. He didn't mind.'

Of course he didn't, thought Patrick. Infatuated Amos, the Admiral's guinea-pig, whose bed had rattled too often on the floorboards above for him ever to suppose that he would have preferred secrecy or even discretion. 'Do we know how he died?'

'In the saddle,' said Downey.

'Actually doing it?'

'If I understand Cassandra correctly.'

So the Senior Centrefold had gone out with a bang. He wondered whether *The Fogey* would make it a matter for celebration or regret. Either way it was unlikely that the silence of the grave would be maintained. There were too many interested parties for that.

In the entrance hall to the flat two men in overalls were propping a life-sized portrait of Amos on to a gilt stand. It was one of the set of pictures taken for *The Fogey*. Amos stood facing the camera. His hands rested on his hips. The rest of him hung free.

'We'll do the interviews here,' said Cassandra.

'What interviews?'

'The news. Television.' Her tone was patient as though she was telling a backward child how to get dressed.

Downey cleared his throat. 'You know how sorry we are.'

'Yes, yes. Thank you.' She allowed them a brief, professional smile. 'We need to get things sorted out. People will be arriving soon.'

'What people?' asked Patrick.

'Reporters. Interviewers. I phoned the agencies before I called you. We've missed the noon edition, but we'll make the afternoon bulletins.'

For a moment Patrick thought, quite seriously, that Cassandra had gone mad. Perhaps he had misconstrued her relationship with Amos. Perhaps she was unhinged by shock. 'Cassandra,' he said gently. 'The body's barely cold.'

She showed them the same brief smile she had rehearsed earlier. 'Life goes on.'

'Not like this.' He indicated the portrait.

'People will expect it.'

'What people?'

'Readers,' she said. 'Viewers. It's how they saw him.'

'What they will expect to see,' said Patrick, 'is a grieving woman. Not lost for words maybe, but certainly not banging on about how great it was to fraternize with Amos.'

'You don't know what I'd say.'

'I can imagine.'

She gave him an odd, appraising look. 'Maybe.'

Although Amos had died unexpectedly, she could not be said to have been caught napping. She was wearing what he had heard her describe as 'my little black Jean Muir dress', and, although it was appropriate, it could hardly be described as mourning apparel. It was as though she had been holding it in reserve for a fitting occasion. Her only jewellery was a gold chain around her neck and a ring he recognized as one he had chosen in the amber shop at Southwold where they had once spent a cold summer weekend. He leaned forward and sniffed suspiciously, but the scent she had on smelled of roses and rain, the essence of regret. He nodded his approval. Cassandra had the essentials right. But that was not the end of it. What they comprised was a point of departure. The real show was yet to come.

She led them through into the living room. The flat overlooked the Heath and through a window which ran the length of one wall he saw girls exercising dogs, children throwing balls and riders in hard hats pretending that the shabby turf poached by their horses' hoofs was somewhere wilder, lovelier, more remote. 'What I want to do,' she said, 'is an Open Heart special. Amos deserves it. Viewers loved him. They wrote and said so. They identified with him. He stood for something.'

'Maturity,' said Downey. 'Virility. The unquenchable life force.'

Each affirmation clunked like counterfeit in Patrick's ears. But he recognized the Admiral's buzz words and saw where Cassandra was heading. Whatever it did for the dead, the programme would certainly help to sustain the living. 'Can you do it in time?' he asked.

'I don't see why not.' She flicked open a desk diary. 'Today's Monday. The show goes out on Thursday. There's lots of Amos on film. We'll reprise the Centrefold stuff. We can line up some tributes. And I'll say my piece.'

'Saying what?'

'I shall describe the man I knew,' said Cassandra. 'What he signified. How he refused to submit to age. What a great lover he was.'

'Ardent?'

'Exactly. And something about his spirit. His stubbornness. There was a poem you used to quote.'

'Do not go gentle into that good night,' said Patrick.

'That's the one.'

'Very moving,' he said. 'That should do the trick.'

'Of course, it needs putting together,' said Cassandra. 'I need someone to write it. You knew Amos. You were his friend.'

It was a day on which too many words were being used indiscriminately, thought Patrick. 'Sort of,' he said. 'More friend than enemy. But not close. Not really.' He stared out of the window and saw that one of the hard-hatted girls was having trouble with her horse. She whacked it with her crop as it strolled into a bed of nettles. 'What you're really looking for is a commercial,' he said.

'No I'm not. Who for?'

'You. The Admiral. The Life Force. It hasn't got much to do with old Amos.' Except, he reflected, that it was his pursuit of the Life Force which had done him to death. It was not the Worst Fuck in the World, but it had certainly been his last. 'In any case,' he said, 'I can't write it. Won't write it.'

Cassandra put her hand to her mouth and pinched her bottom lip. 'Do it for me.'

He shook his head. There was no point in itemizing his reasons for refusal. There were too many and there was not enough time. The list went back for ever.

'Do it for yourself then,' said Downey.

Patrick shook his head again. Something momentous was taking place and his only regret was that the Admiral was not there to share it. They had all been through so much together: insults and bullying, humiliation and deceit. It was a pity that the author of so much that had happened was not there to see the end of it.

'You're throwing away your job,' said Downey.

No forecast could have sounded sweeter. Its fulfilment had been a long time coming. 'I meant to tell you earlier,' said Patrick. 'I resign.'

★

The world did not end overnight. No one telephoned to beg him to reconsider. The sun shone brightly and the pavements were free of dog shit as Patrick walked to the corner shop to collect his morning papers. On the front page of Felix Benn's paper there was a famous photograph of the Admiral. Taken in his fighting prime it showed him wearing a baggy pair of shorts, crouching behind an enormous pair of boxing gloves. The headline said LOW BLOW SCUPPERS LEGEND. There were photographs of Harry Miller, Nora and Lady Larkin and blow-ups from the knockout sequence in the newsreel.

Patrick read the small print as he walked home. No one had warned him that the story was about to appear, but the timing could not have been better. The revelations were bigger and more punishing than he had ever imagined; when it came to telling all, Cassandra had nothing on Harry Miller. The fight had been a fix, the decision a travesty and he had been bought and paid for to keep quiet for half a century. Now he was coming clean. The Admiral's reputation as a sportsman, a philanthropist and a friend lay in rags. It was hard to imagine the degree of resentment that lay behind such a comprehensive trashing. Harry Miller had taken his Judas money, but he was exacting another payment in blood. Three more days of it were promised. DEALS WITH BLACK DICTATOR said the trailer for tomorrow's instalment. GOOD TIME GIRLS AND THE GOLD-PLATED ROLLS. It was the day of dog eat dog. Once upon a time Fleet Street would never have savaged one of its own so fiercely, but traditions had changed with the geography. It was a different world in which proprietors stood naked in the dock.

He phoned Benn to offer his congratulations. 'I heard you were back,' said Benn. 'What's going on?'

'Not much apart from Amos.'

'Poor old sod. Was he really on the nest when it happened?'

'So I'm told.'

Benn whistled respectfully. 'Did you have a good trip?'

'Eventful.' Patrick gave him a quick run down. 'So I resigned,' he said.

'Wasn't that a bit drastic?'

'No alternative.'

'You'll get redundancy.'

'Not a penny.'

There was a shocked silence at the other end of the line. Few disasters, Patrick had observed, touched journalists more keenly than learning that money had been cut off at its source.

'What are you going to do?' asked Benn.

'Ask around.'

'There might be something here.'

'I'd like that.'

'What about the panda story? Will it stand up?'

He had already given the matter some thought. As things stood, he emerged with no credit and very little credibility. He was everyone's dupe. What he had to do was find another point of view. 'There are no pictures,' he said cautiously.

'Pity,' said Benn. 'But it might be good for a follow-up after Harry Miller. Let me have a word with my people. I'll get back to you.'

Patrick put down the phone and listened to the silence. What he was missing, he realized, was the clatter of Amos's typewriter. There would be no more of that, just as there would be no more twanging of the bedsprings in the small hours. Amos had always let his presence be known. The irritation had been constant and its absence was uncanny.

He re-invented a routine. Mr Bassett, the osteopath, agreed to see him that afternoon and he walked across the park to collect his car. In his absence the garage had conducted an MOT and done extensive repairs. Patrick winced at the size of the bill.

'You said we should do what was needed,' said the mechanic.

'Four new tyres?'

'They were all bald.'

'Windscreen wiper?'

'Worn out.'

'Exhaust pipe?'

'Rusted right through. Wonder it hadn't dropped off.'

Patrick raised no more objections. He was not an expert. His part in the transaction was to believe what he was told and pay up.

His relationship with Mr Bassett was just as simple. He stretched out on the leatherette couch and felt the strong, white hands alight on his spine.

'Someone's been meddling here,' said Mr Bassett.

'I don't know what you mean.'

'Doing something different. I can tell.' He tapped Patrick's lumbar region as if he was expecting it to make music. 'Have you consulted someone else?'

'There was an emergency.'

'You could have phoned me.'

'I was in North Korea,' said Patrick. 'I collapsed in the street. They took me to hospital.'

'I see.' He sounded reproachful rather than sympathetic. 'What did they do?'

'They gave me a going over. I couldn't stand.'

'Injections?'

'One injection. Very painful.'

'There has also been manipulation.'

'How can you tell?'

'The alignment,' said Mr Bassett cryptically. 'Things are not as they were.'

'Is that bad?'

'Not necessarily.' His fingers explored the guilty vertebrae. 'Pure luck, I imagine. But we will persist.'

Which meant, thought Patrick, that Lottie's massage had been on the right lines. He decided to say no more about it. After so long without achieving a result himself, Mr Bassett probably felt aggrieved. He was not above taking it out on the customer.

'Miss Flynn has left us,' he said.

'Why's that?'

Mr Bassett bent forward to breathe in Patrick's ear. 'Strictly between ourselves. Some patients found her distracting.'

'Is that so?' His own response had been fairly spectacular, he remembered, but he was not one to tell tales out of school. 'I never really noticed,' he said.

★

Lottie came to see him the next day. It was early evening and he was sitting on the floor of the bedroom attending to the last of his unpacking. The dirty laundry went into black plastic bags. The bottle of ginseng, brought back for Amos, went on to the drinks trolley. The notebooks, the tapes and the tape recorder were stacked on the bottom shelf of the bookcase. From the bottom of the valise where it had been lurking he retrieved the packet of paper underpants. He had not worn them during the trip and he knew now that he never would. When Lottie rang the door bell he dropped the packet into the trash bin and closed the lid. It was like burying a former self.

'Why didn't you tell me you were going to resign?' she demanded as he opened the door.

'I didn't know.'

'What made you do it?'

He spread his hands. 'It all got too much.'

'I've resigned too,' she said.

He drew her into the hallway and closed the door behind her. 'Not because of me?'

'I don't know. Partly, I suppose.' She looked around her. 'This is cosy. Are we going to stay here?'

He shook his head, confused. He felt breathless as if he had run too far, too fast. 'Of course not. I'm sorry. It's straight upstairs.'

As he followed in her wake he smelled her perfume, something fresh and woody. He tried to remember what state the flat was in. At least he had got rid of the underpants. He realized that he wanted to make a good impression.

'They were such sods,' she said. 'They didn't even say they were sorry.'

'Of course not.'

'Is it always like that?'

'Not always,' said Patrick. 'Sometimes it gets really bad.'

'I thought I might sue them.'

'What for? False pretences? Breach of contract? Don't waste your time. Just show them what they've let go.' He lifted the whisky bottle. 'Some of this?'

'Yes please.' She opened her shoulder bag. 'I've brought your mail from the office. They gave me your address.'

'I'm surprised they even knew it.'

'I had to ask around.' She stood by the window and watched the traffic streaming south. 'Is it always so busy?'

'Early morning, early evening.' He skimmed through the envelopes. One of them was large and hand-written and bore a Leeds postmark. He knew no one there. He ran his finger beneath the flap. 'Surprise, surprise,' he said. 'It's from Frobisher in textiles.'

'Which was he?'

'You remember,' said Patrick. 'Not Morgan in plastics or Lumsden in metal alloys.'

'I remember,' said Lottie. She sipped her whisky. 'Thank God we're not there.'

'Nor is he. He left just after we did.' He glanced through the letter and shook the envelope. A smaller envelope fell out. 'Jack Blazer asked him to pass this on. He couldn't post it himself.'

'I suppose not.' She led him over to the settee and sat beside him. 'Go on, then. Read it.'

'Aloud?'

'I'll look over your shoulder.' She clasped her glass between both hands and inched closer. He had never smelled anyone so clean and he breathed deeply as though he was inhaling oxygen.

Blazer's letter filled a single page from an exercise book. The writing was copperplate and there were no crossings-out or revisions. It was dated five days earlier, the day they had left North Korea.

'Dear Patrick,' it began.

No one else is going to tell you what's going on, so I suppose it's up to me. As the Bishop said to the actress. Or vice versa. The thing is, Lulu's found herself a friend. You remember that roaring you thought you heard? Well, it wasn't your imagination. We've got another one, home-grown, and that was his call of the wild. All that bollocks about bringing one in from Beijing and we needn't have bothered. Christ knows where he's come from. Further north, we think, and the vet says there are bound to be more. Mr Kim says that we now have a breeding colony of giant pandas which gives us zoological status. You can see his point. Zoological status equals political status. Lots of chat with interested parties, governments even. All we have to do is track the buggers down and Bob's your uncle. We've left a few of the lads behind to keep the bed warm and I'm going back with another expedition in a day or so. I suppose they'll announce the good news when they're good and ready, but this is just to keep you in the picture. Keep it to yourself, this letter I mean. But I thought you deserved to know. Remember me to the lovely Lottie and take good care of her. She's a right little cracker and don't tell me you think differently. Love to her and don't let the bastards grind you.

After his name in large, looping characters, he had added a PS. 'Mr Lee knows I'm sending this. He wants you to know that all's Sir Garnet.'

Patrick passed the letter to Lottie and got up to pour them another drink. 'Fancy that,' he said.

'Bless his hairy ears and whiskers,' said Lottie. 'Are you going to tell the Admiral?'

'Not exactly.'

'What do you mean?'

He told her what Benn had suggested. 'A nice little series,' he said. 'But they're worried about pictures.'

'What a coincidence,' said Lottie. She hummed a tune as she picked up her brief-case and struck a pose as she pulled down the zip. 'Ta-rah!' she said and spilled a sheaf of glossy prints on to the table top.

Patrick saw the burning helicopter and Blazer with blood striping his face. He saw Mr Lee sprinting towards the flames and Lulu cowering behind the bars of her cage. He saw someone wrenching the wire free and realized that it was himself. He was not a good subject, he thought. He looked frightened and desperate and he needed a shave. 'Where did these come from?' he asked.

'I kept a roll back.'

'How?'

'I hid it.'

'Where?'

'Nooks and crannies,' said Lottie. 'Female parts.' She grinned widely. 'It's all right. Don't be embarrassed. It's what ladies do. It's an old tradition. Not comfortable, just convenient.'

'Why didn't you tell me on the plane?'

'No point until I knew what we'd got.'

'The Admiral's not seen them?'

'You're the only one who's seen them. I was taking them in when I heard you'd resigned. I changed my mind.'

He felt himself smiling as he had never smiled before. It was as though someone with strong and certain fingers was remoulding his face. There were curves and angles which were entirely new. Someone should take a picture now, he thought. There was no doubt that he would need a new likeness for his passport. He was transformed. He was a happy man.

'You'll use them?' said Lottie.

'If that's all right.'

'It's perfect,' she said and kissed him. The last time she had done that, he remembered, was after he had set the panda free. This time he was ready for it. He kissed her back.

They lay on his bed and watched television. The bedroom was where the set was and she told him not to move it. There were five minutes to go before Open Heart, and a man wearing dreadlocks told his backing group how love would burn them like fire and freeze them like ice. It was the kind of non-musical turn which used to drive Amos into a frenzy. 'I'm sorry about this,' he said.

'It doesn't matter.'

'Would you like another pillow?'

'I'm fine.'

He reached across her and tilted the bedside light away from her eyes. 'That's nice,' she said.

It was nice, thought Patrick, because it was simply companionable. Everything else was on hold. There were no flying cats. No one was giving orders or setting a sexual menu. There were no expectations to live up to. There was nothing to prove. In fact, there was no shopping list of any kind. For better or for worse, nature was going to take its course. He breathed in a wisp of Lottie's hair and blew it out. She stirred against him and he felt himself stiffen, not painfully, but in hope of things to come. It might never happen, he warned himself. There were hangups he had to dissolve. He would have to explain about Cassandra.

'About Cassandra,' he began.

'There she is,' said Lottie.

The programme had come on unannounced. There were no satin hearts, no fanfares; simply a black and white set on which Cassandra stood beside the portrait of Amos. She wore the Jean Muir dress and the amber ring. The simplicity was arresting. Perhaps it will be all right, thought Patrick; perhaps the Bigness has abated. But the moment that she spoke he knew that all his apprehensions were justified. 'This was a man,' said Cassandra and somewhere, offscreen, an organ pealed.

He had been expecting the worst but nothing had prepared him for the sheer banality of the event. It was like watching a pop video on which Cassandra was the lead singer and the accompaniment was an audio syrup which parodied true feeling, making it absurd. 'He was strong,' said Cassandra, and the organ growled an electronic echo. 'He was gentle,' she claimed, and the organ squealed agreement. 'He was loved,' she sighed and the organ throbbed its vibrato. Her chalky face filled the screen. Her eyes were liquid, her mouth tremulous. As the camera pulled back it took in details of the portrait beside her and Amos's large and gnarled penis loomed into focus by her right elbow.

'He met every demand that was made on him,' said Cassandra. 'Age was an irrelevance, vitality his trademark.' She laced her fingers into a neat, white basket filled with air. 'We were lovers,' she said proudly. 'Tonight my arms are empty, like my heart.'

She had written her own script, Patrick decided. No one else could have devised such impeccable crap. It combined bathos and boasting, prurience and cant. In the black museum of TV performances it was an instant classic. Tributes were tributes, with an inbuilt licence to go over the top. But this was a star vehicle in which the departed was merely a prop and the survivor was the object of compassion and desire. The organ pealed and Cassandra stood bathed in studio limelight, like a special offer.

He felt the mattress shaking and looked at Lottie with alarm. Could she possibly be crying? Her back was turned towards him and he could not see her face. 'Are you all right?' he asked.

She nodded violently, but her shoulders continued to heave.

'You're sure?'

'Quite sure,' she gasped.

'What's wrong?'

She rolled on to her back. Her face was crimson and she was fighting for breath. 'That woman,' she said. 'Is she always like that?'

'More or less.' Even now he felt strangely protective.

'Then how could you stand her? Why did you ever need her?'

He ignored the question.

'You were laughing,' he said.

'Of course I was laughing. She's laughable.'

'I never thought she was funny,' said Patrick.

'Do you need her now?'

He shook his head. 'It's all over.'

'Think about it.'

He did as he was told. He thought about falling in love and falling out of love and the Worst Fuck in the World and how, beyond all reasonable doubt, there was more to life. He saw Cassandra, still posed in a halo of light, but even as he watched her, another part of his mind projected an image which was simpler, stronger, more compelling. A large boulder began to roll down a hill. It started slowly, but soon gathered speed. At one point it hit a rock and bounced into the air, turning at a tangent to present another damp profile before trundling to a halt on clear ground. It seemed to have taken very little time to have made such an important journey. He felt as though a curse had been lifted. His body was lighter. His chest was filled with helium.

'I don't need her,' he said. 'I don't even need to talk about her.'

'What a relief,' said Lottie.

She aimed the zapper and the screen turned blank. He opened his arms and she rolled into them.